Elizabeth,

I hope you enjoy!

Best wishes,

JoAnne Keltner

Possessed

(Pagan Light Book 1)

Previously published by Solstice Shadows as
Goth Girl Virgin Queen

By
JoAnne Keltner

Previously published as *Goth Girl Virgin Queen*
by Solstice Publishing, December 2015

Published in the United States of America

ISBN-13: 9781791657413

Interior Book Design: Marci Clark

Prologue

In Holy Resurrection Orthodox Church, while the gathering sang the cherubic hymn, the candles in front of the Virgin of Vladimir icon had begun to cry. At first, Jackie Turov thought someone in the congregation was crying, but the flames flickered in sync with the sobs as if they were moved by a mournful breath.

Father Dmitriev was preparing Holy Communion behind the iconostasis—the majestic wall of icons of Christ, the Holy Mother, and the saints. The wall, trimmed in gold, its painted icons radiating bright blues, reds, and yellows, had always drawn Jackie closer to God, and every time she gazed at its Holy Doors, she felt as if she were standing at the entranceway to heaven. But now, the sobbing drummed against Jackie's ears, making her stumble over the words of the hymn and fall a beat behind.

She looked at Grandma to see if there was any hint in the way her gaze met the iconostasis that she heard it too, but Grandma's gaze was fixed on the Holy Doors as she sang.

She looked to Prababulya, her great-grandmother. Her head was bowed; her black scarf knotted tightly beneath her chin. She seemed to be mouthing a prayer, rather than the words to the song.

As Jackie moved her lips wordlessly and out of time with the rest of the congregation, an overwhelming sadness split her heart in two. She pressed her palms to her ears.

"Jackie. Stop that," Grandma whispered. She tugged Jackie's fingers to pry her hand from her ear, but Jackie squeezed tighter.

Prababulya rubbed Jackie's shoulder and then hooked her stubby finger around Jackie's pinky. Jackie lowered her arms, but the sobs continued, and her chest ached so much that tears broke from the corners of her eyes.

The altar boy passed through the Holy Doors holding a golden candlestick, and then came the deacon, swinging a smoking decanter of incense. Father Dmitriev followed behind them, carrying the cloth-covered chalice. Jackie wanted to burrow her face against Prababulya's plump arm or stand behind her so that Father Dmitriev wouldn't see her cry. She didn't want her behavior to embarrass Grandma and Prababulya. She wiped her face with her dress sleeves every time new tears formed.

Father Dmitriev and the congregation volleyed prayers back and forth, and then Grandma coaxed Jackie to go before her. Jackie entered the line for the Holy Eucharist and slowly progressed to the front until she was staring into Father Dmitriev's dark eyes. He seemed to be looking through her as if he were lost in thought.

Tilting her head back slightly, Jackie opened her mouth and poked out her tongue. Her prayer-folded hands trembled; her knees weakened. Father Dmitriev dipped the spoon into the chalice, spooned out a lump of wine-soaked bread, and dropped it onto her tongue. Expecting a cool, soothing sensation, she was shocked when the bread seared her tongue. Without thinking, she spat the hot mass to the floor. Father Dmitriev's eyes widened; his mouth dropped open. The wine-soaked bread lay at his feet.

She drew her hands to her quivering lips.

"Clean this up," Father Dmitriev said to the deacon.

Behind Father Dmitriev, the flames from the crying candles caught onto the Virgin of Vladimir icon. Jackie pointed to the iconostasis and screamed, "Fire!"

The flames disintegrated the Virgin's face and crawled upward to consume the icons of the saints. Canvas curled into charcoaled scrolls and dropped like hot ash to the floor, catching the Oriental carpets.

Father Dmitriev turned toward the iconostasis. "What fire?" He turned to Jackie. "How did you—"

Grandma tugged Jackie's hand. "Enough."

The flames spread upward, rising from the top of the iconostasis and forming a fiery wall in front of the Virgin painted in the apse. The Virgin's arms were spread open as if she were embracing the flames that touched the Christ Child in her womb.

Fire caught the hem of Jackie's skirt and, in a single sweep, enveloped her. Thousands of hot needles pricked her nerves and sent excruciating pain through her body. She slapped at the flames and let out bloodcurdling screams as the stench of seared flesh filled her nose.

Prababulya restrained Jackie and chanted a prayer in Russian. Jackie screamed and writhed in her arms, but Prababulya's touch was as cool and comforting as salve and soon Jackie's screams turned to sobs.

The chattering congregation grew silent. The iconostasis was once again bright with yellows, reds, and blues—the Virgin and the saints unharmed.

Jackie's shoulders shrank inward. Nothing she had felt or witnessed was real.

Father Dmitriev's face was ghastly white. "She's possessed," he said.

Grandma put her hand on Jackie's forehead. "She's sick. She has a fever. Feel," she said to him.

"She's broken the Divine Liturgy," he said to Grandma. "Get her out of here!" Father Dmitriev said something to Prababulya in Russian.

Prababulya threw her hands up and ranted at him in the

same language—a language Jackie couldn't understand.

"Mama!" Grandma said to Prababulya.

Prababulya held Jackie protectively.

"*Net*, Mama, *net*." Grandma pled with Prababulya, but Prababulya and Father continued to argue. Over what exactly, Jackie didn't know.

Afraid that Father Dmitriev would throw Grandma, Prababulya, and her out of the church for good, Jackie broke from Prababulya's arms and said, her voice mousey and trembling, "Stop, please. I'm not sick." With her heart pounding, she pointed to the Virgin of Vladimir. "She spoke to me. She showed me a sign."

Prababulya covered her face with her hands. Her fingers were spread; her eyes, cast downward.

Jackie turned to the congregation, neighbors and friends who huddled near the back of the nave, the spaces between them so tight they were shoulder to shoulder, toe to heel, whispering among themselves.

She stood before them, hugging her arms and digging her fingernails into her flesh. "The Virgin," she said, her voice echoing in the hollow of the church, "she spoke to me. She showed me a sign." She told them this over and over, her words gradually turning to pleas for them to believe her, even though she knew it was a lie.

They stared at her, mouths hung open, silently, breathlessly.

Chapter 1

The medicine cabinet mirror—dotted with rust and turning gray—made the powder foundation on Jackie's face look ashen and her jet-black hair, blurry. She looked like a shadow of a girl. She smeared black lipstick on her lips and shook out her shoulder-length hair. Her straight-cut bangs veiled her mascara-lined eyes, and the layered ends of her hair stuck out in defiant wisps.

Some of the kids at school—the ones she didn't hang out with—called her Goth Girl. Some, whose memories wouldn't die, called her VQ for Virgin Queen.

Jackie preferred Goth Girl, to be one of the living dead, to be numb to the emotions that plagued her. But this was what she *wanted*, not what she got.

Goth Girl or Virgin Queen, she was a freak, absorbing the emotions around her like a sponge. Sometimes the emotions made her sick. Sometimes they made her see things.

Because of this, she kept to a tight-knit group of friends—Jason, Zeta, and Trish—and avoided social activities. She attended Ravenwood High only because Mom wouldn't let her homeschool. Mom was afraid she'd hang with Babu all day, making piroshki and doing needlepoint instead of studying. Jackie, afraid of what life offered a freak like her beyond high school, had to admit that hanging with Babu all day was tempting.

Typically, Fridays were movie nights for her best friend, Jason, and her, but tonight would be different. Tonight, she'd subject herself to a hodgepodge of emotions from crowds and rides and the very ground she'd walk on to protect him. For this, she would need physical and spiritual strength, which she sought these days from Babu.

Babu's door was cracked, and Jackie slowly pushed the door open. "Babu?" She had quit calling her great-grandmother "Prababulya" years ago, and instead shortened her name to Babu.

The room smelled of beeswax and down. A candle burned on the shrine on the dresser. The flickering flame animated the icon of the Virgin of Vladimir and cast shadows across the picture of Babu, Grandma, Mom, and Jackie. Although Babu didn't speak English, and Jackie didn't understand much Russian, Jackie knew Babu kept that picture on her shrine to pray for Grandma, who passed away several years ago; for Mom, who divorced Dad; and for the girl who saw the Virgin when she was twelve—for the girl she had become as a teen.

Babu sat in bed, a country quilt spread over her legs, her thumb pressed against a knot of her prayer rope, her head bowed sleepily, and her lips wording prayers.

"I wanted to say good-bye," Jackie whispered.

Babu crossed herself and then smiled at Jackie, her gold eyetooth shining from the light of the bed-stand lamp She patted the empty space beside her. "*Sadis.*"

Jackie sat down beside Babu at the edge of the bed and took Babu's hand in hers. Babu's hand was warm and knotted with arthritis. Jackie rubbed her thumb over the bumps on Babu's knuckles. Her black fingernails were a sharp contrast to Babu's pale skin.

She wasn't afraid to touch Babu's hands and absorb her emotions. Jackie got a good feeling from her. Babu filled Jackie's inner vision with white light. She renewed her spirit. And this is what Jackie needed for the commitment she had made for tonight.

"*Kuda idosh*" Babu asked.

"I'm going out, with Jason," Jackie said as if Babu understood her. This is how they communicated—Babu telling her stuff she couldn't understand and Jackie telling Babu stuff she couldn't understand. Somehow they carried on fine this way.

"*Vsevo kharoshevo*," Babu said in a comforting tone. She cupped her hands around Jackie's face and pulled her forehead to her lips. Jackie imagined Babu's kiss imprinted on her forehead and carrying Babu's blessings and love with her tonight.

In the front room, Mom was watching an old horror movie on TV and eating tortilla chips and guacamole.

Jackie unhooked her black trench coat from the coat rack.

"Jesus, Jackie," Mom said, her mouth full. "Do you have to go out like that?"

Jackie stopped, one arm in a coat sleeve, and gave Mom a look like she had to be kidding.

"My friend at work keeps asking if you're in a cult or something," Mom said.

"My friends keep asking if you're crazy or something. I mean, who rollerblades anymore?"

"I'm just worried about you."

Jackie could say anything to Mom. It was one of Mom's good qualities.

"You're not on drugs, are you?" Mom asked.

"Would I be pulling a 4.0 GPA if I were?"

"Maybe on coke."

Jackie rolled her eyes as she buttoned her coat. "If I were doing coke, I'd be rollerblading against traffic, like you."

"I'm not on coke."

"How do I know?"

"Sorry, I never know what's going on with you. You're always so... to yourself. Hey, where're you going anyway? It's the weekend. Shouldn't you be in your room socializing via text?"

Jackie shrugged. "I'm going to the Oktoberfest."

Mom's brow creased. "That's *this* weekend?"

"Yeah. Where've *you* been?"

Mom's eyes narrowed like she was thinking seriously about something.

What was up with her? "You okay?"

"Yeah," she said, her voice higher pitched, retreating. "I'm fine."

Jackie fished her keys out of her satchel and then hung her camera around her neck. The camera was a secret she had discovered in Photography 101 last year. Looking through its lens was the only way she could truly look at people without feeling what they felt. She was counting on it and the light she absorbed from Babu to get her through the night without passing out.

"Be careful," Mom said, which sounded odd coming from a person who rollerbladed like a runaway shopping cart.

Jackie stepped outside and into the cool, damp air. The evening sky had turned light gray.

Her Oldsmobile was parked in front of the house. It used to be Grandma's, which was hard to keep secret because of how old the car was and the *Pray the chotki every day* bumper sticker. Jackie had been trying to remove it, but it was one of those papery stickers that just didn't want to come loose. She had managed to scrape off most of the letters. The only ones visible were the *the*, the *o* from *chotki*, and *ry* from *every*. So now, it read "theory," underlined with a string of prayer-rope beads.

She drove slowly down the block as she headed toward Main Street. Soggy leaves carpeted the sidewalks and curbs, and the small-town Victorian homes were decorated for Halloween—Indian corn bound to lampposts, plastic tombstones studding yards, and paper witch heads and scary Halloween cats taped to windows. All but Dad's house—her old house. His front lawn was packed with autumn leaves, and a rain-beaten newspaper was caught in the prickly branches of the rosebush by the front porch steps.

That rosebush had been in bloom when people from nearby churches gathered on the front lawn, holding candles, singing, praying, begging for Jackie to come outside to pray for them, touch them.

She pressed on the gas pedal. The circus was over, and she swore it would never come to town again. Still, her stomach churned and squealed as she followed Main Street out to Route 6, toward Jason's house. She didn't know why she even looked at her old house. The memories were too painful. Maybe she worried about Dad. She hadn't talked to him since her birthday last March, and even then, they didn't say much. Crazy, isn't it? But she really didn't think he wanted to talk to her. She was his past, something he needed to get over and forget.

Jason's driveway was two tire tracks with grass in-between. She parked behind his shitty truck and honked the horn.

Doh! She forgot it pissed off his dad. She really shouldn't have to do anything but keep this clunky motor running. The car had what Jason called a rough idle—coughing and wheezing like Babu with bronchitis.

Jason came down the front porch steps, angled bangs curtaining half his face, a black, leather jacket zipped to his chin, black jeans, and combat boots. He had a special way of climbing up and down steps, always forward on the same foot. It was kind of like he was unsure of himself, like maybe he fell once on a flight of stairs.

The passenger door squeaked when he opened it. He slid onto the front seat. "You forgot."

She glanced at him. "Sorry." She never looked Jason directly in the eyes, at least not for longer than a second or two. He carried a lot of baggage, and she preferred not to share his load.

"You should have heard what my dad said he wanted to do with that horn."

She winced.

Driving to the Oktoberfest, Jackie focused on the road. Sometimes she looked at Jason but focused only on his mouth or his jacket. When he was around her, his aura turned from black to reddish purple, almost like his spirit had been bruised. She interpreted it as a mixture of pain and love—the love he felt for her pouring over his pain like salve. Yes. She sensed Jason was in love with her. But this relationship worked out well for the both of them, she supposed. Jason liked to suffer. It made him feel alive. Though, she knew he'd never admit it. And she was comfortable being around him, not just because he allowed her space, but because he accepted her as she was. He made the guilt she carried more bearable.

Jason fidgeted with his wallet chain. "Dad didn't give me my allowance yet. All I got's a fiver... I'll pay you back."

"Hmm. So is this why you wanted me to come to the fest? 'Cause I'm the only one with funds?"

"That's not true. It's just that—"

"Jason, I know, and I know you'll pay me back. You always do." She shook her head. "But I tell you, I gotta take care of you like my own child."

He pounded her thigh with his fist. "I'm not a child. I'm seventeen and just two months younger than you."

"I'm teasing. And I completely understand why you're afraid to be alone with Trish. Once she gets it in her head she wants something, she doesn't let up."

She pictured herself being squeezed between Trish and Jason.

"Just be easy on me. This body needs space." She wasn't so much worried about Trish and Jason as she was the thousands of other people and emotions that would be packed around her.

At the Ravenwood Oktoberfest, music came at Jackie from

all directions—hip-hop from the roller coaster, rock from the Tilt-a-Whirl, pop from the Himalaya. Red, blue, and yellow bulbs blinked in rhythmic patterns; rides spun and jetted outward; and voices screamed and boomed over loudspeakers. The contrasting movements and sounds clashed in midair. She wanted to close her eyes and press her palms to her ears.

Relax, Jackie.

But she couldn't.

As they walked down the main path of the carnival, surrounded by a drove of people, emotions swirled around her and she couldn't distinguish one from the other. It was one huge cauldron of sensations churning inside her.

The camera strap tugged at her neck, and the camera bounced against her stomach. She wanted to hold the lens to her eye and shield herself, but she figured she'd trip.

Jason reached for her, like he wanted to put his arm around her shoulder. But then he hesitated. "You okay?" he asked.

She nodded and sucked in a deep breath.

Zeta waved at her from behind a group of boys in baggy pants and hoodies. "VQ," she called. Zeta was the only person who could call Jackie V without making Jackie cringe. Trish was with her. The two of them looked like total freaks: Zeta in black tights, pointy-toed boots, and a red-and-black striped sweater, a fuzzy scarf tied around her neck; Trish in a black tutu over her jeans, a short, black leather jacket, and multiple ponytails sticking out all over her head.

Nearing the two, Jackie stumbled and grabbed Zeta's arm for support. Stung by raw emotion, Jackie pulled her hand away like she'd touched a hot burner. Zeta was pure electric, switching on and off sporadically and so fast that she was neither happy nor sad, but energetically sassy. Trish was usually cool to the touch, her predominant mood: melancholy. Her mind was like a snowy TV station, the images faint and ghostly.

People stared at the four of them. Though, usually, not many people ever recognized Jackie with her makeup and black hair—not many people outside of school, that is. She no longer had to worry about them tugging on her or touching her. She only had to worry about what she touched and where she stood.

Every time Trish started to walk in front of Jackie to get close to Jason, Jackie stepped up her pace and casually blocked her. When Trish bumped into her, Jackie was stung by Trish's anger and unquenched desire.

"Let's go on the Ferris wheel," Zeta said. "Maybe we'll get stuck on top."

"Not me," Jackie said. "I'll probably barf. I'm just getting used to being here."

"I'm hungry," Jason said.

"Chow sounds good." Trish caught Jackie off guard. She crossed in front of Jackie and squeezed next to Jason.

Jason's eyes widened in terror. He moved behind Jackie and to the other side so that Jackie was in the middle again.

Before anyone could make another move, a woman, with red hair wrapped loosely in a cornflower blue scarf, stepped in front of them and locked her boney hands around Jackie's.

"What the..." Jackie tried to slip her hands free, but the woman tightened her grip.

The woman was tiny, yet overpowering. Her face was narrow and fox-like. "I know who you are," she whispered.

Jackie knew who the stranger was too, and she couldn't pull away. It was like a magnetic force had bound their hands together.

The woman's beady eyes looked straight into Jackie's. "Interesting."

What was weird was, Jackie couldn't read her, but she knew the woman was reading her.

Zeta shoved the woman's shoulder. "Leave her alone, you psycho."

The woman's eyes darted toward Zeta, allowing Jackie to

yank her hands free.

Jason and Trish gathered on each side of Zeta. The three of them glared at the intruder like guard dogs.

The woman smiled, as if satisfied that she had gotten what she wanted. She walked away and sat down at a table in front of a tent with a sign that read, "Psychic Reading $20."

"Just great," Trish said. "That's Madam Sophie. We're all cursed now."

"What do you think is brewing in her psycho brain?" Zeta asked.

"Maybe she just wanted to read your fortune," Jason said calmly.

"Against Jackie's will?" Trish rubbed her hands front and back against her tutu as if Madam Sophie had locked hands with her.

Dizzied, Jackie dropped down onto a picnic table bench in the food tent. "I don't feel good. I need a sugar fix." The thick smell of fried onions and grease gave her something solid to breathe in.

"Jackie?" Jason asked.

She handed him her satchel. "Just take it."

A sheepish look covered his face. "I'll pay you back."

"I know, Jas."

"I have money," Trish said.

"I'm good." Jason set Jackie's satchel on the picnic table and dug into it.

Trish pursed her lips and turned abruptly. As she marched to the food stands with Zeta, her multiple ponytails wiggled like the snakes of Medusa.

Zeta brought Jackie a sugary elephant ear with a half-inch topping of powdered sugar, just how Jackie liked it.

"Maybe she was testing the competition." Zeta sat across from Jackie, a green basket containing a fat gyro and a wad of napkins in front of her. "Who?" Jackie asked.

"Madam Sophie."

"I'm not psychic, well, not like her."

"Yes, you are," Jason said. "You predicted—"

"Trust me," she said, intentionally cutting him off. "I'm just really sensitive to everyone's emotions. All I do is piece together the impressions I pick up... kind of like working a jigsaw puzzle. The images tell me things about a person's past and about the present."

"Uh, because you're psychic?" Zeta bit into her gyro. Cucumber sauce rolled down the side of her mouth. She grabbed the wad of napkins and dabbed her face.

Trish's lips turned upward into a devilish smile. "Will and Sandra are here," she sang.

Zeta reached across the table for Jackie's hand, but Jackie recoiled. "You going to be okay?"

"Yeah," she said, but already, her insides were burning. Not that she still had feelings for Will, it was just that he and Sandra were the perfect pair in their varsity jackets—Will, the class president, and Sandra, the head cheerleader. Gag!

Sandra had one tiny taco in a paper wrap. Will had a plate full of chicken and vegetables. Jackie feared her black lips were powdered white from devouring the elephant ear. She self-consciously patted her mouth with a napkin.

"Well, if it isn't VQ and her circus crew." Sandra slapped her thigh. "O-M-G, that rhymes."

Will tugged Sandra's arm. "Come on."

Somehow, Jackie always freaked Will out. She thought it was because he was afraid she was going to throw a curse on him for dumping her.

"VQ, I'm surprised you're not working your own booth," Sandra said. "Give Madam Sophie a little competition."

"Maybe you should set up a booth yourself," Zeta said. "I hear you're a pro."

Will angrily looked at Sandra, as if she'd been keeping her promiscuity a secret from him.

"A-building, boys' room, second stall," Zeta said.

Sandra appeared all huffy and glowered at Jackie like she was the one reading all her dirty secrets. "Weirdo," she called her. "Come on, Will, we don't need to watch this freak show."

As they walked away, Will questioned Sandra.

"It's written in black marker," Zeta yelled. "You'll never get it off—but then, maybe you will."

Jackie leaned forward and eyed Zeta. "Did you make that up?"

"Make what up?"

"You know."

"Hell, no. Last basketball game I sneaked under the bleachers to smoke a cigarette, and I caught her with Sean Perry. Then, I added a little advertisement in the boys' bathroom in A-building—no charge, of course."

"No shit," Jason whispered. He looked really interested.

"Looking to take a number?" Jackie teased.

Jason blushed.

Trish glared at Jackie and then switched to sulk mode.

After they ate, they dumped their garbage in a blue barrel and walked the grounds. Together, they were one. A freak show maybe, but this show drove everyone away from them—well almost everyone.

Carnival lights swirled around Jackie, dizzying her as emotions rose through her feet. She stopped and pressed her eye to the camera lens. The lens washed the emotions away, stilled and silenced the mayhem. She could see everything like a normal person. Maybe if she had camera lens contacts she could be normal.

She shot pictures of the Viking boat, the merry-go-round, and even Madam Sophie. She was still shaken over their encounter. She was certain Madam Sophie hated her. She couldn't blame her, though, not after what had happened. And she wouldn't be surprised if Madam Sophie knew the truth.

For Jason's sake, Jackie went on the Ferris wheel, the

Himalaya, and the Tilt-a-Whirl, absorbing the emotions from the people who previously sat in the rides, which made her sicker than the spinning and twirling. She was physically and emotionally sapped and wanted to wrap her arm around Jason and lean on him, but she couldn't. She was all alone with this disease.

As they walked down the main path of the carnival, heading to the parking lot, the lights dimmed and the rides slowed. Motors hummed and drained of power. The four of them stopped walking, and everyone around them stopped in the middle of what they were doing.

The carnival fell silent.

After a few seconds, the power resurged. Transformers buzzed, the lights illuminated and blinked in rhythmic patterns, and music boomed. Carnies restarted rides, and people went about what they had been doing—the carnival once again filled with sound and movement.

"Would you look at that?" Zeta pointed to the sky.

But it was the ground and the minute vibrations surging through the soles of her boots and up her legs that Jackie was focused on. Her shins ached and tickled—the same feeling as hitting a funny bone—and they were too weak to support her. She dropped to the damp ground, onto the mud-dried hay.

"Jackie, you okay?" Zeta knelt beside her.

Jackie rubbed her shins. "Did you feel that?" The nerve endings throughout her body tingled, and blue washed over her eyes and faded to black.

Chapter 2

When Jackie opened her eyes, white, ghastly faces with blackened eyes and lips stared down at her. Had she died and gone to hell?

"Guess the carnival was a bad idea," Trish said sarcastically.

"Holy blazing balls of fire," Zeta said. "Don't tell me solar storms set you off too."

"What?" Jackie said.

Zeta pointed up. "Look."

Swirls of red and green spread across the night sky. "Was there an explosion?"

"Kind of, but it happened several days ago. All these energized particle thingies from the sun just reached the Earth now. It's all Miss Gut Tree's been yapping about for the past month. I had to write a freaking report."

Jackie had Ms. Guthrie last year. She was always working current scientific events into her lesson plans. Not having Ms. Guthrie this semester, she missed this one coming. "I don't think I can get up. I feel like I've been struck by lightning."

"Magnetism," Zeta said. "That's why the lights dimmed. Screws up homing pigeons big time too." She bent over and reached out her hand.

"No, I can do it." The last thing Jackie needed was to get zapped again. She carefully rose up. She stayed bent over, her hands on her thighs, until she felt stable enough to stand up straight.

Zeta picked up Jackie's satchel and dusted it off.

"My camera!" She felt for it. It still hung around her neck. There was a little dirt around the bottom edge and the lens where it had hit the ground. She rubbed the dirt off with her thumb.

Zeta handed Jason the keys to Jackie's car. "Here, you drive Jackie home. Trish and I will follow."

Trish reached for the keys. "No."

Jason locked his fingers around them before Trish could. "I'll do it."

"Relax," Zeta said to Trish. "He's just driving her home."

Trish's face was red, her emotions scalding.

Zeta tugged Trish's arm. "You're making Jackie sick. Let's go." She led Trish to her car.

Trish turned and glared at Jackie.

In front of Jackie's house, Jason parked the car along the curb behind Mom's Jetta and cut the clunky engine. The silence was a relief to Jackie. The weight of the passenger door as she pushed it open made her feel like some creature pushing open the lid of a vault in one of those black-and-white horror flicks Mom watched.

She swung her legs around, mummy style with knees together. Her feet touched the curb. Her shins still tickled. She didn't know if she could stand up without her legs giving out, let alone climb the cement lawn-steps and the eight steps to the front porch.

Jason leaned over. His angled bangs swept across his face. "I could have opened the door," he said meekly.

"Sorry."

He awkwardly reached out, his fingers a hair away from

touching her arm.

She broke a sweat. Her shoulders tensed.

"You're going to have to let me help you," he said.

"This means we have to touch?" She sighed. "All right."

Jason anchored his arm under hers. She wrapped her arm around his shoulder. He tugged her to her feet. The scent of cold leather from his jacket filled her nose.

"We'll take one step at a time," he said.

"Okay, then." She knew this was more to his benefit than hers. Getting up these stairs was going to take all night following Jason's method of stair climbing.

They climbed one step—stopped—took another step—stopped.

Jason's emotions passed from his body to hers like mutual induction. Pain cut through her. Not physical pain, but emotional pain. "You okay, Jas?"

"Yeah." His fingers loosened from around her shoulder.

Crossing the sidewalk, they moved at a faster pace. But then they started their excruciating climb up the front porch steps.

Zeta blasted the horn. Or maybe it was Trish.

"Ignore her," Jackie said, but she was really hoping he'd speed things up.

By the time they made it to the front porch, she was trembling like a scolded puppy.

She slipped from Jason's embrace and leaned against the house near the door. "That one," she said, pointing to the gold key with the square-cut loop. She inhaled the brisk night air of fall leaves and smoke-filled fireplaces. The pleasure she found in this diluted the throbbing in her chest.

Inside, the house was silent, the front room lit by a night-light that was plugged into the outlet by the stairs. As Jason helped her up the stairs to the bedrooms, she used the handrail for support so she didn't have to throw her full weight onto him. The hallway was dark, but she left it that way so she wouldn't wake Mom. She didn't want her mother to make a big deal about this; although, it was probably too late. Her clunky car and the horn blowing were enough to wake the dead.

Inside her room, Jackie flipped on the light and then quietly closed the door. Jason walked her to the bed. Her legs felt as sturdy as cooked noodles.

She dropped onto the mattress and sat at the edge with her hands on her knees and fingers spread.

Jason squatted in front of her and raked his fingers through his angled bangs, pushing them out of his face. His big, fawn eyes gazed at her. His skin was smooth, young, and innocent, like he was fifteen instead of seventeen.

She lowered her eyes and studied the wide zipper on his jacket.

"You want me to take anything off?" he asked. "I mean, like your shoes," he said, nervously.

She laughed. "I'm good."

His cheeks flushed.

Nice going, Jackie. "Hey, tell Trish and Zeta I'm sorry for all the excitement," she said, trying to lighten the mood.

He stood up and burrowed his hands in his jacket pockets. He looked downward at the floor. "Sorry I made you come."

"You didn't make me do anything. I wanted to go. I know the way Trish is. You deserve better than that."

He looked at her and cracked a hopeful smile. "Thanks."

She smiled awkwardly back. "You're going to have to ride home with her."

"I know." He looked downward again. "Could I, maybe, stay here, with you?" he mumbled.

"What? Uh, no, not a good idea."

He closed his eyes for a moment. "Sorry. It's just that you said... I mean, I thought..."

"I didn't mean that we should be... you know... if that's what you meant."

He turned abruptly and headed for the door.

"Jas?"

He stopped.

"The stair thing. If you ever want to talk about it, I'll listen."

He looked at her and grimaced.

"Or not," she said

He walked out.

She felt like an idiot. It wasn't a best friend he was looking for.

She let the thought sink into her head—her and Jason as girlfriend and boyfriend? Her stomach quivered.

Chapter 3

Inside her bedroom, Trish unzipped her leather jacket and whipped it across the room. It hit the thin chains that hung from the ceiling lamp and plopped onto the bed. The chains clanked against the fixture as the lead singer of Death's Child, from a poster above her bed, stared at her with heavily-mascaraed eyes. His puckered, blood-red lips told her that she had totally fucked up this evening.

A pang rose in the center of her chest and caught there and burned like desire smacking against fiery rage. She clutched the lace of her tutu and, thinking of Jackie blocking her from Jason, pulled at it as if she were tearing at Jackie's hair. If Jackie would quit getting in the way, she could make Jason fall in love with her. She slammed the toe of her boot into a heavy book bag and pouted.

Like a switch clicking on in her head, she realized the place where she might find an answer. She trampled over a pile of clothes lying by the closet door. Inside, she ruffled through a toppled stack of games and pulled out a crushed Ouija board box. She flung the box top. It sailed through the air, crashed against the wall, and plummeted to the bed.

Sitting cross-legged on the floor, she rested her fingertips on the triangular pointer, the planchette, and concentrated on a single question: How can I get Jackie out of the way so I can get close to Jason?

With short hot breaths puffing from her nose, Trish eyed the needle that dangled from the center of the planchette. She waited for the pointer to move, repeating the question inside her head until her brain burned. Her fingers tingled and the hair on her arms rose. The air popped and crackled as if filled with electric energy. Electricity arced from her fingertips. She jerked her fingers from the planchette and examined her hands. The pointer veered to the left and slid off the board.

Around the room, bluish sparks arced from object to object. From garment to garment in the clothes pile. Handle to handle on the dresser drawers. Base to socket on the dresser lamp. Between the ornate scrolls on the headboard. From carpet to bed skirt.

Energy pulsed through her fingers and sent chills across her shoulders.

She set the planchette in the center of the Ouija board and rested her fingers on top. A continuous flow of energy ran between her fingers and the pointer. She focused on the dangling needle, breathlessly reading each letter the needle paused over: I-C-A-N-H-E-L-P-Y-O-U-M-A-Y-I-E-N-T-E-R.

She grouped the letters into words and swallowed their meaning.

"Yes," she whispered, triumphantly.

Chapter 4

Jackie checked her cell phone the next morning. Nine missed calls from Jason. The last call was at one in the morning. Sweat broke across her forehead. Maybe he just wanted to talk about the stair thing. God, she hoped he realized their relationship was fine the way it was.

Jason had obviously been up late. She decided to let him sleep until eleven and call him then. She slipped the phone into her pajama-pants pocket.

Babu was watching TV in the front room. A glass of warm water and an empty egg holder on the end table told Jackie that she had already eaten breakfast.

"Morning, Babu," she said.

Babu didn't hear her. She was busily flipping channels. What did she get out of that TV? She didn't understand English, maybe just a word or two. Maybe the TV just kept her company.

Jackie started a pot of coffee and checked the front porch for the newspaper. Actually, she checked the bottom step because the paper never quite made it to the porch.

Inside, she tossed the newspaper onto the kitchen table and waited at the counter for the coffee pot to make its final gurgle and hiss.

Mom meandered into the kitchen, dazed. She opened the cabinet that held the aspirin and took two. She must have tied one on last night.

"You look like death warmed over," Mom said.

Jackie remembered she didn't wash her face last night before she went to bed. She probably looked like a raccoon. But Mom's eyes were puffy and her face pale. "At least my death look is washable."

She poured a cup of coffee for Mom, who had beaten her to the paper.

"Huh," Mom said. "There was a stabbing last night at the Oktoberfest. You know anything about that?"

"No. Must have happened after we left." She poured herself a cup, added a little cream, and sat down.

Mom spoon-fed her the news. "'Michael Jenson, seventeen, of Colby, stabbed Sean Perry, eighteen, of Ravenwood, on October 7th at the Ravenwood Oktoberfest.'"

"Sean Perry?"

"You know him?"

"Not personally. I mean, we're not friends."

"'Sources say that the confrontation was due to an altercation that had occurred last Friday night at a football game at Ravenwood High.' Did you go to that game?"

"Mom, do I ever?"

She creased her brow. "Darla called this morning, frantic. Said George Hanson hung himself last night. He lives right next door to her. Thank goodness his daughter lives with him. Otherwise, he might have been hanging there for months. He went to school with me and Darla, you know. Was there a full moon?"

"You believe in that?"

"Well, yeah. Statistics show—"

"Actually, they don't. Scientists have proven that the moon's gravitational pull has no effect on humans or animals. Besides, if full moons drove us nuts, wouldn't everyone be affected? Wouldn't there be total mayhem every time there was a full moon?"

"Maybe most of us have better control of our brains."

Jackie's cell phone rang, startling her. It had to be Jason. She fumbled through her pocket for the phone.

"Hey Jas," she said.

"I've been trying to call you all night," he said.

"Sorry. Had my cell on vibrate."

"I've been freaking out."

She swallowed. "Don't worry about it, Jas. It was an emotional evening."

"No, not that. When I came home last night, the police were there. Two squads. My dad went berserk. Slapped my Ma around and shit. I mean, he just lost it. He hadn't done that in... years. Mom wouldn't press charges. She just wanted the police to make him stop. I spent the whole night worrying Dad was going to freak again."

"Jas, I'm sorry. If it ever happens again, you're welcome to come here and spend the night." Why did she say that?

"Thanks, Jackie." Her offer seemed to have perked him up.

"So how's your dad this morning?" she asked, intentionally changing the subject from sleeping arrangements.

"I don't know. I've been keeping my distance. Ma too."

Worried about his mom, Jason passed on their normal weekend routine—caffeine buzz at the coffee shop, snacks and loitering at the pharmacy, and movies at her house. Maybe it was good they didn't see each other. A day or two apart should cool things down between them and get them back to normal; although, she felt uneasy about him being home with his dad.

Maybe Mom was right—a scary thought. Maybe it was a full moon that had caused so many traumatic events to happen in the same night. But then, Zeta had said something about the solar storm affecting homing pigeons. Had the solar storm affected Jason's dad, Michael Jenson, and Mom's former schoolmate?

She made a mental note to do a little research at school Monday, maybe pay a visit to Miss Gut—Miss Guthrie. Knowing half the town was going berserk—especially Jason's dad—was a onetime event would put her mind at ease.

Chapter 5

With her Ouija board tucked under her arm and the hood of her red velvet cape pulled over her head, Trish knocked on Mr. Davis's door.

He answered bare footed, donning a plaid robe. A confused look washed across his face.

"Hey, Mr. D.," she said.

"It's Saturday morning," he said, groggily.

"I know, but it's *uber* important."

"Tutoring hours are weekdays after school."

"It's not about homework. It's about your second-hour lit class. I have a proposition to make."

Chapter 6

Monday morning, Jackie called Jason, but he didn't answer. She couldn't wait to see him in American Lit today. She needed to know that he was okay.

At school, everyone was talking about Sean Perry's stabbing. Nervous energy bombarded off metal lockers and cinderblock walls, and a cyclone of emotions whirled inside her. She headed to class with her books tucked to her chest and her head down, trying not to make eye contact or bump shoulders with anyone.

Speculation buzzed in the halls—speculation that Michael Jenson was in a gang, speculation that his gang member friends were going to come for the rest of the Ravenwood-High football players, speculation that Sean would never be physically well enough to play again, speculation that there was a dark cloud over the school.

Her logic told her two hotheaded guys collided that night, but her body was soaking up the gossip and the negative emotions, making her stomach queasy and her legs fatigued. Still, she found it hard to believe that so many traumatic events could happen on the same night in the same small town. There must be a scientific explanation. She reminded herself to stop by Miss Guthrie's classroom after school.

In her first-hour American History class, minds settled down, tuned out, shut down, or slept. Rebecca fantasized about Nick.

Her aura glowed bright red like a toxic radish. Her emotions exuded passion and lust.

And there was Pete. He had been slighted in every way possible to man. He wore braces and glasses, and he was a scrawny five foot one. He lacked strength, self-esteem, and sometimes, common sense. His days were spent being slammed into lockers, picking up scattered books and papers, and having his butt kicked. He shriveled, mentally and emotionally, in the back row. Although she sat as far away from him as she could, she felt his pain and shame. She wanted to give him a year's membership to a gym, but he probably didn't have the sense or gumption to use it.

His feelings drained and depressed her.

She finished a quiz and turned it over and then folded her arms on top of the blank side of the paper and rested her forehead on her arms.

This was her last year of high school, but then what? Would she go into hiding? And what about college? She definitely wanted to be a photographer, but she'd be limited to studio work. She couldn't possibly shoot weddings and events. Surrounded by emotionally high, energetic people, she'd pass out on the job. Maybe she should just study anthropology and photography and get a job where she could be alone in the Congo like Dian Fossey, socializing with gorillas and taking their pictures.

She imagined portraits of gorilla families hanging on trees.

In American Lit, she fidgeted in her chair as she waited for Jason to walk through the classroom door.

Finally, he entered, his head down, his hair covering his face, and his books hooked loosely in his hand.

"Jas," she said, happy to see him.

"Hey," he said through a veil of hair. He slipped into his chair and slouched.

She leaned forward. "Is everything okay?"

Jason turned and looked at her, his expression sullen. "Yeah,

I'm okay."

He was lying. Something was wrong. Before she could ask him, Mr. Davis started class.

Mr. Davis was overly rumpled. The back of his corduroy jacket heavily wrinkled. His eyes were cupped with purple half rings, and his crow's-feet clawed deeply around his eyes. He started a discussion on "The Yellow Wallpaper" but kept losing focus. His aura was so dark, she couldn't tell if it was a deep purple or just black.

"But what if it *was* the wallpaper that drove her crazy?" Jason asked.

She rolled her eyes, but Mr. Davis narrowed his. He didn't shoot Jason down. Maybe because it was the first time Jason had ever participated in a class discussion. It took Jackie by surprise too.

"So you're saying that the wallpaper had some force, some power to control the mind of the narrator to drive her insane, and not the fact she was suffering from postpartum depression?" Mr. Davis asked.

"Sure," Jason said. "I mean, that's why the author named the story 'The Yellow Wallpaper.' Because it's about the wallpaper."

The class laughed, but Mr. Davis was serious.

"Does anyone else think it's possible for an object to hold some force, to exude an emotional effect on a person?" Mr. Davis asked the class.

"You're joking with us, right?" Sandra said.

Mr. Davis was always so analytical, so scientific in his approach to examining the intent of a literary work. But now he wasn't even quoting from the text to prove his point. He was just throwing out a hypothesis.

"Jackie, what's your take on this?" Mr. Davis asked.

Sandra, who was sitting in the first row, craned her head around and sneered at her.

Oh great. What am I supposed to be, the expert on paranormal activity? Ask Jackie. She's the freak who saw the Virgin at twelve and predicted the fire at Holy Resurrection. She sighed. "The narrator was obviously suffering from postpartum depression. In the text—"

"Fine," Mr. Davis said. "But what I'm asking is, do *you* think an object can affect a person's mood?"

She felt that all eyes were on her, breaths held, while the class waited for Jackie's response—the guru of strange and amazing things. If she said no, they'd think she was lying. If she said yes, they'd confirm their belief that she was some psychic freak.

She closed her book. "This sounds more like a question for Miss Gut—Miss Guthrie. She's the physics expert."

Mr. Davis grimaced. "Thanks. Looks like Jackie's not going to help us out with this one."

Holy shit. Now he's pissed at me. What was his problem? Staying up too late, watching reruns of *The Twilight Zone?*

The bell rang, thank goodness. She gathered her books. Jason looked agitated.

"What?" she asked.

"Nothing," he said. "See you later."

"Wait. I want to ask you—"

He dissolved into the group of students exiting the classroom. By the time she got out the door, Jason was nowhere in sight.

On her way to study hall, she discovered that the bathroom in C-building was out of order. Besides reading the "Out of Order" sign that was written in black marker and taped to the cinderblock wall, she knew it because she felt that something was wrong—like emotionally broken. Curious, she went inside. The janitor was stooped beneath a sink trying to shut the valve off as water flowed over the side of the porcelain bowl.

"You're getting your shoes wet," he said.

The top of the water was level with the toe of her boot.

She wanted to go over to the sink and touch it so she could read it. The room was overflowing with hopelessness, and she wanted to know why, but the janitor kept looking at her like she'd better get the hell out of here—*now.*

"You're going to slip and fall, and it's going to be my fault," he said. "Find a dry bathroom."

She nodded and backed out as she studied the emotions. Had Mr. Davis seen this? Is this why he was so fixated on the question, can objects have an emotional effect on people—drive them crazy? They did on her when they stored people's emotions. But she'd be damned if she was going to tell him this. Let him be pissed.

In study hall, Trish was sulking. With her notebook flipped open, she doodled in pen on the narrow-ruled paper. The page was filled with hexagrams, eyes, and Gothic crosses. Trish was no doubt pissed at Jackie for keeping her away from Jason.

She sat next to her and then flipped open her trig book. "Studying art?" she asked, trying to make conversation.

Trish flipped the pages of her notebook and pulled a sheet of paper out of the pocket.

"Look at this. Mr. Davis gave me a frickin' *C.*"

Trish had Mr. Davis third hour. She, Jason, and Trish had tried to get into the same class when they had registered, but only she and Jason wound up together in second hour. Trish had been a spaz ever since, always putting Mr. Davis down in some way.

"I really got into that story too," Trish said, "and I put a lot of work into this essay."

"Yeah, the whole two paragraphs of it." Jackie tugged the paper from her hands. "Let me see this."

In red pen it read, among other things, *Needs further development.*

"There's more red ink on this page than content," Jackie said.

Trish ripped the paper out of Jackie's hand and wadded it up into a ball. She tossed it four feet to the garbage can by the window. Then, she picked up her pen and traced over and over one of the hexagrams in her notebook. "I hate that class. I hate

Mr. Davis."

"See if you can doodle quietly. I got a trig exam I need to review for."

"I thought you were going to be a photographer. What do you need trig for?"

"In case I fail to make a living at it and have to be an astrophysicist instead."

Trish looked at her like, get serious.

"I don't know," Jackie said. "Somehow I wound up on the college track."

"You don't have to be. Why don't you work as a psychic for the Ravenwood Police Department or something?"

The word *psychic* made her cringe, and Trish knew it. "First of all, the emotions I pick up make me sick, and second, Ravenwood doesn't have any crime."

"It does now."

"And three, I don't want to put Madam Sophie out of business. I caused her enough harm back in the day."

"It's not like it was your fault the town wanted to burn her at the stake."

"No, but I created the whole frenzy."

"That's true. I remember my mom dragging me to church. I never went to church before in my entire life. I had to wear a frickin' dress. It was pink. I still hate you for that."

"Thanks, Trish. From you, I take it as a compliment. At least you're thinking of me."

Trish glared at her. It was more than a pink dress that had her feathers ruffled.

As soon as the final bell rang, Jackie headed toward Ms. Guthrie's classroom. Walking against the flow of traffic, she was knocked about by book bags and elbows and saturated with a hodge-podge of emotions—excitement, worry, passion. At Ms.

Guthrie's classroom door, she closed her eyes and tried to clear her head. Her heart was pounding, and her stomach was queasy.

"Jackie."

She opened her eyes. Ms. Guthrie, dressed in a black smock and black stretch slacks, stared at her with a concerned look on her face. She held a whiteboard eraser as if she'd stopped moving the moment she saw Jackie.

"Hey, Ms. Guthrie," Jackie said, out of breath.

"What brings *you* this way?" Her brow creased. Ms. Guthrie had always worried about her—ever since her freshman year when she saw her transform from a quiet girl with an odd past to a goth girl. She always looked at her with curiosity. Once, out of the blue, Ms. Guthrie told her that there was a scientific explanation to every phenomenon, and if there wasn't, they just haven't found it yet. Jackie knew she was saying there was a scientific explanation as to why she was such a freak.

Jackie entered the classroom, her heart thumping heavily. She covered her chest with her hand, trying to still it.

"Sit down," Ms. Guthrie said.

Jackie slid into the first desk chair she saw and took a moment to catch her breath. There was no use beating around the bush. She had already wasted Ms. Guthrie's time trying to control her emotions, so she got straight to the point. "This is going to sound crazy, but I was wondering, could a solar storm cause a person to commit suicide or act violently?"

Ms. Guthrie stepped closer to the desk. "Are you okay?"

"Yeah, I'm okay. I was just worried about a friend, and Zeta mentioned your lesson on solar storms affecting homing pigeons and stuff."

"Hmm..." Ms. Guthrie studied her. "Well, scientists, like Professor Raymond Wheeler and Alexander Chizhevsky, have correlated major violent events to the sunspot cycle. I'm not sure how accurate their research was." Her eyes beamed at Jackie as if she were reading deeper into her question. "You shouldn't overlook the deeper problems of what may cause a person to do those things."

"I know. And normally, I wouldn't think anything of it. But, it's just that a lot of crazy things happened last night."

Her eyes softened, creased with pity. "I'm going to write down a few topics for you to research. You may find the answers to what you're looking for."

Ms. Guthrie scribbled onto a green Post-it and handed it to her. "You're a good person, Jackie."

"Thanks, Ms. Guthrie. It means a lot."

In the hallway, she read the Post-it, which she had stuck on the tip of her index finger. It read, "Electromagnetic effects on the pineal gland" and "Mirror neurons." She knew what mirror neurons were. They were the neurons in the brain that allowed people to feel empathy. Ms. Guthrie must have thought that she was the friend in trouble.

Chapter 7

Babu rolled dough for piroshki, her hands pressed flat against the wooden roller handles. Flour was sprinkled on the counter, the edge of the counter, the cabinet door, and Babu's toes, which were poking out from her slippers.

Babu was eighty-eight years old and still insisted on cooking. Jackie couldn't blame her. What else did she have to do? Sit around and wait to die? But Mom was afraid she was going to catch her sleeve on a lit burner and burn the house down.

Stephanie Yarrow, the housekeeper at Holy Resurrection, had caught her sleeve on a lit candle in front of the Virgin of Vladimir. It happened on a rainy, Saturday morning two weeks after Jackie had the vision. The fire burned the iconostasis, it burned the Virgin in the apse, and it burned Stephanie beyond recognition.

Her stomach shrank. "Let me," she said to Babu, and gently placed her hands on top of hers. Babu's hands were warm. Boney. Her light flowed from her hands into Jackie's, making Jackie's stomach muscles relax.

Babu slipped her hands from beneath hers. Jackie pressed her palms against the wooden handles and rolled forward, backward, to the sides. The edges of the dough stretched and retracted with each pass of the roller.

Babu babbled in Russian as she mixed fried onions and mushrooms into day-old mashed potatoes.

When Jackie finished rolling, she cut circles in the dough and placed them on a baking sheet. Babu spooned filling onto each circle, and Jackie folded them over and pinched the edges together. She loved cooking with Babu.

Mom hadn't come home from work yet. She was already an hour late. So, since she and Babu needed their strength, as soon as the piroshki were done baking, they went ahead and ate.

Jackie was washing dishes when Mom walked in. Mom had this spacey expression on her face and didn't seem to notice that Jackie was cleaning up dinner dishes and that *she* was late.

"Where've you been?" Jackie asked, trying to cut Mom's fog.

"Me?"

"Well, yeah. You're the only other person in this room."

She hung her coat on a hook and then looked at Jackie like she was contemplating whether or not to tell her why she was late. Finally, she threw up her hands and spouted, "I went to see Madam Sophie."

Jackie's mouth dropped open. She felt betrayed and at the same time confused. Mom was one of those who signed a petition against Madam Sophie, who picketed in front of her place of business. "Did she recognize you?"

"If she did, she's forgiven me. She was overly generous and kind."

Jackie wiped a soapy arm across her forehead. As the bubbles on her skin popped, she imagined Madam Sophie in her head, sucking out her thoughts.

Mom opened the cabinet door. "Where's my glass?"

"In the rack, drying."

Mom ripped two paper towels from the roll and dried the king-sized rock glass she had gotten from a Florida vacation.

"So what'd she tell you?" Jackie asked. "Some tall, dark, handsome guy is going to sweep you off your feet and make your life all better?"

"No," she snapped, as if pissed that she had guessed it.

"So what possessed you to go?"

She shrugged. "I don't know. Things around town have gotten kind of freaky. Maybe I just wanted to know if anything terrible was going to happen to me. It's scary when you see your peers dropping dead around you. It makes you realize how mortal you are."

"Mom, it was just one peer, and he didn't just drop dead. He killed himself."

"Still, it's freaky."

She hosed the inside of the pot with scalding water and watched the opaque, pink skim of soap spread from the pot's surface and turn it to steely blue. Mom was always so extreme. Once she got a notion in her head, she obsessed with it. Like the time the residents of Ravenwood were signing petitions against Madam Sophie, trying to run her out of town. Jackie didn't know why Mom jumped on that bandwagon. Mom threw her horoscope and yoga books away. Jackie wondered what had caused this obsessive swing now. Her intuition told her it was something deeper than George Hanson hanging himself.

"So what did Madam Sophie say?"

"Well, really, it was kind of weird. Her hands locked on mine, and it felt like she was reading more than she told me because she was quiet for the longest time."

"So what'd she tell you?"

"Oh, you know, the usual. That I'd live to a ripe old age."

She rolled her eyes. "How corny. There's a fifty-fifty chance of that. If I had to guess, I'd go the other way on that one. All I have to do is count empty gin bottles."

"She said other stuff too, but it's kind of personal."

"Personal?" Jackie laughed.

Mom will pop, eventually. She always did, sometimes telling Jackie more than she cared to hear.

"Hungry?"

Mom filled her rock glass with crushed ice and then poured

it full of gin. "Not right now."

"How old did she say you were going to live to?" she rinsed the sudsy plates.

Mom sipped her martini and then leaned against the kitchen counter, cupping the icy glass in her hands. "She asked about you."

Jackie released the handle on the hose. The spray of water abruptly cut off.

"She wanted to know what you were doing with your gift," Mom said.

"Did you tell her I returned it?"

"I didn't know what to tell her. You never talk to me. I mean, really talk to me. I don't know what's going on inside your head."

"Good." She really didn't mean it as cruelly as it sounded. She just didn't want Mom wrapped up in her problems, obsessing over her. She destroyed Mom's marriage with Dad. She didn't want to ruin Mom's life anymore. "Mom, I think it's really neat you went to a fortune-teller. I mean, I want you to be happy. To do whatever makes you happy. Even if my friends think you *are* crazy."

Her eyes creased with dread.

"Mom, I was just kidding. They never said anything about you. Well, Zeta did say that she wished when she's your age,"— actually she had used the word *old*, but Mom didn't need that piece of information—"that she'll act as young as you."

Mom's eyes grew wide with delight. "She did?"

Jackie nodded and left Mom on that note to research electromagnetic effects on the pineal gland. From what she read, she learned that electromagnetism can affect the pineal gland, which in turn affects the circadian production rhythm of melatonin. In short, a decreased level of melatonin could cause, among other things, loss of sleep, depression, and bipolar disorder.

She came to the conclusion that Jason's dad going berserk

could or could not have been caused by the solar storm. In fact, all the violent events occurring in the same night could have just been a coincidence, and maybe Jason's dad just happened to return to his old ways of being an abusive dickhead.

Worried even more about Jason, she called him and let the phone ring until the call cut out. It occurred to her that maybe Jason's dad was being a dick and had taken away Jason's phone. She texted him just in case he didn't.

Miss you. Please call.

Chapter 8

Jackie spent the evening with Babu doing needlepoint. Her light had already washed the negative emotions away and eased Jackie's worry over Jason.

Babu patted Jackie's thigh and smiled. *"Ochen' khorosho."*

This, Jackie knew, meant very good. "Thanks, Babu."

The doorbell rang. The loud and boisterous sound of the bell annihilated the silence, splintered the peace. Jackie wove her needle through the canvas squares and set the tiny canvas on the couch.

Through the etched glass of the door window, all she could make out were fragments of someone dressed in dark clothing. Every time she moved her head to get a better look, the fragments shifted, and she couldn't assemble the whole person. Whoever it was, looked too tall to be Jason.

She unlocked the door, but left the chain connected. Her eyes locked on the black cassock. Tiny pins prickled her nerves, and perspiration rose beneath her eyes.

"Good evening," said the young man dressed like a priest. His eyes were deep-set and downturned, and his cheeks were flushed from the cool evening air. He couldn't have been older than twenty-five. "I am David Davidovich." His accent was foreign. Russian?

She studied his cassock and wondered why he wasn't addressing himself as Father.

He smoothed down the breast of his garment. "You are confused," he said. "I am a seminarian, not an ordained priest." The sides of his mouth dimpled when he spoke. "We must wear a cassock when on official business."

Official business? What could be official about this visit? Had the church finally come to burn her at the stake? She squeezed the door handle.

"Please." He passed her a business card through the crack.

She glanced at the card and read, "Holy Resurrection Russian Orthodox Church." Her muscles hardened.

He wrinkled his nose and brushed his fingers through his closely-clipped sandy-colored hair. "I am looking for Jackie Turov."

"She's not home." She wanted to shut the door in his face, but he was looking at her with those dreamy, mesmerizing eyes. She pressed her fingers to the business card. She was having a hard time reading him. She only got a feeling of him being hung in a balance, but maybe that was her.

"Do you know when she will be home?"

Hmm... He doesn't know who I am. "She works late at the soup kitchen," she lied, figuring it was what he'd like to hear about someone who supposedly saw the Virgin.

"It is important she contact me."

"Why?"

"I would rather tell her myself. She would understand. You will give her my card, yes?"

"Yeah. Sure."

"I am sorry. I did not ask your name."

"Fiona," she spouted. "Jackie's evil twin." She raised the corner of her mouth in a sinister smile.

He smiled humbly and nodded. "Thank you, Fiona. May the blessing and the mercy of the Lord be with you."

"And with your spirit," she automatically said and quickly closed the door. Heat rushed to her cheeks. Her heart raced.

"Dork! Why did I say that?"

Through the front room window, she watched him put on his helmet and mount his motorcycle.

"*Kto byl?*" Babu asked.

"It's no one Babu. He had the wrong house."

In the kitchen, Jackie stepped on the garbage can pedal and held David's business card above the opened can, but for some reason she couldn't let go. She took her foot off the pedal. The garbage can lid snapped shut. She read David's name, which was written in blue ink. There was a line through Father Dmitriev's name. She wished it meant that Father Dmitriev was no longer the rector of Holy Resurrection, but she knew it most likely meant the church was saving money on new business cards. She stuffed the card in her jeans pocket and rejoined Babu in the front room. As she sat down, the business card bent in her front pocket.

She picked up where she left off on her needlepoint. Her heartbeat had slowed to a normal pace, but she couldn't concentrate. What did David Davidovich want? What would the church want with her? To the congregation, she was just a vague memory, "that girl" who had "the vision," who slipped away from God and into the folds of society. She didn't think any of them could pick her out in a crowd. With that thought, she relaxed. But soon, the curiosity of why David Davidovich was looking for her ate at her again. Was there an investigation or something?

The thought of going back to Holy Resurrection Church or having any kind of connection with it made her stomach sour. Her fingers trembled so much, she couldn't get the needle through the tiny holes in the canvas. She dropped the needlework to her lap and sighed.

Babu looked worried, like she sensed something was wrong. "*Chto ne tak?*"

"I don't feel well, Babu. I'm going to go lay down." She tilted her head onto pillowed hands so Babu would understand.

Babu shooed her with a flick of her hand. "*Idi, idi.*"

Wanting to wash away the dread that had saturated her, she filled the claw-foot tub with hot water and immersed herself in its warmth. Cold porcelain cooled her neck, and the water gently rocked her shoulders. She closed her eyes and listened to the slow rhythm of water dripping from the spout.

Her thoughts drifted to when Father Dmitriev had tried to cleanse her with holy water. He had stood before her in front of the iconostasis with an open prayer book in his hand. "Did the vision come from God or Satan?"

She froze. Grandma warned her that whatever Father told her to do, to go along with the program. Jackie considered telling Father what he wanted to hear as going along with it.

"From God," she said. "I mean, from the Virgin. She showed me the fire." She lowered her head. Her thoughts and lies were as entangled as the pattern of vines in the Oriental carpet beneath her feet. She knew in her heart that what she saw in the church wasn't a heavenly vision. The Virgin didn't appear in a bright light before her. She didn't appear at all. There were no cherubs with trumpets or holy beings in white light.

Father Dmitriev leaned forward, lifted her chin, and pinned his eyes on her. "What else did you see?"

Her knees trembled. "Nothing. Just the flames burning the iconostasis."

His brow lifted. "Even the devil can appear as an angel."

"The girl said it was from God," Grandma snapped.

It surprised her that Grandma would speak to Father that way.

Father locked his hand around Jackie's wrist, his stern eyes searing whatever was left of her innocence. Her wrist grew hot. She tried to free herself from his grip, but his fingers were strong.

"You know it's against the law of God to divine. Have you been playing with a Ouija board or tarot cards or having séances?"

She shook her head. His accusations did not sting as hot as his hand on her wrist. It hurt like sitting on a hot car seat in her shorts. She gritted her teeth to keep from screaming and tried to pull her arm away, but Father wouldn't let go.

Her sleeve caught fire. The fabric curled and dropped like hot embers to her feet. She took it as a sign that she was going to burn in hell. She screamed and twisted her arm, finally freeing herself.

Babu wrapped her arms around her, and the burning stopped.

Father Dmitriev raised the open book. "O God of gods and Lord of lords," he read. "Grant that this my exorcism being performed in Your awesome name, be terrible to the Master of evil and to all his minions who had fallen with him from the height of brightness."

He picked up a sprinkler, and, whipping it forward, he hurled a spray of holy water at her head.

She raised her hands in front of her face to block the spray, but some of it hit her forehead and dripped down her nose.

"Drive him into banishment, commanding him to depart hence, so that no harm might be worked against Your sealed Image." He raised his arm.

She shielded her face. Her hands and arms were wetted this time.

"And, as You have commanded, let those who are sealed receive the strength to tread upon serpents and scorpions, and upon all power of the Enemy. For manifested, hymned, and glorified with fear, by everything that has breath is Your most holy Name: of the Father, and of the Son, and of the Holy Spirit, now and ever and into ages of ages. Amen."

The "Amen" lulled her into a false sense of security, and she didn't raise her arms. Father whipped the holy water at her, hitting her in the eyes. The water rolled down her face like tears, and a drop had gotten into her right eye, blurring her vision. She rubbed her eye and wiped her arm across her face to dry it.

A heavy hand on her shoulder startled her. She uncovered her eyes to see his dark beard and probing eyes close to her face.

He leaned closer to whisper into her ear. "You'll do well, my child, to keep silent, lest God cast your soul into the fires of hell," he whispered.

She believed that even Father Dmitriev had the power to cast her soul into hell.

With her lips pressed shut, she nodded. Her body had knotted up tighter than a bead on a prayer rope. She had wanted to go home and never ever come back to church again, for fear she'd evoke the wrath of God and the wrath of Father Dmitriev.

Jackie slid down in the tub until the water's surface tickled her nose, and she took a deep breath and slipped under the water. Silence was magnified. It quieted her memories, calmed her emotions. She wanted to stay there forever, immersed in silence, but her lungs pushed outward, begging for air. She tried to ignore their plea, but they pressed hard against her chest.

Just as she couldn't hold her breath any longer, she emerged from the water. Gasping for air, she sucked in the water around her lips and nostrils and coughed until her mouth and throat went dry. With her hands, she squeegeed the water from her face. She let out a hard, final cough and stood up, her heart pounding.

She patted her face dry with a white, fluffy bath towel and put on her black pajamas. Besides being extremely comfortable, they made her feel invisible.

In bed, she pulled the covers to her nose. *I'll never call you, David Davidovich. As far as I'm concerned, the Jackie you are looking for doesn't exist.*

Chapter 9

The next day in American Lit, Jason didn't show. Jackie could see him being sick, but why didn't he call? He always called if he wasn't going to be at school.

At lunch, she called him, but he didn't answer. For the rest of the school day, she watched the clock. At the end of the day, she practically ran home to get to her car, and then she drove to Jason's. His truck was parked in front of his dad's. Wet leaves plastered the hood and windshield as if his vehicle hadn't moved in days.

On the stairs, she caught herself doing the Jason thing, taking one step at a time. She poked the doorbell button. A timbre as rich as a pipe organ resounded through the house. A minute passed, but no one answered.

Finally, the door opened. Jason's dad was in a pair of gray sweat pants and a white T-shirt. A half inch of stubble covered his face. His cheeks were sunken, and his eyes bloodshot like he hadn't slept in days. Shouldn't he be at work? What? Was the whole family on a quarantine holiday?

"Is Jas here?" she asked.

He stared at her and then craned his head to the side. "Jason," he yelled and walked away, leaving her outside.

After about five minutes, Jason came to the door, his hair draped over the side of his face. For some reason, he looked different. He had parted his hair in the other direction.

"Hi," he said, sleepily.

"Hey, Jas. You guys don't have the flu or anything, do you?"

"No," he said, the one eye she could see, lowered. Of all the times she wanted Jason to look her in the eyes it was now.

"Can I come in?"

"Yeah, sure," he said in a low voice. "Let's go to my room. It's... safer."

Safer? What the heck was going on?

She followed him, even though she knew he wasn't allowed to have girls in his room. How safe was it going to be when his mom and dad found out?

Jason closed the bedroom door and then plopped down on his bed. Elbows on his spread knees, his chin tucked to his neck.

She plopped down beside him. "Are you mad at me?"

Jason shook his head.

Why wouldn't he look at her? He was hurting. She felt it. Her throat tightened, and her chest became sore, like she had been crying for hours. She touched his face.

He jerked his head away. "Don't."

She managed to see a tinge of purple through some of the parted strands of hair.

Her cheek stung and then burned as if someone slapped it. "Who did this to you?" she asked, even though she knew the answer.

Jason was silent.

She reached out again to part the veil of hair covering his eye, but he pushed her hand away.

"I'm all right," he snapped.

A faint nervous energy occupied the room. "What's going on?"

"My dad's not feeling good lately."

"You know, this is child abuse."

He dropped his head into his hands. "He just lost it for a second. That's all. Don't tell anybody. Okay? The school thinks I got the flu."

"You can't let your dad abuse you like this. You need to report him." Or she would.

Jason's dad's voice rose from downstairs. "Don't start," he yelled.

A weak, trembling voice flailed in the background—Jason's mom.

The nervous energy in the room intensified. Her stomach quivered. "It's not safe here, Jas. You have to get help or get out."

Jason's face was as white as his socks. "If I told anyone, he'd kill me. He'd hurt Mom too."

"Come home with me then. You can sleep over until this thing cools."

"There's no way—"

"You can't leave the house?"

He shrugged. "I didn't ask, but he's on my ass about everything. And there's no way he's going to let me spend the night."

"Tell him we have to work on a project for school. Then later, at my house, we can make up some excuse why you can't come home. My mom will vouch for us. I know she will. She doesn't think much of your—" She decided not to go there. Jason didn't need to develop any more of an inferiority complex because of his family.

Jason grimaced. Too late. He knew where she was going with that.

"He'll know I'm lying," he said.

"Then I'll lie. I'm sure I'll be good at it," she muttered. "You got to get out of here." She stood up. "Pack your things."

He jumped up. "No, Jackie. Don't."

"Jason, you can't—"

"What about Mom?"

"She's a big girl. She can protect herself."

She left Jason standing in protest, and she followed the

sound of the TV, which was coming from below.

In the basement, violent, nervous energy crackled. Jason's dad was sitting in a recliner, his fingers burrowing into the worn fabric of the chair's arms, staring at the flat-screen TV by the fireplace.

Her stomach was jumping like it wanted to get the hell out of there. The hair on her arms rose.

What if he went ballistic on her?

She'd call the police. Press charges.

Her hands locked into fists.

She hoped he'd snap.

He was staring at the TV, dazed, like he wasn't really watching it.

"Mr. C.?" she said to get his attention.

He slowly turned his head to look at her. She wondered what he was thinking. He hated her, she knew it. He thought she was a fake, a slut, pond scum. He had never liked her. He was going to like her even less now. "Would it be all right if Jason came over my house?" Her voice trembled. "We need to get moving on a project that's due, like, Monday. We've kinda been putting it off, so we don't have much time."

"Jason's not leaving this house. He's got chores to do."

"Yeah, but, he's a student too. He can't keep missing school. I can help him catch up with his homework."

"You deaf?" he bellowed.

Jason was right. He wasn't going to let him leave the house.

She walked away, but stopped at the foot of the stairs. What if he took his anger about her asking out on Jason? What if, when she left, he beat the holy hell out of him? She couldn't let that happen. She'd die if something terrible like that happened to Jason, especially if it was her fault.

She turned around and headed back to Mr. C., her heart pounding. Nearest him, the violent energy was strongest. What little courage she had became brazen. "You're not keeping Jason here so you can abuse him," she spouted. "I know what you did. If Jason and Mrs. C. won't report you, I will. Jason's coming home with me. You've got three days to get your act together." *Wow. Go, Jackie.*

He flew up and swung an open hand at her.

She ducked and then straightened up.

Doh! She missed her opportunity. *Stand up to him. Let him hit you. You can call the police right now and get him the hell out of here.*

She looked him straight in the eyes, trying not to blink.

His fingers curled into a fist.

"Do it," she said.

His shoulder and arm made small jerky movements as if he was caught between restraint and the forces of kinetic energy.

She met him eyeball to eyeball. "Do it." There was no calling bluff because she wasn't bluffing. "Come on, Mr. C. Show me what you got."

His fist slowly unfolded, finger by finger as if he was taking great effort to do so. He stood there, tight-shouldered, his open hand slightly curved, his fingers rigid, the vein near his wrist jumping.

"Three days," she said.

If looks could kill, she would have been dead right then.

With an open hand and a sour look on his face, he nodded.

She exhaled, which surprised her because she didn't recall breathing at all during the whole ordeal.

Walking toward the stairs, she could feel his eyes boring holes in her back. "Jas," she yelled as she ran up.

Jason was at the top, hiding behind the partially-closed basement door.

"Let's get out of here," she said.

Jason stared at her wide-eyed. "You stood up to him?"

"Yeah. I can't believe it myself."

Chapter 10

It didn't take much of an argument to convince Mom to let Jason spend the night. At first, Jackie told her that Jason needed to stay so she could help him catch up with homework. But when Mom, having suspicions about what they really intended to do, didn't buy it, she told Mom the truth, that Mr. C. was abusing Jason and his mother. Something in Mom clicked. She went to school with Mr. C. She knew what a hothead—not the word she used—he could be. If there was ever a fight at school, Mr. C. was involved. He had even beaten up a boyfriend of hers. This last note was TMI for Jackie, but she was glad Mom finally agreed.

Mom wasn't much of a homemaker. She was more of a slapdash kind of housekeeper, but she had actually made the effort to wipe the dust off the dresser and nightstands in the spare bedroom and started the space heater. Jackie could only imagine how cold and dusty those sheets were, but maybe Jason would be too depressed to notice.

Babu was in the front room watching *Wheel of Fortune* while Jackie sat with Jason at the dining room table and helped him catch up in American Lit. In the last two days, while Jason was absent, Mr. Davis had jumped from the Realistic Period to Transcendentalism, mixing things up a bit.

"You're supposed to have read the excerpt from *Walden* and write an essay on how Thoreau conveys the movement of Transcendentalism," she said to Jason.

"Trans what?" Jason asked.

"Transcendentalism. It was an artistic movement that diverged from Romanticism. Its followers believed a person can find truth within themselves instead of from God."

"Sounds sacrilegious."

"Sounds like inner happiness."

"So were they doing yoga and shit?"

She smiled deviously. "Actually, they were watching naked, young men bathe in ponds. Like Walt Whitman... *The Leaves of Grass?*"

Jason blushed and dropped his eyes toward his open book.

The doorbell rang, startling her. "I'll get it."

Babu lowered the volume on the TV, which reminded Jackie that, this Christmas, she planned to get Babu the wireless headphone set so she could listen in private.

Jackie peeped through the etched glass of the front door window and saw the same dark fragments she saw the other day. Great. She would have to lie again. She opened the door, hesitantly.

David Davidovich smiled half-heartedly, dimpling only one corner of his mouth, as if he knew he wasn't welcome. "I was passing your house."

She rolled her eyes.

"*Da,*" he said. "I went little out of the way. Thought I would check if Jackie was home. She did not call. You gave her my message? Yes?"

"Yes, she got the message, and no, she's not home."

"Please. It is very important I talk to her. All I want is that she come to church and look at something. Give her—uh—impression."

"Impression? Sounds like a job for Madam Sophie."

He smiled, sheepishly. "Madam Sophie is fortune-teller, which is against the teachings of church. You are—"

Busted!

"I mean," he said, "Jackie is special because her vision came from Holy Mother. Maybe Holy Mother can help her again?"

She scrunched her shoulders.

"For the church?" he added.

"Okay. I confess. I'm Jackie."

He smiled. "So you will come?"

"No."

His smile faded, and a pensive look washed over his face. "I hear it has been a long time since you came to church."

"What exactly would I be giving my impression of?"

"You have to see for yourself."

"In the church?"

"Yes."

"No. Can't. Sorry."

"Please, Jackie."

"No. Absolutely not. I have stuff to do. So, if you don't mind." She closed the door slowly, hoping he'd go so she wouldn't have to close it in his face.

He pressed his hand against the closing door. "All right, but please, tell me Jackie, why the change of heart? I do not understand."

For some reason, her name coming from his mouth made her heart pound. The sound of it was—too personal. Yes, he was just getting too personal. He was stepping on sensitive territory here. How dare he come to her door and confront her about her spirituality? Who did he think he was? A Jehovah's Witness or some Bible-thumping Baptist? She opened the door wide enough to see his face and looked him in the eyes. "It's really none of your business."

"Please."

"I'm sorry. I can't. Bye." She closed the door and hooked the chain. Through the etched glass, she watched the dark mass of him disappear down the stairs. She felt horrible. She didn't like hurting people.

"*Kto byl?*" Babu asked.

"Jehovah's Witness." She rejoined Jason at the dining room table and slid her trig book in front of her.

"Was that guy a priest?" Jason asked.

"Seminarian." She flipped open her textbook to the page marked with a torn piece of loose-leaf paper.

"What did he want you to come to church for?"

"He wanted my impression of something. So, did you read *Walden?*"

"I'm not a fast reader."

"Well, read it. I'll work on my trig homework. When you're done, I'll help you plan your essay."

Jason leaned into his American Literature anthology and rolled the outer corner with his fingers, curling the pages. "So why don't you go?"

"Just forget it, okay?"

"Why are you so put off from church? Not that I want to go or anything, but you—I mean—shit, if I saw the Virgin Mary, or even an angel, I'd probably commit to celibacy."

"You kind of are celibate," she said, hoping to put an end to this conversation.

He wrinkled the corner of his mouth. "Not intentionally."

Ignoring him, she opened her trig book and searched for her homework exercises. Jason's gaze was on her. She felt him staring.

"What?" she said.

His innocent eyes stared into hers. He sucked in a breath and closed his eyes. "I love you, Jackie."

The words hit her like a torpedo, totally knocking her off guard. She swallowed. "I... I care about you too."

He grimaced.

"I don't know what else to say. You kind of took me by surprise."

He slouched over his book and cupped his hand over his

bruised cheek.

Ugh. Not what he wanted to hear. "Where is this coming from?" Wrong words. She burrowed her forehead into her hand. "It's just that I never thought of us... uh... like, you know, boyfriend and girlfriend."

"Whatever," he said.

Now you did it. You hurt him again. "It's not you. It's me."

"S'okay."

She tried to get her mind on her homework, but the mood was awkward.

"Jason," she said.

He didn't look up.

Great. He'll sulk all night, like Trish. She couldn't handle that emotionally; it would make her sick. She wondered how she could get him back from the dark, sullen corner inside himself.

She opened up to the energy around him. She got inside his head and put herself in his place. Her intuition told her he needed to know that she was vulnerable too. She needed to tell him something embarrassing that happened to her. Jeez, where to start? He knew she was teased in junior high for wearing Orthodox clothes. He went to the same school. He also knew about the vigils held on her front lawn and how people used to grab her hands or her clothes just so she would bless them. She had talked about that a zillion times with him. Although, he never ever got why that bothered her. He knew picking up everyone's emotions and experiencing their maladies made her sick, but he didn't know that what really bothered her was deeper than that. She hadn't told a soul. If she told him, maybe he would understand why she was so "put off" with church. And maybe he'd quit sulking.

Jason was staring at his book and mutilating the corners. It didn't look like he was reading because his eyes weren't moving. They had been fixated on the same spot for the past two minutes.

She took a deep breath. "Jas? There's something I need to tell you."

His eyes shifted toward her.

"You have to promise you won't tell anyone. Not a soul. Not even Trish or Zeta."

"Promise," he said, sullenly.

"You don't sound convincing."

"I'm not sure I want to hear it."

"It's nothing to do with you. It's me. It's something I did a long time ago. I haven't told anyone, but I think it'll help you understand where I'm coming from. You have to promise not to tell anyone because what I did was really bad."

"You did something really bad? That's hard to believe."

"Promise?"

"Yeah, I promise."

She tapped her pen against the dining room table.

"What?" Jason asked.

She clenched the pen with both hands. "I lied. I lied about seeing the Virgin."

Jason's mouth dropped open. "You're not psychic?"

"That's not what I'm talking about. I mean, I'm not all holy like everyone thought I was. I didn't see the Virgin. I made it up so Father Dmitriev wouldn't think I was possessed and excommunicate Babu, Grandma, and me."

"But, you are psychic? You predicted the fire, didn't you?"

"I saw the fire, but I really didn't know what it meant. I was scared to death. There I was, screaming about a fire that no one else could see, and Father D. accuses me of being possessed. The best I could do was say the Virgin gave me a sign that the church was going to catch fire. But then, two weeks later, it did, and Stephanie died. And everyone thought I was someone special, when all I am is a liar."

"So what? What's it matter how the vision came to you? You saw it. That's what matters."

"Because I lied." She couldn't believe he wasn't getting this.

"And I had this weird experience in a church. I spat the Holy Eucharist to the floor, for goodness sake. I disrupted the liturgy, and then I defrauded everyone. The way I look at it, I'm pretty much going to hell in a hand basket."

"You're such an ass," Jason said. "It makes you special. It makes you gifted. Why do you keep shrugging that off? If I had that ability, my dad wouldn't catch me by surprise and back hand me."

She couldn't believe it. She had risked her integrity, and he brushed it off. "Jason. You don't need this so-called gift to avert your father's anger. You know what you have to do. And I know what I have to do. I gave him three days to go for help. If he doesn't get his act together, I'm turning him in."

"You can't. You promised."

"Sometimes, I think you like being hurt." Why did she say that? Another observation from her great ability?

Jason stuffed his book into his backpack.

"I didn't mean it like that."

"I don't need your sympathy or your confessions to make me feel better." He stood up, hooked a backpack strap over his shoulder, and headed to the front door.

She followed him. "Where're you going?"

"Home." He flung open the front door and walked out into the cold, dark evening.

"Jas, I'm sorry. I didn't mean..."

He awkwardly descended the steps, one foot at a time but faster than usual.

"If he hurts you, call me," she said.

She realized he had a long walk home, so she grabbed her trench coat, satchel, and keys. By the time she started the car and drove off to look for him, Jason was no longer on this block or the next.

She drove slowly down Main Street, but she didn't see him there either. Doubling back down the side streets, she saw him—at Trish's door.

In the middle of the night, Jackie awoke in a cold sweat from a dream about Holy Resurrection. In the dream, she was standing in front of the congregation, lying to them about her vision.

She couldn't fall back to sleep. Her chest ached, and her thoughts shifted to Jason and Trish. A scene played in her head: Trish comforting Jason, wrapping her arms around him. An innocent kiss on his forehead, his cheek, and then near his mouth.

Trish made out with him. Jackie felt it in her soul.

Why was she so jealous? Jason was her best friend. He should be allowed to have a romantic relationship with anyone he wanted.

But what if she lost him for good?

She planned to touch his shoulder tomorrow in American Lit. Then, she'd know if something happened between him and Trish and if Trish was what he wanted. She'd know, too, if she and Jason could still be friends.

Chapter 11

Practically the whole cheerleading squad, including Sandra, was gathered by Sean Perry's black Pontiac in the school parking lot. Sean unzipped his varsity jacket and raised his jersey to show his scar from the Oktoberfest stabbing. The cheerleaders gasped with rapture.

Give me a break, Jackie thought. Never be well again? He looked better than ever, and he was eating this shit up.

Entering American Lit, she paused by Jason's desk. A heavy application of eyeliner was smeared under his eyes to hide his black eye, no doubt. At this moment, she didn't care what went on between him and Trish, she just wanted to know that they were still friends.

"Jas," she said.

He leaned forward and rested his forehead on his folded arms.

With a ton of weight crushing her chest, she slowly reached for him. He felt miles away. When she was an inch from touching his shoulder, Mr. Davis said, "Ms. Turov, do you mind? I'd like to start class now."

She retracted her hand, tears stinging her eyes.

Mr. Davis looked haggard again, and if she remembered correctly, he was wearing the same shirt he wore yesterday.

She tuned Mr. Davis out for the rest of class. Her focus was on Jason. As she fought back tears, she told herself that this day was bound to come, that he would find himself a real girlfriend. She didn't expect things to end badly between them, though. She really screwed up.

In study hall, she sat down next to Trish, but not too close. Jackie didn't want to know what went on between Trish and Jason. She had seen enough through her own imaginings.

Trish was reading a romance novel. She looked at Jackie with narrow, heavily mascaraed eyes and then redirected her gaze to her book.

There was no use in her and Trish not being friends. Trish won fair and square. "Did you do the Transcendentalist assignment?" Jackie asked.

Trish's blood-red lips puckered.

"The American Lit assignment, did you do it?"

"What? Are you my mother?" She raised the paperback close to her face and continued to read.

"I just asked. I—Are you mad at me too?"

Trish looked at her like she should know.

"What did Jason tell you?"

"He said you're the coldest, shut-off bitch he's ever known." The corner of her mouth turned upward in a sinister smile.

"Those don't sound like Jason's words."

"I paraphrased."

Okay, you won, Jackie thought. She grimaced and then opened her notebook and trig book and started the exercises on page one hundred and thirty, but she couldn't concentrate. Her mind kept going over her conversation with Jason. She was honest about what she had said. Didn't honesty count for anything?

At the lockers, Trish was still gloating.

Zeta pressed her cheek to the side of the open locker door. "What's with her?" she whispered to Jackie. "She's been acting really strange lately. Like, psycho strange."

Jackie didn't want to think about it anymore. The whole situation was making her sick. "Ask her yourself."

Zeta shut her locker and turned to Trish. "Hey, Trish. What's up?"

"Ask Jackie," Trish said.

"I just set Jason straight on what I thought about him," Jackie said to Zeta.

"Ha," Trish spouted. "That he likes to be hurt?" Her eyebrows arched in delight.

Zeta stepped back and leaned against her locker.

"I didn't mean to hurt him by telling him he likes to get hurt," Jackie said. "I was simply stating what I've observed."

"Oh, Ms. Observation. Ms. Don't-Touch-Me," Trish said, moving her hands around for special effect, like a wizard casting a spell. "Ms. Stay-Away-From-Me. Ms. I'm-Too-Sensitive-To-Be-Around-People." Her aura was black, and a devilish glow burned in her eyes. The energy coming from her scared the hell out of Jackie.

Students at their lockers turned around to look at them. Others passing through the hall stopped and watched. Trish was drawing a crowd.

"You're right," Jackie said. "I shouldn't have said anything." She slammed her locker door shut. She was hoping that this would end their little spat and the crowd would clear. But when she turned to head to class, she was blocked by a wall of students who didn't look like they were ready to move.

"You're nothing but a fake," Trish shouted.

Jackie's heart stopped, and the blood in her face plunged to her feet.

"She lied," Trish said. "She never saw the Virgin."

Jason told.

Everyone was staring at Jackie. Their poisonous energy was making her sick. She needed to get out of there.

She shoved through the crowd. As she brushed against rigid

bodies, hostile energy stung her shoulders. In the back of the crowd, she bumped into Sandra. Her aura was black, too, and her venomous eyes locked onto hers.

"Freak," she hissed.

Sandra's toxic emotions surged through Jackie's nervous system, making her heart race. She felt like heaving. She ran to the C-building bathroom, but there was a yellow ribbon stretched across the entrance and a paper sign taped to the wall reading, "Out of Order."

She touched the cinder block doorframe. It was icy cold. Impressions of sadness and lost hope soaked into her hand and seeped through her body, adding to the poisonous energy. Now, she was really going to puke.

She tore the ribbon and splashed through water. The bathroom was cast in a blue hue, even though the walls were painted red. She rushed to the first stall and dropped to her knees. She held on to the cold porcelain as her jeans soaked up water, and she choked on dry heaves. Her body shook violently. She wanted to lie down, but everything was wet.

She was going to die. She had to get out of here. Go to the nurse's office.

With her hands on the toilet bowl rim, she pushed herself up, but her knees were so weak, they folded, and she collapsed into water.

I'll never get out of here.

Blood trickled from her wrists. *How did I...? It's a vision.* She squeezed her eyes shut. "Please, go away," she whispered.

When she opened her eyes, her jeans and the water were crimson, and her wrists bloodied. She leveraged her arm against the toilet paper dispenser and grabbed the edge of the stall to lift herself up. Blood ran down her arm and dripped from her elbow. With her knees trembling, she held onto the top of the stall wall for support and pushed open the door. Just as she let go of the wall and stepped out, her knees gave way. The room went black.

Chapter 12

Jackie was lying on a slab—no, a cot, a thin cotton blanket over her. Her clothes were wet and cold. A poster of the respiratory system hung on the wall above a metal desk. She was in the nurse's office. How did she get here?

"Finally," Nurse Seneca said. She patted a pile of clothes. "Your mother dropped these off."

"My mother was here?" Mom didn't need to be dealing with this. Jackie sat up. Her head was spinning. She clenched the edge of the cot to keep from tipping over.

"Relax," Nurse Seneca said. "It's not like you're in the dean's office."

She checked her wrists, which were totally unscathed, thank goodness.

"You need to get out of those wet clothes. I can help you, if it's okay. I don't want you falling over and cracking your head open."

Jackie's teeth clattered. She eyed the sweater that Mom had brought. "I can do it. Is she still here?"

"No. She had to get back to work. She said to call her when you're ready to go home."

"I wish you hadn't called her."

"Sorry, those are the rules."

Jackie tugged her shirt over her head, but she could only pull it square with her elbows. She was stuck and in the dark, until

Nurse Seneca tugged the shirt and handed it to her.

Nurse Seneca looked at her curiously. "When was your last menstrual period?"

It took Jackie a few seconds before she realized what Nurse Seneca was insinuating. "Whoa! I seriously doubt I'm pregnant, unless it's an immaculate conception."

"I thought, maybe, because you didn't want your mom involved you were..."

"Not the problem." She tossed her wet shirt to the side and then slipped her arms into warm sweater sleeves.

"Can you stand up?"

Jackie nodded. She adjusted her sweater and scooted to the edge of the cot. Her head spun when she looked at the floor. "Still woozy."

"Let me help." Nurse Seneca held Jackie's arm while Jackie slid off the cot.

Jackie's bare feet pressed against the cold floor. Using Nurse Seneca for support, she peeled off her jeans. Her thighs were splotchy and cold. With Nurse Seneca's help, Jackie stepped into her dry jeans, one leg at a time. Then, Nurse Seneca helped her back onto the cot.

Jackie worked her cold, damp foot into a dry sock while Nurse Seneca stuck a thermometer in Jackie's ear.

It beeped.

"One hundred point one," she said. "You really should follow up with your doctor."

Like he'd have a cure for her problem. "Sure," Jackie said. She put on her other sock.

"You might be coming down with something. If you're still sick Sunday, I suggest taking Monday off. We don't need an epidemic at Ravenwood High. We're already having a hard time stretching our funding. I'll call your mom."

"Great."

Nurse Seneca made Jackie rest on the cot until her mom

showed, which wasn't until four forty-five when the after-school activity buses were lined up.

At home, Jackie sat in bed with her cell phone by her side. She wondered if Jason had heard about what had happened to her. Even if he was still pissed, he could at least call and apologize for telling Trish her secret.

By now, the whole school must know that she lied about seeing the Virgin. She couldn't believe Jason told when he promised not to. Maybe it just came out when he was crying on Trish's shoulder—another scenario Jackie tried to push out of her mind. But Trish told out of spite. What had gotten into her? She was more than her usual, broody self. She was sinister.

Jackie sunk her head into the pillow and closed her eyes, her mind settling into sleep.

A minute later, her cell phone rang, thrusting her back into worry mode. It was Zeta.

"You had me freaked out," Zeta said. "Your face was in the water when I found you. You could have drowned."

Jackie's mouth opened, but no words came out, like there was a concrete wall between her brain and tongue.

"You're not preggers, are you?"

The wall crumbled. "Can't I pass out without everyone questioning my virginity? Everyone's emotions made me sick. I needed to run somewhere and throw up."

"You picked the wrong bathroom. Everybody's saying that you saw the ghost of Julie Dickenson. She committed suey in there in the seventies, high on LSD. Mrs. Stinko told her Home Ec girls about it. Word spread fast."

Why couldn't Mrs. Zinko keep her mouth shut? Like she needed more shit spread about her. "I didn't see anything. I just passed out."

"You know, the janitors can't plug that leak."

"It's not a leak. The faucet won't shut off."

"Because the place is haunted. They say that Julie slashed her wrist and then held it under running water, bleeding herself down the drain."

Jackie felt like passing out, again. "Would you stop?"

"So don't tell me you didn't feel anything when you were in there."

"I felt like heaving."

"Jackie. Why do you do that? Pretend you're like... normal?"

"I don't want to talk about it. Is Jason still pissed at me?"

"He'll get over it."

"His dad's been going ballistic on him and his mom. Could you check on him tomorrow?"

"If I see one mark on Jason, I'll go to his house myself and kick his dad in the ass."

"What we need to do is convince him to go for help."

"Yeah, or that. But if his dad isn't going to stop, he's got to get what's coming to him. Hey, I got another call coming in. Call you later."

Mom pushed open the bedroom door, a bed tray with a bowl of steaming something in her hands. It smelled like chicken noodle soup. "Courtesy of Babu," she said, a bright expression on her face.

Mom had been taking her passing out at school pretty well.

"I should get sick more often," Jackie said.

Mom placed the bed tray across Jackie's legs. "Babu's specialty, cures even a broken heart. That's what Grandma used to tell me."

"Does it?"

"Not really. Only gin does that. If you can, it'd be a good idea if you went downstairs to see Babu. She keeps babbling to me about something. I think it kills her that she can't get up the stairs. Sounded like she was cursing them."

She laughed. "Sure, Mom."

Jackie placed a spoonful of Babu's soup in her mouth. Wide egg noodles, round pieces of carrots, chunks of celery, and slivers of chicken breast comforted her taste buds and warmed her soul. When she bit into a stray peppercorn, her mouth caught fire and radiated through her entire body, melting her shivers away.

Done, she placed the tray to the side, laid her head back onto the pillow, and closed her eyes, letting the soup continue the healing process.

It all seemed so crazy now, that Jason and Trish would be mad at her. And who cared anymore what she saw or didn't see when she was twelve? She was almost eighteen now and a different person than she was back then.

Or was she?

Maybe she wasn't that different at all. If she did change, it was because she was more closed off.

Sandra calling her a freak was just like when they were in seventh grade, after the whole Holy Resurrection incident—the vision, the fire, and the vigils.

"Hey, freak. I'm talking to you," Sandra had said to her.

Jackie had kept her back turned to her as she rifled through her locker pretending to look for something. A hand shoved her back, and she nearly fell into the narrow opening. She grabbed the sides of the locker to steady herself and then turned around. Sandra was standing there with her two friends. Sandra's hair was shorter then, and she wore it in pigtails. She was wearing a pink shirt with a huge sequined heart on her chest and a pair of designer jeans that had been artistically shredded at the thighs and knees.

"Where'd you get that skirt, Goodwill?" Sandra taunted.

The other girls giggled.

Jackie figured that if she didn't answer, they'd go away.

"Look at her knee-highs," the girl with acne said. "Who wears knee-highs?"

"Look at her blouse," the one with the sharp nose said. "It's buttoned to her neck."

"She's the miracle girl," Sandra said.

"Who?" asked Acne Face.

"The one who saw the Virgin Mary, or something, at that church on Main Street. You think you're so special, don't you?"

Jackie's mouth wouldn't move. She couldn't even form words of prayer in her head. Her heart was empty; her head was empty. Feeling abandoned, she pictured God with his back turned to her.

"Say something, freak," Sandra said.

Jackie wanted to say a lot of things, like "What have I ever done to you?" and "Just leave me alone," but her was mouth dry and no words would come out of it. She darted passed them and walked as fast as she could toward her next class.

"Loser," Sandra shouted down the hall.

The next morning, before school, Jackie looked at herself in the mirror. Her white knee-highs disappeared beneath her long jean skirt, and yes, she had buttoned her dorky print blouse to her neck. She looked at herself as if with a stranger's eyes and was ashamed of what she saw. Up until the seventh grade, she was best friends with Samantha, and they dressed pretty much the same. She guessed they may have looked like their own clique. But Samantha had moved to Pennsylvania, leaving Jackie friendless and looking oddly unique.

Jackie unbuttoned the top button so that her shirt made a tiny V at her throat. Then, she dug through her bottom drawer for her work jeans, the ones she wore when doing yard work and helping Mom clean the house. In front of the mirror, she dropped her skirt. It formed a circle around her feet. She stepped into her jeans. The button was snug at her waist, and as she pulled the zipper up, the material at her hips drew tight against her skin. Going up a size this year, she had been in desperate need of a new pair. They were as close to her body as her own skin.

But when she looked in the mirror, she saw an average girl, like every other girl who attended Ravenwood Junior High.

"Oh, my God," Mom had said. She had been standing in the doorway, purse slung over her shoulder, dressed in her postal outfit. "Grandma's going to shit."

Jackie's eyes snapped open. She needed to visit Babu.

Downstairs, Jackie peeked into Babu's room. Babu was standing by her dresser, lighting a candle in front of the icon of the Virgin of Vladimir.

"*Spasibo za sup*," she said to Babu, thanking her for the soup. It was one of the few Russian phrases she knew. Maybe that's why she always made it for her.

Babu motioned for Jackie to come to her. "*Idi syuda.*"

Jackie let Babu smother her in her bosom.

Babu released her from the bear hug and then pressed her hand to Jackie's forehead. She clucked her tongue. "*Sadis*," she said, indicating Jackie should sit down on the bed.

Babu opened the bottom drawer on her dresser and took out a dusty photo album. She sat beside Jackie on the bed and opened the album. The photo album cover rested on Jackie's knee as Babu flipped through pages filled with a mix of color and black-and-white photos. She pointed out a worn photo of three young women dressed in long, black dresses and black headscarves standing in front of a wooden building. Their austere expressions made it look like they had been gathered there for execution. Babu pointed to the second woman and then tapped her chest. "*Eto ya.*"

Jackie pointed to the picture and then to Babu. "That's you, Babu?"

Babu nodded and then babbled to her in Russian. Jackie didn't have a clue what she was telling her. Babu, looking terribly concerned, sandwiched Jackie's hand between hers. Her hands were unusually cold, and a chill ran through Jackie's body.

She was making Babu sick. "I'll be fine, Babu. Don't worry about me. Please."

Babu's round eyes looked at her with pity.

In her room, Jackie checked her phone for text messages and missed calls. Nothing. She lay down but couldn't sleep. Feelings of doom wrestled with her reasoning that things would be back to normal when she returned to school on Monday.

Chapter 13

Trish made a surprise visit to Jason's house. After all, he couldn't refuse to let her in after she came all this way.

Just as she had hoped, Jason opened the door.

"Trish," he said, looking sulky and scruffy, his bangs hanging over that black eye of his.

"Hey," she said. "Thought you could use some company."

Jason grimaced.

"What's wrong?" she asked, even though she knew.

"Why'd you do it? Tell on Jackie like that?"

She puffed hot air out her nose and placed her hands on her hips. "The other day, you were all gung-ho about getting even with her."

"I didn't mean like that."

"Can I come in?"

"I guess. We need to talk."

Jason led Trish through the kitchen, past his mother who was sitting at the kitchen table writing on a notepad. His mother, a tiny wild-haired woman, eyed her disapprovingly and then looked to Jason. "You two stay where I can see you."

"We'll be two minutes," Jason said to his mom. "Please, we need to talk. Privately. We'll be in the basement." As he led Trish down the stairs, he said, "My dad went to the bar, so it'll be safe down here."

"We could go to your room."

"No!"

In the basement, Jason made Trish sit down, but she leaned forward, her clasped hands just inches away from him. She wanted to reach out, pull him to her, but he was angry, and before she could reclaim his love, she had to bring him back to his senses.

"I don't know why you're so worried about Jackie. She made her bed. Let her lie in it."

"Why do you hate her so much?"

She shrugged. "I've never really liked her. She always acts like the mature one, the voice of reason, when she's more f'd up than all of us." With her gaze pinned on Jason, she rose from the chair and put her hands on his tense shoulders. "She even thinks she owns you. How dare she try to keep you away from me, when she doesn't love you like I do?"

Jason slunk away from her. "But, Jackie and I are..."

"Best friends? Is that what you really want? How long are you going to wait for her to come around?" She touched his soft cheek and brushed back his angled bang. "You and I belong together. You and I are birds of a feather. Through thick and thin and stormy weather. You are mine forever." She pressed her lips against his.

Jason squeezed her shoulders and pressed his lips against hers. Yes! The spell the demon taught her worked, again.

"Jason," his mom called. "What are you two doing down there? Come on up where I can keep an eye on you."

Jason pulled away.

Damn her. "No, don't," Trish said.

"We have to."

Behind Jason, electric arcs jumped from the fireplace hearth to the floor, from the floor to the recliner. Trish wasn't sure what it meant, but she figured it must be part of the demon's plan to help her win Jason.

Chapter 14

In the morning, Jackie checked her phone. Not one message from Jason. It was going to be another shitty day.

Mom poked her head into Jackie's room and knocked on the doorframe. She was already dressed in her postal uniform, her hair pinned up, and the ends of her hair—curled?

"Happy Saturday," she said.

Jackie squinted, examining her. "Is that blue eye shadow you're wearing?"

She touched her cheek. "Yeah. Does it look bad? I wanted to use something that would make me look perky, but something that matched the uniform."

"It's fine, Mom. I mean you look, uh, perky."

She smiled. "Thanks. So, how do you feel today?"

Jackie shrugged. "Okay, I guess."

Mom sat down at the edge of the bed and felt Jackie's forehead. Jackie picked up this weird feeling from Mom. Her energy level was super high. It was almost like she was—

"I think you should take the day off from work," Mom said. "It's not like you ever miss. Lean forward."

She cautiously leaned forward.

Mom worked the pillow like Babu kneading dough. "You need a good mental health day. We all need them from time to time. And today, you deserve one. Lean back."

She leaned back. The plump pillow snuggled her head.

Mom caressed Jackie's hand. "I love you, Jackie. I really do." Tears formed in the corners of her eyes, but there was a smile on her face, and her face was glowing. "You have a good day."

Jackie was stunned. It wasn't until Mom was leaving the room that Jackie said, "Yeah, you too."

Since Jackie's incident at school, Mom had been overly motherly. Well, not overly. Just motherly. But since, typically, Jackie was the mother and Mom was the child, Mom taking her rightful role back seemed kind of odd. Not that their roles had always been reversed like this. Their roles didn't switch until a little before Mom and Dad split. Before that, Mom was the quintessential mom, and she had that all-seeing, all-knowing mom sense—especially that day Jackie had the vision.

Mom had been in the front yard raking leaves. When Grandma had stepped out of the car, there was a look on Mom's face like she knew something was wrong. She leaned onto the rake handle. "What? No lunch today?" she asked Grandma.

Grandma opened the car door for Jackie to get out. "Come on, sweetie," she said to Jackie. "Can you walk?"

Jackie nodded.

Before Jackie could get out of the car, Mom dropped her rake and came running. "What happened?"

"She doesn't feel well," Grandma said. "Flu, maybe." Grandma took her hand as she climbed from the backseat.

"Oh, my God." Mom cupped her hand under Jackie's chin. "You look pale. Honey, are you all right? What's wrong?"

Jackie had never been so glad to see her mother. She threw her arms around her neck. "I don't feel good." Embarrassed, she didn't want Mom to know what happened.

"She was fine this morning," Mom said to Grandma.

"Well, sometimes these things just come on," Grandma said.

"Mom, what happened? There's something you're not telling me."

"It's nothing. She just had a little traumatic experience. She'll be fine."

"What kind of traumatic experience?"

"She was sick and she... She threw up the Eucharist."

Mom squeezed Jackie to her side. "Oh, honey. I'm so sorry. Come on. We'll take your temperature."

She wanted to tell Mom vomiting wasn't all that had happened, but she couldn't. If Grandma wouldn't tell Mom, she wouldn't either.

In her bedroom, Mom pulled the thermometer from Jackie's mouth and read the digital display. "Ninety-eight point nine."

Dad leaned into the room. There were bits of sawdust on his arms and pant legs. "What's wrong with her?"

"Sick, I guess," Mom said.

Dad laughed. "Of what? Church?"

Mom rolled her eyes and then shook her head.

Dad left the room.

"Mom, I don't want to go any more."

"Where? To church?"

She nodded.

"Oh, honey. I know you had a traumatic experience. You're going to have a lot of traumatic experiences in your life. Believe me. You just can't quit and hide. Besides, Gram and Babu want you to go. It's important to them." She laughed. "They couldn't do anything with me. You're their only hope, Obi-Wan Kenobi." She rubbed the top of Jackie's head.

"What?"

"Never mind. Before your time. Get some rest. You'll feel better tomorrow. You'll see."

Mom walked toward the door.

"Mom."

She turned.

"Yes, honey."

"What's 'The Force'?"

Mom stared at her, a bewildered look on her face. But Mom didn't come to fully realize what was going on until the church caught fire and the vigils began.

Two days after the fire, a group of people from Holy Resurrection and other people Jackie didn't recognize gathered on their front lawn. They set up a shrine consisting of a large icon of the Virgin of Vladimir, flowers, and candles. She suspected that some of the people were Roman Catholics from Sacred Heart because of the tiny statues of the Virgin and saints that were set before the Orthodox icon.

From a slightly parted curtain in her bedroom, she watched them. As the evening grew on, it looked like a sea of flames flowed from her front yard out into the street. They prayed. They sang. They called for her to come outside to pray for them, heal them.

Mom and Dad were downstairs arguing. Mom was trying to keep Dad from going outside and telling everyone to get the hell off his lawn. Dad was never as kind and accommodating as Mom. Mom wasn't religious, but she respected those who were. She was more than tolerant. She lived by the motto, "Live and let live."

Jackie stood in the middle of her room, prayer book in hand, and recited the Prayer of Saint Basil, trying to expel her demons, trying to set everything right.

In the morning, nothing had changed. Mom followed behind Dad as he dragged a lawn debris bag across the front yard and tossed flowers, statues, and stuffed animals into it.

"Stop it," Mom said. "This stuff doesn't belong to you."

"It's in my yard. What am I supposed to do? Mow over it?"

Mom stood there, her hair up in a ponytail, her arms limp at her sides, and her hands clenched in fists. She looked much younger than Dad, like a little girl who wasn't getting her way.

"You think the neighbors like seeing this?" Dad rubbed his hand over his forehead and clenched his hair. "Why can't she just be normal like every other little girl?"

His words slid down Jackie's throat like a handful of nails. In her room, she knelt in front of an icon of the Virgin and prayed that Mom and Dad would stop fighting. Then, she prayed for God to take her keen awareness of emotions away.

She prayed the Prayer of Saint Basil often, dousing herself with the Holy Water Grandma had given her the previous Easter, but her senses grew keener to the point where she was getting sick when exposed to too much emotion. It was like becoming nauseated from too much wind and sun.

She was withdrawing too and was too sick to go to school. She could tell that Mom was feeling helpless. Fighting with Dad every day had drained her. Mom seemed to be losing her capacity to think straight. She didn't know how to help Jackie. Dad had told Mom that she could help her by keeping her away from Grandma, Babu, and church. Mom went along with him. But still, Jackie was withdrawn. She didn't want to go to school. She didn't want to go anywhere. She just wanted to hide in her room.

One day, Mom insisted she go to the grocery store with her. When they entered, the cashier and manager stared at her as if they were afraid the ceiling would fall in or some other disaster would occur. At the meat counter, Mom picked through packages of ground beef.

Something lightly touched Jackie's arm, and she swatted it thinking it was a bug. A woman stood beside her, a scarf tied around her shaved head and her clothes hanging on her like they were two sizes too big.

"You're the Holy Resurrection girl, aren't you?" the woman asked.

Jackie shook her head and stepped closer to Mom.

"Yes, you are," the woman said. "I saw your face on the local news."

Jackie looked at Mom for help.

Mom brushed the back of Jackie's hair. "Yes, she is," Mom said, "but she's tired. She's been through a lot."

"Could you please lay your hands on me and pray that I'll get well?"

Jackie was pinned between the woman and the meat counter.

"Please?" The woman knelt before her and grabbed her hand.

Mom stepped toward the woman, but the woman wouldn't budge.

"Please help me," she said.

Jackie had a feeling that the woman had cancer. Her disease tasted like soured milk. The back of her throat tightened. She tried to hold back the urgency to gag.

Mom put her arm around Jackie's shoulder and pulled her close. "Let go of my daughter."

Not letting go of Jackie's hand, the woman stood up. "Please, heal me."

"Let go of her," Mom yelled. "Manager!"

Some of the shoppers peered out from the aisles.

Jackie's bones tickled, and she envisioned them turning to mush. She couldn't hold back the feeling to gag.

Mom pushed the woman. "Let go of her."

The woman clawed at Jackie's jacket trying to hold onto her.

Jackie slipped out of her coat and dropped to the floor. The pressure in the back of her throat made her heave. Bent over on her hands and knees, she spewed bits of Lucky Charms and milk onto the polished floor. Saliva dripped from her mouth. Her eyes were wet from the force of heaving, and her vision was blurred. She looked up at the woman, who crossed herself and then disappeared down an aisle.

In the car, Mom leaned her head against the steering wheel and cried. Jackie squeezed a wad of paper towels in her hand and vowed she was going to go to school on Monday and go about with her life as normally as she could. If anything happened or was bothering her, she would keep it inside, hidden from Mom.

It was out of her control when Nurse Seneca had called Mom. Jackie had expected Mom to fall apart again. But she didn't. There was just something weird about her mood. Almost like she was overjoyed to be a mom again. Almost. Jackie couldn't help but sense that there was something else going on with her. It was almost like she was—in love.

Chapter 15

Mom's glow ignited a spark of hope inside Jackie that Jason would show up after her shift at Photo Junction and things would be back to normal between them. She was going to go to work today.

While Mom examined her eyes in the bathroom, Jackie took it as the perfect opportunity to beat her to the paper.

The front porch and stairs were wet from dew, and the paper was miraculously lying on the landing. She stooped to snatch it. Standing up, she noticed streams of toilet paper hanging from the maple tree in the front yard.

At the base of the tree was a shrine of the Virgin Mary propped upside down. It looked like the neighbor's cement shrine, the one with the Virgin inside the grotto. Surrounding it were three plastic devil spears shoved into the ground, prongs sticking upward. On the tree trunk, written in red spray paint, "Liars go to hell."

Without thinking, she made the sign of the cross like Babu did when she saw something spiritually disturbing. Jackie didn't want Babu to see this. She held onto the rail and moved as quickly as she could down the wet steps in Babu's old, slick-bottomed house shoes. She slipped and came down hard on her butt, and her back hit the edge of a step. She had forgotten that the third step from the bottom was always extra slippery when wet because of the algae that had accumulated there.

"*Bozhe moy!*" Babu cried.

Standing on the front porch, Babu crossed herself just like Jackie had done. Babu threw her hands over her heart and ranted in Russian, gasping in between ecstatic phrases.

"Babu, go back in the house. I'm okay. Go, Babu."

Mom poked her head out the door. "What's going on?"

"Take Babu inside," Jackie said. "I'll take care of this."

Mom put her arms around Babu's shoulder and steered her inside the house.

Jackie pulled the spears out of the ground and threw them onto the wet lawn. Streams of toilet paper waved over her head.

She tried to lift the shrine. Her fingers scraped against its rough surface. It was made of concrete and was too heavy to lift. She tipped it over, thinking that maybe she could roll it to the side of the house so Babu couldn't see it. It just missed her toes and landed with the Virgin facing the ground.

She dropped to her knees; the moist ground soaked into her pant legs and cooled her skin. There must have been quite a few people involved in this, male, at least, and strong. The only man she had to call for help was Dad, but she couldn't. Not for this. This was all he needed to start a war between him and Mom again and to make him hate Jackie more.

"Jackie," Mom screamed. She was in the doorway—phone in her hand. "Babu's having a heart attack."

Jackie darted up the stairs, slipped on that same slick step, and banged her knee, but her adrenaline was pumped, so she really didn't feel a thing.

"I called 9-1-1," Mom said.

Inside the kitchen, Babu was pressing her hands to her chest and wheezing. Sweat beads dotted her forehead and temples.

Jackie didn't think Babu could make it to the couch without overexerting herself and making things worse. "Can you lie down?" she asked her, tilting her head onto pillowed hands and pointing to the floor so Babu would understand her.

Before Jackie could take Babu's arm and help her to the floor, Babu crashed to her knees and fell onto her shoulder. Jackie stooped and rolled Babu onto her back. She put her ear by Babu's mouth and nose. Then she pressed her ear to Babu's chest. Her chest was silent; her body, lifeless.

"She's not breathing!"

Suddenly, the air was sucked out of the room. When Jackie breathed, she couldn't fill her lungs enough to satisfy them. Fingers spread on thighs and head lowered, she fought the shortness of breath that was overtaking her.

"Jackie, don't panic," Mom said. "You can't help Babu if you panic." She stooped beside her and rubbed her back. "Relax, Baby. You have to relax."

Jackie knew what Mom was worried about. Mom was worried she would take on Babu's ailment and have a heart attack, too, or lose consciousness. And she was right. That was exactly what was about to happen, and Mom, not knowing CPR, wouldn't be able to help either of them.

She shook the thought of Babu dying and instead, filled her inner vision with giving Babu CPR and reviving her. She took deep, full breaths until she gained control. Then, she pressed the heels of her hands into Babu's chest and pumped.

Feet trampled the front porch steps. Mom directed two paramedics with huge, blue bags into the kitchen.

"Let me in," one paramedic said.

She jumped out of the way and let him take over CPR as the other set up the heart monitor.

The paramedic pressed the palms of his large hands against Babu's chest. Ribs snapped and popped.

Jackie grabbed her chest and dropped into a kitchen chair. Her ribs ached, and her chest tightened. The heart monitor flatlined. The paramedic leaning over Babu continued to pump her chest while the other inserted a needle into her arm.

They worked on Babu's lifeless body—one giving her CPR,

and the other administering drugs to get her heart going. Mom touched Jackie's shoulder, but Jackie, her body numb, couldn't feel her.

The heart monitor bleeped, and then continued to do so, steadily.

"She's breathing," the paramedic who'd been giving CPR said.

Jackie caught her breath.

The other paramedic put an air mask over Babu's nose and mouth.

"Thank you. Thank you so much," Jackie said to the paramedics.

They ignored her gratitude and worked quickly to lift Babu onto a stretcher and strap her down. As they hauled her down the front porch steps, Jackie warned them about the third step. When they put Babu into the ambulance, she rushed to get dressed, and then she and Mom drove to Mercy Hospital.

At the hospital, Jackie and Mom sat in the ER waiting room.

"Who would do such a thing?" Mom asked.

On TV, a woman was punching another who had slept with her boyfriend. The other woman made a protective shell around her head with her hands.

"I don't know, Mom."

"Have you made any enemies lately?"

"Obviously."

"Well, who? We have to tell the police."

"Oh, I don't know. Let me go down the list: I pissed off Jason the other day. He's not talking to me now. Trish sided with him. Called me a cold-hearted bitch, or something like that. Sandra thinks I'm trying to steal Will away. And God knows who else I may have pissed off when I passed out in the C-building bathroom—the janitor maybe?"

"You've been busy."

"I move people in mysterious ways. I'm gifted like that."

A nurse approached them. "Can either of you speak Russian?"

She and Mom shook their heads.

"We'll have to call an interpreter, then," the nurse said.

"This won't hold up Babu's treatment, will it?" Mom asked.

"No, not at all. We're monitoring her heart now, but we'd like to know how she's feeling. We also need an interpreter to present her with her options."

"Good luck with that," Mom said. "You're going to need more than an interpreter."

About a half hour later, they followed the nurse through two huge automatic doors and into the emergency area. Along the perimeter were curtained rooms. The nurse pulled back a curtain by the room labeled 2A. Babu was lying in a hospital bed. Her sleepy eyes looked up at them. Wires ran from her chest area, under the blue hospital gown, to the ECG machine. The machine rhythmically bleeped.

Jackie rubbed Babu's hand. It was cold, and the light she always saw around Babu was dim. "I'm so sorry, Babu."

"The doctor will see you in a bit," the nurse said.

When the doctor came in, he told them he wanted to run other tests. Jackie and Mom sat for nearly an hour while Babu was wheeled away for an angiogram. After the staff wheeled her back into the room, Jackie and Mom waited for the angiogram and blood tests to be processed and reviewed by the doctor.

They had to keep telling Babu to relax. She wanted to go home. She didn't trust doctors.

Finally, the doctor told them that Babu had high cholesterol, one of her coronary arteries was narrowing, and they would need to do surgery to open it up.

All this because of some vandals, Jackie thought. All this because she lied five years ago about seeing the Virgin.

Mom explained to the doctor that Babu was nearly ninety years old and she has been healthy as a horse until now, that having surgery may kill her, and no one is available to explain this to Babu.

The doctor said that the interpreter was on the way.

Jackie and Mom sat with Babu another hour and a half, waiting and discussing Babu's options between themselves. The funny thing was, they knew what Babu was going to say. No pills. No surgery. No hospital.

Finally, the curtain parted and the nurse walked in with the interpreter. A mixture of surprise and dread socked Jackie in the gut.

David Davidovich, dressed in a cassock and black slacks, looked at her and smiled, the corners of his mouth dimpling in delight. "The Lord works in mysterious ways," he said. "Yes?"

She grimaced. No. Definitely not. It was just that her life had turned to shit.

"Ms. Turov," the nurse said to Mom, "this is David Davidovich. He's our volunteer interpreter."

"Pleased to meet you," Mom said. By the look in her eyes and the sound of her voice, Jackie believed she was very pleased to meet David. "Uh, this is my daughter, Jackie."

His knowing eyes focused on Jackie. "We already met."

Of course he'd be honest.

"You have?" Mom looked at her and then at David and smiled.

David directed an open hand toward Babu. "So, this is your great-grandmother, and neither of you can communicate with her?" He clucked his tongue.

It felt so weird to be on the same team as Mom. She felt like a complete flunky.

"*Zdravstvuyte*," David said to Babu. "*Menya zovut David Davidovich.*"

Babu's tired eyes widened, and she glowed with delight. She started talking and stopped only to let David get in a quick word or two here and there.

What is this? Mom and Babu are infatuated with David.

When the doctor came in, he and David worked together to explain Babu's health to her. Babu waved her hand like she didn't want to hear about it. Like it was nothing. Like her heart attack as no more than a hiccup or yawn.

Jackie sidled beside David, but kept enough distance between so they wouldn't touch shoulders. David exuded a lot of energy. It was empowering, but too strong at a close distance. "What's she saying?"

"She wants to go home," he said. "No surgery. No doctors."

She sighed. Maybe they should let Babu say what's best for her. After all, she'd lived this long. But what if something happened because she didn't go for surgery? She couldn't forgive herself, or Mom, if it did.

"*Ya lyublyu tebya*, Babu," she said to her in Russian.

"I thought you could not speak Russian," David said.

"I can't. Pretty much all I can tell her is 'I love you' and 'thank you for the soup.'"

Babu reached under the fold of her hospital gown and tugged at the plugs on her chest.

"No, Babu." She grabbed Babu's hands to make her stop. "You have to stay. David? Tell her." His name sounded awkward in her mouth. Calling him Father would have been worse.

A slight grin formed on his face, and he peered at her with raised eyebrows.

She diverted her gaze to the bed rail. "Could you tell her she has to stay a day or two?"

He didn't answer, so she looked at him.

"How about this?" he said. "If I do this for you, you do something for me."

"You're going to bargain with me?"

Mom touched her shoulder. "I'll be in the waiting room."

"Mom!"

Mom waved at her and left the room.

Holy shit! She left us together.

"Your impression," David said.

"You know this isn't fair. I mean, you're the translator here. You're supposed to do your job."

He pressed his hand to his chest. "I do this service out of the goodness of my heart. I am a servant of God. Perhaps you will do something, not for me, but for God."

How dare he go there? "I really don't think God needs my services."

"Why?"

"Trust me with that."

Babu started ranting in Russian and moaning every time she tried to sit up.

"Babu, no," she said. "You have to stay."

David touched the curtain.

"I don't believe this. You're actually going to leave?"

Babu pointed to the plastic bag on the hook across the room that was stuffed with her clothes and said something to her in Russian that sounded like an imperative.

"No," she said. "Absolutely not. You're staying here."

"You have my card," David said. "Call me if you change your mind." He disappeared behind the curtain.

"Ugh! You bastard."

Babu commanded her again in Russian.

"All right," she hollered. "I'll go."

The curtain parted. David stepped back into the room—a sly smile on his face.

What a devil. He knew she'd change her mind.

"Allow me." He stood beside the hospital bed and worked his charm on Babu.

At that point, Jackie really didn't care what she had bargained—anything was worth saving Babu.

Chapter 16

Jackie and David walked down the hospital corridor.

"You really have a way with Babu," she said. "I thought, for sure, we'd have to restrain her."

"She is stubborn, like you." He winked at her.

She grimaced.

Mom was in the ER waiting room watching a soap opera.

"I'm going to grab a cup of coffee," she told Mom. "I'll meet you at home."

Mom looked at David and then at her. "With—"

Jackie signaled with her hand for her stop. "It's just coffee."

Outside, David led her to a silver Honda.

"No bike?" she asked.

"Too slippery this morning. Father Dmitriev let me borrow the car." David opened the passenger door, grabbed his backpack from off the seat, and held the door for her.

She felt like she was being lured into a trap, but she got in anyway.

David adjusted his cassock as he slid into the driver's seat. He set down his phone on the center compartment and turned down the volume on the car's audio system. He was young and too handsome to ever become a priest. Like, what a waste. She tried to imagine him in street clothes. He turned the key in the ignition and smiled at her. She was glad he couldn't read her thoughts, but still, she had to be careful. She was sure he was having no problem reading her body language and facial expressions. He seemed very intuitive, very people centered.

David drove the Honda out of the hospital parking lot. "So why the change of heart?" he asked.

"You set me up, that's why."

He laughed. "No. I mean, why the black clothes and fingernails?"

She looked at his cassock. "*You* have a problem with *black*?"

"I guess the color of clothes does not matter, but something has turned you away from God and church."

How dare he ask? She turned away and gazed out the window at the small-town shops they passed. The most excitement this town had ever known was due to her. How much did David already know?

"You do not want to talk about it," he said. "That is okay. Maybe another time."

She forced a smile. "So, what's on the playlist?"

"Judas Priest."

Her mouth dropped open. Judas Priest may be way before her time, but she knew they played something like heavy metal.

He laughed. "I am joking."

She felt like an idiot for taking him seriously. She typically wasn't easily duped. It must be the cassock that made her believe every word he said.

David made a left onto Lancaster and then parallel parked in front of Holy Resurrection. It was a modest building with a white canopy over the entrance, narrow arched windows, and three gold cupolas, a cross on each one. Her stomach tightened.

David cut the engine and unlatched the doors.

The blood drained from her face.

He opened the passenger door. "Jackie? What is wrong?"

"I can't go in there."

"It is just a church." He stooped so that they were pretty much eye level with one another. "I will not let anything happen to you. I promise."

She tried to smile, but her facial muscles had turned to stone.

"Please." He reached out his hand. His energy was so strong, it made her believe he meant what he said. For Babu, she reminded herself, and she took his hand and let him help her out of the car.

He kept his hand on her shoulder as they climbed the church steps and approached the carved entrance doors. The last time she climbed these steps was the day of her exorcism.

"You are not afraid the church will fall down on you, are you?"

"Ha-ha. Very funny." His joke slightly eased her tension.

He pushed open the church door and motioned for her to go in before him. She took a deep breath and then stepped inside the vestibule. When she took another breath, the scent of incense and beeswax filled her nose. It was both comforting and haunting.

David touched her arm. "Come."

It felt sacrilegious for her to leave the vestibule and enter the nave. She hesitated.

"It's okay. You are not a stranger to this church."

Maybe she did believe the church was going to fall in on her. She cautiously followed David through the arched entranceway and into the nave. Sparsely decorated, it was tranquil and clean. A large Oriental rug covered the polished wood floor in the center of the nave. Smaller Oriental rugs covered the outer areas. The candles in the choir areas were lit. She didn't remember ever seeing the church without people. She could still feel their energy and their foreboding stares.

David climbed the platform steps and then pointed to the iconostasis. "It is here." A drop cloth covered the left half.

She froze at the steps.

"It is okay, Jackie. Come."

"But..."

"Please."

As she climbed the steps, she had an eerie feeling that the floor was going to open up, and she would plunge straight to hell.

David fingered back the drop cloth, revealing the charred icons behind it. "What do you think?"

She swallowed, but her mouth was dry. "I don't know what you're asking me."

"We found it like this one day. We thought the candles were too close, that it caught fire and burned itself out. So, we replaced the icons and didn't light the candles. Within hours, it looked like this again." David made a quick sign of the cross.

"So, what do you want from me?"

"I thought that maybe you would have another vision."

"You think the Virgin is going swoop down and tell me what's up with the iconostasis?"

"I really did not think about how this was going to work. I only know that you were warned once about the fire in the church. I thought that maybe if this meant any danger to the church, you would be warned again."

"You don't know anything about me."

His eyes lit. "I know that you saw the Mother of God and that she spoke to you. I know that Stephanie's life would have been spared if Father Dmitriev would have listened to you."

"Says who?"

"The congregation. They still talk about you."

"Do they talk about how Father Dmitriev made me stand right here as he performed an exorcism on me?"

"They know."

"Why don't you tell Father Dmitriev to work his holy spells on this?"

"He has. I have prayed too. It does not seem like God is listening to us."

"He's not going to listen to me, either." She started for the platform stairs.

"I wear black to mourn the evil in this world and for those who are suffering," David said. "What do you wear black for?"

He was really crossing the line here. She turned to David. "I wear black so people will leave me the fuck alone." She felt bad about letting the f-word fly in church, but this place was really getting under her skin.

"Is that what you want Jackie? To live your life alone?"

She lost Jason. She almost lost Babu. Yes, it did frighten her to be alone; however, doing a psychic reading inside a church wasn't going to win her friends among the congregation. David needed to know what he was dealing with.

"I need to touch the icon to pick up an impression. Is that what you want me to do inside this church? I don't know what they taught you in seminarian school, but what you're asking me to do is against the laws of God. Divining, I believe the church calls it."

David fell silent for a moment. His eyes appeared to be studying her as if he was accessing her integrity. Then he said, "Do what it is you have to do. You were warned before for a reason. I believe that warning came from God. The congregation believes that too."

"What if it didn't?"

"What if it did?"

"Fine. I'm doing this for Babu. Not for you." She walked back to the iconostasis and reached for the drop cloth. As she did, her arm brushed the candlestick. Tiny vibrations tickled her arm bones and then spread across her chest.

"What is it?"

"I don't know." She wrapped her fingers around the candlestick. The energy poured from the holder into her hand. Sadness filled her, and her heart began to ache. Within seconds, her heart ached so much, it was ready to crack open. She let go of the candlestick to stop the pain, but the energy was so strong, it clung to her. She covered her face with her hands. Tears pricked her eyes. She sniffled.

"What is it?" David draped his arm over her.

She nuzzled her face against his chest and breathed in his scent.

"Are you all right?" He squeezed her shoulder.

She had this terrible need for him to hold her, to love her. She clenched his robe.

He pressed his cheek to her head, and his arm tightened around her. His energy combined with the energy binding her, transforming it from unquenchable desire to pure bliss. Her vision filled with white light.

"What's this?" Father Dmitriev boomed.

The spell was broken. White light crumbled into thousands of tiny stars, and then the stars disintegrated, leaving her and David standing in Father Dmitriev's shadow.

She backed away from David.

Father Dmitriev was standing by the Holy Doors like an icon of God's wrath. His fuzzy beard was grown out to his chest, and his dark eyes fossilized into an accusing stare.

Even she was horrified by what she had done. She had been holding David like she was—in love with him. She felt like crawling into a hole and never coming out.

"I-I brought Jackie to assess our problem," David stuttered.

"Are you mad? Get her out of here."

"But this is the girl who saw the Holy Mother and warned of the fire. Surely, she can help us."

"She's a heretic, a diviner. See her for what she is, my son."

David studied her as if he was trying to see her in a different light.

"It's okay," she said, her voice quivering. "I'm done here."

She jumped off the platform and bolted through the church and out the entrance doors.

Outside, she took long strides and alternate side streets to avoid being followed. No matter how fast she walked or how sporadic her path, David's scent rose up from her trench coat, and she could still feel his arms around her.

Chapter 17

Jackie rushed to her room so she wouldn't have to explain to Mom how her "coffee date" went. She dug an oversized sweater and a pair of black yoga pants out of her top drawer and then dashed to the bathroom and started the shower.

When the steam rose over the shower curtain, she stepped inside and let the water rain over her body. She imagined David's scent slipping over her shoulders, her hips, and her feet, trickling down the drain. She held the mesh bath sponge to her nose and smelled the remnant of shower gel, trying to get David's scent out of her head. She squeezed more shower gel onto the sponge, and starting at her shoulders, scrubbed her skin raw.

A rap on the door startled her. "Jackie? Is that you?" Another rap. "Jackie?"

Speak, Jackie. She almost had to remind herself how to form words on her lips. "Yes, Mom. It's me." Who else would it be? Some bum off the street desperately in need of a shower?

She dried off and then got dressed. Her skin was pink and smelled like strawberry, but she could still feel David. She needed to see Babu, to cleanse her spirit with her light.

In Babu's room, she searched the dresser drawers and found a scarf with a paisley pattern. She tied the scarf around her head like Babu always did, the ends drawn to the back of her head and knotted over the back flap. Then she grabbed Babu's satchel, dumped the contents on the bed, and filled it with clean underwear, socks, a housedress, and a warm sweater. She dropped Babu's chotki in the satchel, too, and put their needlepoint supplies on top.

"Mom," she yelled. "I'm going to bring Babu some clean clothes."

Mom was standing in the kitchen doorway. She wrinkled her brow at the sight of her. "I thought we'd go together, later."

"I don't want to leave Babu alone."

"Fine by me."

Jackie opened the front door. Her dad was lifting the shrine into a wheelbarrow. She closed the door. "What's *he* doing here?"

"Who else was I going to call?"

"You called Dad?"

"Jackie, your father doesn't hate you."

She could see him like it was yesterday, clutching his hair and looking miserably frustrated at the clutter on his front lawn, asking Mom why their daughter just couldn't be normal. "He does."

Mom's brow furrowed. "He divorced me, not you."

"Yeah, right."

The front door opened. Dad stopped at the threshold—knit hat pulled over his ears, Carhartt jacket open, and jean pant legs crumpled over his boots.

They stared at each other as if they didn't expect to meet head on. She felt like she was an evil force keeping him from crossing the threshold.

"I'll let you two talk," Mom said and left the room.

Jackie didn't want to talk. What was she supposed to say? Oh, thanks for coming out, Dad, to take care of my mess—once again.

He looked at Babu's satchel. "I hear Babu's in the hospital."

"Yeah, I was just going to bring her some things."

"Want to tell me what happened?"

"Babu had a heart attack. Besides that, no."

He put his hands in the pockets of his jacket and nodded. "I pulled down some of the TP. You'll have to wait for a heavy rain to bring down the rest of it."

"Thanks."

"All right then. Well, say hello to Babu for me." He lifted his hand, fingers spread, to say good-bye and then turned and walked out the door.

She parted the curtain on the narrow window. Dad's truck pulled away from the curb and drove down the street, devil spears poking out from the truck bed.

At the hospital, Jackie treaded down the corridor looking like a refugee in her boots and yoga pants combo, the paisley scarf tied around her head. She found it strange that people were staring at her more now than when she was in full goth attire.

Babu was thrilled to see her. She smothered her in her bosom and kissed her on both cheeks, three times. Jackie scooted a chair close to the hospital bed, and she and Babu continued with their needlepoint as if they were at home in the living room. Babu's light was dim, so Jackie tried not to absorb it. But just being with Babu made her feel good inside. David's energy had just about faded. Perhaps the only thing sticking to her was the distasteful memory of what had happened between them that day.

Then, David walked into the room.

He stopped when he saw her.

The needle slipped from her fingers and dangled by a thread from the canvas.

He nodded. "Jackie."

"David."

Babu was all smiles. She called him to the bed and took his hand in hers and kissed it. He was going to think they were both nuts, Jackie thought.

David pulled up a chair and glanced at her several times while talking to Babu in fluent Russian.

In between glances, she fled to the bathroom, locked the door, and sat on the edge of the toilet, waiting for him to leave. After about ten minutes, she pressed her ear to the door, hoping for a lull in the conversation, for the sound of closure.

She hoped he wasn't waiting for her to come out. Seeing each other was not a good idea. Besides being totally embarrassed about what happened that day, she was scared to death of the way he made her feel. She barely knew him, and yet, she wanted him more than anybody could ever want another human being. That feeling had to have come from the candlestick. But then, the candlestick exuded sadness. What she felt for David was more than sadness.

After another five minutes or so, she heard the conversation come to an end.

There was a rap on the bathroom door. No!

"Good-bye, Jackie," David said.

Just go.

"Are you okay in there?"

"Yeah."

"I would really like to talk to you. Tomorrow, maybe?"

Would you just go away?

"Jackie?"

No way in hell.

"Okay then. Call me."

Sunday, Jackie missed Jason more than ever. She wished things could be normal between them again. She called Zeta.

"Have you seen Jason?" she asked her.

Silence.

"Is he okay?"

"Looked fine to me. At least what I could see with Trish hanging all over him."

A hot breath escaped her lips. She had sighed so heavily, it came out as a low growl.

"Jackie?"

"Do you know where they were Friday night?"

"Trish said something about going to Jason's house."

"Those dogs."

"Are you jealous?"

"Someone vandalized my front yard. Babu saw it and had a heart attack."

"Is she..."

"She's fine. Mom picked her up today. She's supposed to be on medication."

"I know Jason. He'd never hurt you like that."

"I hope you're right."

Ironically, she brooded for the rest of the day. Her hope that by Monday everyone would have forgotten about her lie and she and Jason would be friends again was looking bleak. In fact, she got a bad feeling that things were going to get worse.

Chapter 18

Jackie's intuition was dead on. Monday morning, she was greeted by "Burn, witch, burn" spray-painted onto her locker door. The energy these words exuded pounded like fists against her chest.

"Whoa!" Zeta said.

Jackie quickly turned the tumbler on her lock, thirty-five left, two to the right. The lock released with a twelve to the left. She opened the locker door wide enough to hide the hideous words. Inside the locker, dropped onto a pile of books and stuff, was a tarot card.

Zeta picked it up. "The Hanged Man. This is just plain mean."

Jackie's name was written across the man hanging upside down from a tree by one foot. The other leg was bent, forming a triangle with the hanging one. His arms were drawn behind his back, and a halo surrounded his head. He looked like a crucified saint.

People were moseying around their lockers and staring at her as if waiting to see her reaction.

Zeta took a step toward them and stomped her thick-heeled Mary Jane to scatter them. "Why don't you take a freaking picture?"

It worked. A few of them burrowed their heads into their lockers; others scurried down the hall.

Zeta studied the tarot card again. "What moronic maniac would do this?"

"Any one of them, I guess. Everyone hates me."

"Count me out. I can never hate you. You're too weird to hate."

"Thanks."

"What are friends for?" Zeta smiled, her devious eyetooth showing. "Hey, too bad they didn't dump the whole deck in here. I can use a set of tarot cards."

"Seriously?"

"No. Come on. I'll walk down to the office with you. Maybe they can trace fingerprints or question the local hardware stores to see who recently purchased black spray paint."

"I'm not going to the office." The only thing she wanted to know was that Jason didn't do it.

"You can't go the rest of the school year with a vandalized locker either. Besides, the graffiti is bringing down the value of the hallway."

Jackie slammed her locker shut. "I'm sure when Mrs. Zinko comes out of her hole, she'll make sure someone takes care of it."

"Be that way. Leave it for Mrs. Stinko."

Jackie headed toward B-building for American History. On the B-building stairs, she hugged her books to her chest and kept her elbows tucked to her sides to avoid physical contact with the other students. She wished she could carry all of her books with her so she didn't have to return to her locker for the rest of the day, or for rest of the school year.

At the top of the steps, some jock pushed Pete, the kid who was in her American History class. Pete's notebook flew out of his arms and papers fluttered in the air and dropped onto the steps and landing. People laughed and trampled his papers. He stooped to pick his things up. A girl shoved him with her knee.

Jackie reached for a paper, but then stopped. She was a victim too, and if she touched his papers or touched him, she'd take on his pain and maybe his low self-esteem.

He glanced at her and shrunk into the corner.

You dope. I'm the last person you should be afraid of. I'm not the evil person you think I am. Well, not that evil. Not like the people who did this to you.

When she came out of the stairwell, Will shot her an awkward look and then strode down the hall and disappeared around the corner. Students glanced at her and moved away like she had a contagious disease.

In American History, she slouched in the hard desk chair and wondered who vandalized her front lawn and locker. She imagined the scene, how it would have been last night, first with Trish and Jason, which broke her heart, and then with Sandra and her cheerleading team, which totally made her skin crawl.

"Miss Turov," Mr. Sheahy said. "You're being paged."

"What?"

"The intercom. You're wanted in the office."

Some of the class snickered. As she walked down the aisle, someone called her a liar and another, a witch.

In the B-building stairwell, she dropped down onto a step and sat there a few minutes to regain her emotional and physical strength. Homeschooling crossed her mind and the fact that she would probably get blamed for this locker thing.

Inside the main office, the secretary was on the phone verifying an absence, and Principal Mraz was shuffling through some papers on her desk. Jackie stood unnoticed for a minute or two.

Finally, Principal Mraz noticed her. "Miss Turov," he said, a bored look on his face.

She was kind of insulted. Her life and problems were more than routine.

"Come on in my office."

She followed him. The back of his suit was wrinkled. Grandma always said that was how you could spot a cheap suit.

"Close the door." He sat down in an executive-style chair.

She closed the door, shutting her problems inside a tiny office with a man who was about to process them.

"We've already filed a police report on the vandalized locker," he said. "It's a crime against the school more than it's a crime against you."

"Thanks." Did he really think that was going to make her feel better, or did he actually not care?

"Do you know who would have done this?"

"No."

"Don't lie."

"It could have been anyone. I'm not going to make accusations."

"There was a message written on the locker door. You must have some idea what it was supposed to mean. It was obviously for you, along with the witchcraft card."

"Tarot card."

"Don't get smart."

She huffed. She wasn't typically a huffer, but she couldn't believe this guy's attitude.

"Miss Turov!"

She wasn't even going to argue her point. "Listen, I don't know if you know anything about me." She really didn't want to bring this up. With her luck, she'd piss him off too.

"Should I?"

How was she going to say this without sounding weird, without him sending her to sessions with the school psychologist? "I am—I mean, I was the girl who predicted the Holy Resurrection fire," she said, making finger quotes as she said the word *predicted*.

He looked at her like he didn't know what she was talking about. He was obviously not from around here. She wondered how long he'd been employed at this school. Surely, he'd heard rumors. "Shrine girl? Virgin Queen? Anything ring a bell?"

"The fire at Holy Resurrection was about what? Four years ago?"

"Five. I was twelve."

"Yeah. I heard it got kind of crazy around here."

"Yeah, it seems I evoke either the worst or the best in people."

"So you know who would have done this?"

She shook her head. Even if Jason did do it, she wouldn't want him getting in trouble. "Can I go?"

"For now. The police might come by your house later asking questions."

"Wonderful."

Her hand on the doorknob, she considered asking if she could go home for the rest of the day, but then thought against it. Going home would make her look weak, which was what everyone wanted.

"Miss Turov, if it happens to come to you who would have vandalized your locker, come see me."

"Yeah, sure." *Yeah, right.*

She sat on the steps in A-building and waited until the passing bell rang. American Lit was next. She was excited and nervous at the same time about seeing Jason. She'd know if he did it. He knew she'd know too.

In American Lit, Jason peered at her from under the thin veil of hair angled across his face. His aura was murky.

Mr. Davis walked up and down the aisles, handing back essays on *Leaves of Grass* and transcendentalism. She wondered if Jason ever finished his essay. As Mr. Davis walked down her aisle, he accidentally bumped the corner of Jason's notebook, and it fell to the floor.

She practically dove for it. Jason too. Both of their hands were on the notebook. She looked Jason in the eyes as she let the emotions flow from his body, his hand, through the notebook, to her.

A deep feeling of anxiety rushed through her.

Jason let go of the notebook. "I didn't do it."

With the notebook in her hands, she tried to read more. She didn't sense that he was the one who TP'd her yard and vandalized her locker. She also didn't pick up any physical abuse.

"Do you mind?" He held out his hand.

Everyone looked at her and Jason, even Mr. Davis.

She handed the notebook to Jason and then leaned back in her chair and tapped her pen on the desk as if nothing was wrong.

"Someone's feeling feisty today," Mr. Davis said to Jason. "I don't recall seeing a paper from you. Did you turn one in?"

"No," Jason mumbled.

"You know, you lose a whole grade for late turn-ins," Mr. Davis said. "I'd be concerned since you typically don't have much of a grade to start with."

Everyone laughed.

Jason leaned his head against his hand and let his hair curtain his face.

Touché.

Chapter 19

As students slowly filed into Mr. Davis's third-hour American Lit class, Trish slumped in the desk chair. Mr. Davis, looking god-awful, shot her an agitated look and then wiggled his index finger. "I need to talk to you. Now."

She glared at him, but got up and followed him out into the hall. "I don't know what you did, but I want you to make it stop."

The corner of her mouth turned upward into a half smile. "What?"

"You know."

"Switch my lit class."

"I told you, I can't. Second hour is filled to capacity."

"Then switch me with someone."

"I can't just pull someone out of second hour and stick them into third. I don't have that power."

"Then, I don't have the power to fix your problem either."

"You brought something in with that Ouija board." He looked around like he was afraid someone might hear. "Was that even my wife we were talking to?"

"Ask Jackie to help you."

Chapter 20

When Jackie got home from school, Babu was at the kitchen table peeling potatoes.

"You should be resting," she said to Babu. "I can do this."

Babu waved her hand at her, indicating to let her be, and issued a few words in Russian.

Jackie pointed to the front room. "Go."

Babu reluctantly laid down the paring knife and half-peeled potato. Then, she wiped her hands on the dishtowel and ambled out of the kitchen.

Jackie picked up the knife and pared the half-peeled potato. Taking up another potato, she noticed that Babu's prescription papers were shoved between the salt and pepper shakers. Mom was supposed to have gotten those filled yesterday when she picked Babu up from the hospital.

She washed her hands and then dialed Mom.

"Why are Babu's prescriptions sitting on the kitchen table?"

"Because I forgot to throw them away."

"Throw them away? Mom!"

"She's not going to take them."

"She'll take them if I ask her to. I'm going to get them filled."

"Do what you want."

"Dinner will be on the stove."

"I'm going to be a little late today."

"Madam Sophie?"

"No. Not Madam Sophie. I just have some things to do." Her voice insinuated that she didn't want to explain what those things were, but Jackie knew. Still, she couldn't believe she didn't care about Babu—not enough to try to get her to take her pills. Grandma had a heart attack about two years after Jackie had the vision. She wondered if Mom didn't get on Grandma either about taking her medication and had just let her die. She also wondered if Grandma would have had heart problems if it weren't for the church incident.

When dinner was ready, Jackie set a plate of mashed potatoes, green beans, and reheated pork roast from Sunday's meal on a TV tray so Babu could watch *Wheel of Fortune*. She didn't know what Babu got out of that show. She didn't understand English. Maybe she just wanted to see what Vanna was wearing, like the rest of America.

She waved the prescriptions at Babu. "I'm going to get these filled."

Babu ranted.

She patted her chest. "For me. Take these for me."

Babu threw her hand, like *just go away*.

Inside the pharmacy, Jackie gave the prescriptions to the pharmacist and then moseyed toward the candy aisle. Sean Perry and his teammate John Taylor were by the cooler. John reached inside for a cold drink.

Sean shot her a look like she was some freak. "John," he said, "don't look now, but I think we're being invaded by zombies."

John emerged from the cooler, two Red Bulls in hand. "Hey, zombie chick."

She ignored them and continued to the candy aisle where she snagged a bag of Lindor Peanut Butter Truffles. She wished Jason wasn't pissed at her so they could enjoy these together, like they always did.

By the time the pharmacist filled the prescriptions, Sean and John were gone.

When she came out of the pharmacy, they were sitting on the bench by the potted tree. She needed to pass them to get to her car. She anticipated more comments, like, "Hey, vampire girl, bite me."

A red Mustang pulled along the curb beside them. Sandra rolled down her window and talked to them.

Wonderful. Jackie took a deep breath and continued down the sidewalk, keeping her eyes focused straight ahead of her, pretending she didn't even notice them.

"Hey," Sandra shouted.

Jackie kept from looking at her, even though she knew Sandra's call was directed at her. She wished Sandra would grow up and learn how to tolerate others who were different from her, but that probably wasn't the core of her problem. Jackie didn't know why, but she thought Sandra suspected Will was still hot for her. Guess Sandra was just stupid.

"Hey, VQ, I'm talking to you," Sandra said. "I rhymed again!"

As Jackie came nearer, the hairs on her arms rose and the back of her neck tingled.

"Don't ignore me, bitch," she said.

That's it! "Why don't you get a life and quit bothering me?" Jackie yelled.

"Ooh," John and Sean said at practically the same time. They were sitting at the edge of the bench as if waiting to see two chicks fight.

Sandra flung open the car door and pounced to the sidewalk. "Because I have a problem with you."

Great. She's going to put on a show.

Sandra pointed her finger at her. "You think you're so special. You're just a fake, looking for attention."

Jackie wanted to grab Sandra's finger and break it, but it was

Sandra's rage she was feeling, not her own. *Let it go. Get the hell out of here.* "You're right. I just want attention." She continued for her car.

Her coat tightened around her neck, stopping her in her tracks. Sandra had grabbed her hood. Jackie worked her fingers at the edge of the fabric to keep it and the top button from digging into her neck and choking her, but she couldn't get her fingers under it. It was too tight against her skin.

Tugging the coat's hood, Sandra pressed her mouth close to Jackie's ear. "Which one of your bitch friends wrote my name and phone number in the guy's bathroom?"

Oh, shit. That's what this is about. It would have been funny if she didn't feel pain in her throat. She grabbed the sides of the hood and spun around. They stood toe to toe. "I don't have time for this. My grandma's sick and needs her prescriptions. Take this up with my *bitch friends.*"

"No. I want to take this up with you."

"Grow up."

"You grow up." She grabbed Jackie's coat sleeve.

This girl wants to brawl.

Sandra's anger flowed through Jackie, tightening her muscles, making her heart race.

Control yourself. Walk away.

Jackie jerked her arm and turned away from Sandra. An impact hit Jackie's back and she fell to her knees. Her satchel strap slipped from her shoulder. The heels of her hands scraped the sidewalk. As she started to get up, Sandra kicked her in the side.

Jackie couldn't believe Sandra was doing that. How could a person be so mean? She didn't even look like Sandra. Every crease in her face was deepened, her eyes dark, and her lips contorted.

She knew she was going to have to kick Sandra's butt to get out of this, but her muscles had slackened as though Sandra's hateful emotions had weakened her. "Look at what you're doing. This isn't you."

Sandra kicked her in the stomach. Jackie doubled over.

"Bitch," Sandra snapped. "Have any visitors at your new shrine? We didn't have any fancy banners to hang, so we used toilet paper instead."

John and Sean laughed.

Sandra drove the toe of her shoe into her side and then kicked her in the face.

Jackie rolled into a ball to protect herself, but Sandra continued to kick her. She couldn't get up. When was Sandra going to stop?

John and Sean were egging her on.

"Get away from her," someone hawked, "or I'll drop a curse on you so fast, your pretty golden hair will fall out right here, all over the sidewalk. And you two, you call yourselves men? You'll be nothing more than castrated pigs when I get through with you."

Car doors slammed, tires screeched. A small, boney hand touched Jackie's cheek.

Chapter 21

A tiny woman with a fox-like face and wild, red hair bent over Jackie. A crystal rod dangled from her necklace.

"Wicked," Madam Sophie said. "How can people be so mean? Can you stand up?"

"I don't think so," Jackie said.

"It takes its toll, doesn't it?"

She didn't understand what she was talking about.

"The emotions," Madam Sophie said.

Jackie nodded.

Madam Sophie put her hand under Jackie's arm and helped her up from the sidewalk. "Come upstairs. You need to get your strength back."

Jackie glanced at the "Psychic Readings" sign in the third-floor apartment window. How many times had she seen Madam Sophie watching her from behind the parted curtain when she was on her way to work or walking to the coffee shop? It always freaked her out. Now, she was in her clutches, and she had been invited up.

"I'm not going to harm you. And I don't throw curses. It's bad karma."

There was no way Jackie could drive or walk home at that moment. Her emotions had been pushed beyond limit, and her face and side hurt like hell. She needed to lie down for a while. "All right," she said.

Madam Sophie led her to the apartment building. Jackie still felt like she didn't know what hit her, or why.

"You feel so much," Madam Sophie said. "You know, you don't have to suffer like this."

In the apartment building stairwell, Jackie leaned on Madam Sophie for support and held onto the handrail as they climbed three flights of stairs. On the third-floor landing, Jackie was ready to drop.

Madam Sophie pushed open her apartment door. Inside, it was dim and dusty, lit only by candlelight. It smelled like cinnamon. The front-room walls were painted burnt orange. A grouping of astrological signs painted in purple and surrounding a flaming yellow sun filled the back wall. In the middle of the room, two tapestry loveseats faced each other, separated by an antique coffee table. By the window was a round table covered with a red tablecloth, a thick candle in the middle. Two red panels curtained the window.

Madam Sophie helped Jackie out of her trench coat and hung it on a hook that was shaped like a quarter moon. A whole row of quarter moon hooks were mounted to a strip of wood with white stars and yellow astrological suns.

She led her to one of the loveseats and leaned a pillow against the arm. "Rest here while I get you something for your bruised skin and spirit."

Jackie dropped onto the couch and slowly moved her aching body into a reclining position. Madam Sophie draped a throw over her. Jackie pulled it up to her chin, closed her eyes, and envisioned Babu.

The shrill whistle of the teakettle woke her. She must have dozed off.

After several minutes, Madam Sophie set a steaming cup of something and a tiny silver canister on the coffee table. Then she brought an ice pack.

Jackie pressed the ice pack to her cheek just below her eye.

"Your great-grandmother will be fine, but not if she sees you like this. Can you sit up?"

She nodded and then swung her legs over the couch edge and tucked the throw into her lap, letting it drape over her legs.

Madam Sophie sat beside her. Her face was narrow, and there were dark rings under her eyes. She could really use some concealer.

"Don't be afraid. There's no reason to fear me. I mean you no harm. I never did." She smiled. Her bottom teeth were crooked and layered. "My bark is worse than my bite."

Jackie tried to smile, but she didn't feel comfortable in Madam Sophie's apartment. It carried a lot of emotional baggage, like it was full of people.

Madam Sophie lifted the steaming cup and pressed it into Jackie's trembling hands. "Drink this. It'll heal your spirit."

The liquid shivered in the cup. Jackie couldn't believe she was sitting in Madam Sophie's parlor about to drink some magical concoction.

"People like us can easily spark extreme hatred in some people," Madam Sophie said.

Jackie hoped Madam Sophie hadn't lured her here to get even for the petitions the town made against her.

"It's not your fault," she said.

"It kind of is. I dated her boyfriend a long time ago, and my friend Zeta—"

"No. I mean, what happened to me. You know, back when you made quite a splash with your gift."

Jackie's eyes grew wide. "I'm really sorry," she said, in both sincerity and fear.

"I said it wasn't your fault. It wasn't your fault, either, the way people were falling all over you, tugging at you and draining you emotionally, spiritually."

"How'd you know?"

"Who didn't know in this county? It was in the local

newspapers."

"No, I mean about me feeling emotionally and spiritually drained."

"I'm psychic. I know exactly how you felt. Drink."

She took a sip. The temperature was hot, but drinkable. "What is this?"

"Jasmine tea."

"Oh," she said, surprised. She had thought it was some special concoction. "It's good."

Madam Sophie picked the silver canister from the table and removed the lid. "This, my dear, is marigold salve. It will heal the bruising."

"Really?" She wondered if Babu knew of any home remedies she could share with her. She must have used stuff like this back in the day when she lived in the old country.

Madam Sophie smiled. "Your great-grandma has a lot to teach you. But you don't understand her, do you?"

"How do you do that?"

"What?"

"Read my mind all the time."

"You're easy to read. You have so much energy. Your thoughts are always out there, hanging in the air."

Great. Her mind was an open book.

"You're thinking I'm a freak, aren't you?" Madam Sophie said.

Jackie shook her head. After all, she wasn't the one to throw stones here. Okay, maybe she did think Madam Sophie was a littler weirder than she.

"Don't lie," Madam Sophie said. "You think I'm different from you. You don't really know what you're capable of. I'm not sure if you don't know, or if you're just in denial. I think your intuition has been trying to tell you, but your denial keeps silencing it." She rubbed her finger over the top of the salve. "Lift your shirt."

Jackie did, but just enough to bare her stomach and waist

where Sandra had kicked her. "I think I've seen enough of what I'm capable of. I pissed off a lot of people in the past week. People have either been red-hot or ice-cold toward me."

Madam Sophie touched Jackie's side with her index finger. The salve was cold, and Jackie flinched. "You have to learn how to protect yourself." Madam Sophie rubbed the salve all over Jackie's sides and stomach.

Jackie coughed. A sharp pain sliced through her side beneath her ribs.

"Some Tylenol will help too," Madam Sophie said and then disappeared into the kitchen. When she came back, she dropped two Tylenol into Jackie's cupped hand. "That girl that hurt you, there's something evil about her."

"You're telling me." She popped one Tylenol in her mouth, took a drink of tea, and swallowed, and then did the same for the other Tylenol.

"I don't mean it metaphorically. You had to have sensed it." Madam Sophie raised her eyebrows.

"She's just plain mean."

"She has an inner tendency to be mean. A combination of her core being and her life experiences. But she's also one of the susceptible, and her urgency to be mean is stronger."

"The what?" Jackie really wanted to get up and go home more than she wanted to know the answer to her question.

"The susceptible. Some people in this town have been severely influenced by the solar storm. The energy particles are still in the air. The particles disrupt the circadian rhythms of the body and can make the suicidal more suicidal, the violent more violent, and the mentally ill more ill. Spirits and demons feed off this energy too. And there's nothing to stop them from taking advantage of the susceptible."

Jackie believed what Madam Sophie was saying about the solar storm disrupting the circadian rhythms of the body, but she drew the line on spirits and demons. Talk of spirits and demons was nothing more than psychic mumbo jumbo.

"This isn't psychic mumbo jumbo. It's nature. But tell me, why is it that you have such avarice toward things of the supernatural? You've put up this wall. You're making yourself sick because of it. You're half the person you're supposed to be. Why are you doing this to yourself? Is it out of ignorance or lack of guidance?"

"I really appreciate you helping me. I never knew you were, like, nice. But I really have to get home and give Babu her medicine."

She nodded. "I'll drive you."

"But I drove. My car is parked by an expired meter."

"I'll drive your car and walk home."

"I live about five blocks from here."

"I know where you live."

Oh, jeez. She knows where I live. Everybody knows where I live.

"I walk," Madam Sophie said. "At night. A lot. I find the cool, damp air to be cleansing and energizing."

Jackie didn't want to deny her a walk or the opportunity to do another good deed. Never refuse a gift. That's what her grandma used to tell her. "All right."

Madam Sophie put on her coat—a pink, quilted jacket with a belt that cinched her waist. It clashed horribly with the crimson paisley of her maxi dress. She helped Jackie into her trench coat and hooked her satchel over her shoulder.

In her car, it was really strange to see Madam Sophie behind the wheel. She pictured herself at that age—boney, wrinkled, wild-haired, committing serious fashion crimes. *Quit thinking. She's reading your mind.*

Madam Sophie gripped the steering wheel with both hands as she drove her home. Jackie wondered if she did this all the time when she drove or if she was just trying to soak up her vibes to learn more about her.

She parked behind Mom's car.

"Thank you." Jackie was still in shock that Madam Sophie had come to her rescue.

When they got out of the car, Madam Sophie handed her the keys. As Jackie took them from her hand, she wondered how much she had read off them.

"You sure you're going to be okay walking?" Jackie asked. "My mom could drive you home, if you like." She was hoping she'd say no. If she didn't have to tell Mom about this, she wouldn't.

"I'll be fine. But you, the persecution is going to get worse. I know I can't make you do anything against your will, but I strongly recommend you get training, learn how to protect yourself, and learn about your gift."

The wind ruffled Jackie's hair.

"If you don't learn how to protect yourself spiritually and emotionally, you'll be putting yourself in physical danger, worse than what happened to you today. I can help you."

"I don't think so." Jackie really just wanted to go into the comfort and warmth of her house and never see Madam Sophie again.

"See you soon," Madam Sophie said, with certainty, and she turned and walked away.

Chapter 22

Babu's chair was empty, the TV tray back in its rack, and the TV off. In the kitchen, Mom sat at the table eating the mashed potatoes, green beans, and pork roast that Jackie had left warming in the oven for her.

"Where's Babu?" Jackie asked.

"What happened to you?" Mom asked. "Is that a bruise on your face?"

"I tripped and fell. Does it look bad?"

"Well, with the smeared mascara and the swelling, it looks like you've been left for dead. Get some ice on that."

She already had enough ice on it to cause frostbite, but she didn't want to tell Mom that. "Where is she?"

"In her room."

Jackie thought it ironic that Babu included her in her prayers every day, yet her life was slipping down the drain.

"She's got to take these." Jackie raised the pharmacy bag.

"Good luck."

Jackie ripped open the bag of prescriptions, shook a pill out from each of the two containers, and filled a glass of water.

She headed to Babu's room. Listening by the cracked door and hearing nothing, she asked, "Babu, can I come in?"

"*Da*," Babu said.

Jackie pushed the door open with her shoulder and lifted her hand that held the two pills. "Got your medicine."

Upon seeing Jackie, Babu put her hands on her cheeks and ranted.

"I'm fine," Jackie said. She set the water glass on the bed stand and sat down beside Babu.

Babu gently touched Jackie's cheek. *"Chto sluchílos' s toboy?"*

"I tripped." She walked her fingers over her closed fist, which held the pills, and then pressed her knuckles to her thumb. "Tripped," she repeated.

Babu clucked her tongue. Maybe, even she couldn't believe that her prayers couldn't keep Jackie safe.

"I'll be okay Babu, but you, you need to take this." She opened her hand to show Babu the pills and then tapped her chest with her other hand. "For your heart."

Babu threw up her arms and argued.

"But, Babu, this pill will help lower your cholesterol, and this one will widen your arteries."

She continued to rant.

Mom was right. Babu wasn't going to take these pills. Jackie imagined herself slipping them into Babu's food like they did a long time ago for their dog, Buddy. But Babu wasn't a dog. She should know better. It crossed Jackie's mind that the only person who could probably get her to take her pills was David. She pushed that thought far back in her mind.

At about nine at night, Jackie's cell phone rang, and Jason's name and number lit on the display. Maybe he heard about her downtown brawl with Sandra, and he was calling to say she got what she deserved.

"Hello?" she said, even though she knew it was Jason. She wanted to make him work at this conversation.

"Hey," he said. "I'm... uh... sorry. Things have been crazy."

"You're telling me."

"I miss you."

"Apology accepted. I miss you too."

Silence.

"I have a problem," he said.

Of course he does. "Your dad again?"

"Kind of. I don't think I should tell you over the phone. You have to come see."

"I had a really, really bad day myself. If your dad is acting up again, if you think he's going to go ballistic on you and your mom, call the police."

"Uh. No. This is... well, you have to see."

She wanted so badly to put on her pajamas and crawl into bed. Pain shot through her rib cage every time she breathed, and her face hurt like hell.

"Please, Jackie. I promise I'll never get mad at you again. Well, if I do, I'll try not to act like a jerk."

"Hmm. Since you put it that way."

"I think you should bring Babu's chotki or a cross or something."

Was he losing it? "Thanks for the warning. Jeez, Jason, what's going on?"

"You just have to see. Call me when you get here, and I'll sneak you in. I don't want Mom and Dad to know you're here."

"I'm not allowed at your house anymore?"

"No, it's not like that. I just don't want you to get hurt."

Now she was worried.

She dug through her bedroom junk drawer for her chotki and stuffed it into her trench coat pocket.

What am I doing? This is ridiculous. What could possibly be so bad at Jason's house that it would require a holy relic?

Chapter 23

Jackie parked behind Jason's truck in his front yard and called his cell. He didn't answer. She called two more times. Still, no answer.

Worried that something bad had happened to him, she prowled up the front porch stairs and peered through the lace curtains on the front door. Voices, but not a soul in sight.

On the side of the house, the windows were too high to peer into, so she threw a pebble at Jason's bedroom window. "Jas," she called, but he didn't come.

From the back porch landing, she looked into the window. The kitchen light was on, but no one was inside.

On the other side of the house, a light was on in the basement. She squatted and looked in. Through the orange, burlap curtains, all she could see were moving shadows. She pressed her hand against the windowpane. It was warm, like from friction, despite the fact that it was fifty degrees outside. Her palm burned as if she had scraped it against carpet fibers.

The voices were loud. Jackie suspected that the shrill, nervous voice was Mrs. C. The woman screamed, and the shadows moved. Jason yelled and then Mr. C. boomed with accusing tones. Mrs. C. said something and screamed again.

Jackie was about to dial the police, but then thought, what if it was a false alarm? What would she say? She was just snooping around the house and looking in the basement window when she noticed domestic violence about to break out? Besides, Mr. C. would think Jason called, and then he'd really kick the shit out of Jason.

She needed to get inside to make sure Jason was okay. She remembered that Jason always sneaked in through his bedroom window when he was too late coming home. He kept a crate near his window for that purpose.

At Jason's window, she stepped onto the crate. Her nose was level with the sill and her eyes with the bottom of the window frame. She pushed against the window, trying to lift it. It moved slightly so that there was a hairline crack between it and the sill. She jimmied it again and raised it enough so that she could work her fingers into the crack and lift.

When she finally got the window open, she hooked her arms over the sill and pulled herself upward. A sharp pain cut into her side. She slid back down onto the crate. Of all the days for Jason to call and make up with her.

She took a deep breath, hooked her arms over the sill, and then jumped, pulling herself up at the same time. The movement was so swift that she didn't feel anything until she was jackknifed across the window with the sill pressing into her gut and bruise. She had broken a sweat, despite the cold. Pushing against the inside of the window frame, she shimmied her body over the edge and dropped with a *thump* onto Jason's bedroom floor.

She lay still and hoped that no one had heard her hit the floor. The voices in the basement never ceased, so she got up and sneaked into the hall, past the kitchen, and into the front room. The basement door was open.

Creeping down the stairs, she cringed every time a stair creaked. If Jason's parents got upset that she entered the house without being let in, she'd tell them the front door was open, that Jason said to just come in. Jason would either go along with her or not say anything at all, for fear of getting the holy-hell beat out of him.

At the foot of the basement stairs, she watched them—Jason, Mrs. C., and Mr. C.

"I told you, I don't want you seeing him," Mr. C. said.

Mrs. C. moved toward Mr. C. "I didn't," she said.

Mr. C. slapped her face. Mrs. C. screamed.

"Dad, you hit Mom again, and I'll kick your ass," Jason yelled.

Jason yelling? How out of character.

Mr. C. drew a backhand. "Come here, you little shit."

Against her expectations, Jason picked up the iron poker from the fireplace and raised it.

"I told you, I don't want you seeing him," Mr. C. said again to Mrs. C., ignoring Jason.

The poker was back in place, out of Jason's hand. How did she miss that?

Mrs. C. moved in toward Mr. C. "I didn't," she said.

Mr. C. slapped her face. Mrs. C. screamed.

"Dad, you hit Mom again, and I'll kick your ass," Jason yelled.

The same scene happened again. They were caught in a script.

Jackie stepped in closer, but not one of them noticed.

"Jason," she called, but he didn't acknowledge her. None of them did.

As she got closer, the hair on her arms rose, and some of the hair on her head rose too. A tickling sensation wavered through her body like she was passing through the outer edges of some electric force.

A picture on the mantel fell and crashed to the floor, startling only her.

Inches away from Jason, she looked into his eyes. "Jason."

"Dad, you hit Mom again, and I'll kick your ass." Jason went for the poker. Jackie stepped out of the way so she wouldn't get jabbed. Another picture fell from the mantel.

"Jason," she screamed.

The poker was back in the fireplace rack.

"I told you I don't want you seeing him," Mr. C. said.

Mrs. C. moved toward Mr. C. "I didn't."

Mr. C. slapped her face. Mrs. C. screamed.

"Dad, you hit Mom again, and I'll kick your ass." Jason went for the poker.

Jackie placed her hands on Jason's shoulders. "Look at me. It's me. Jackie." The hair on her head shot straight up. The lights dimmed momentarily, and then glowed at their normal intensity.

Whoomp!

The lights went out, and something struck her head.

Chapter 24

When Jackie opened her eyes, Mom was standing over her, a thin curtain drawn behind her.

Mom leaned against the bed rail and touched Jackie's arm. "I didn't even know you left the house," she said.

I'm in the hospital? "What happened?"

"You were hit in the head. They think with a TV," Mom said.

"Mom! That's totally not funny." Her head ached.

"I'm not making that up. It was lying near you on the floor. They arrested that... that..."

"Who?"

"Bob... Mr. C."

Jackie was confused; her mind, blank. She closed her eyes and tried to remember the events leading up to the hospital. She remembered trying to get Babu to take her medicine and then going to her room. Her phone rang. It was Jason. He was in trouble.

Then, memories flooded her mind—Jason and his parents, their repetitious actions and dialog playing like a video on a loop, pictures falling off the mantel, paramedics peering over her.

"The police may come here tomorrow to question you," Mom said.

"They're going to have a long list of things to question me on."

"Oh?"

"They'll never believe this one."

A doctor with bushy hair and square-framed glasses walked into her room, a clipboard and pen in his hands. "Hi, I'm Dr. Zinba. How are you feeling?"

"Like hell," Jackie said.

"Any pain?"

"My head feels like it's being squeezed in a vice."

He made a mark on his clipboard. "Nausea?"

"A sip of water would probably make me blow chunks."

He marked his clipboard again. "You suffered a concussion," he said, casually.

Mom covered her mouth.

"Holy shit!" Jackie said.

"According to the Cantinellis, you were unconscious for less than a minute," Dr. Zinba said, "so it appears to be mild. We'd like to keep an eye on you, though, at least for the next twenty-four hours... just in case anything serious develops."

"Mom, I don't want to miss school." What she really wanted was her life to be back to normal, which included being friends with Jason and going to school every day without being persecuted or harassed by Sandra and her henchmen.

"It's one in the morning," Mom said, "and you're in no condition to go anywhere."

Jackie found her predicament all so weird. Madam Sophie warned her that if she didn't learn how to protect herself, she would put herself in physical danger. It would have been nice of her if she had been more specific. Like, *Hey, don't go to Jason's house today because you're going to get hit in the head with a thirty-two-inch flat-screen TV.*

But Jackie probably wouldn't have listened to her and would have gone anyway. And how the heck could she have protected herself from what happened at Jason's house? It was like she was caught inside a magnetic force. Maybe she imagined it all.

Maybe Mr. C. did hit her with the TV. Her head really hurt. She didn't know what to think. There was an IV in her arm and a full bag on the rack. She really didn't think she had a choice.

"Fine," she said. "I'll stay."

Chapter 25

A staff member wheeled Jackie to a permanent hospital room. Once her head sunk into the pillow, it didn't take her long to fall asleep. In the middle of the night, she was awakened by a nurse taking her vitals. She fell back to sleep, but didn't sleep as soundly as she did before. Soon, she was awakened again, this time by the smell of bacon.

At a little after eleven, a tall, lanky man in a suit walked into the room and flashed an open wallet with a badge. "Hi, I'm Detective Sikes." He pulled a pen and notebook out of his jacket pocket, and after small talk about the weather and how she was feeling, he asked, "Can you tell me what happened last night?"

She wasn't sure what to tell him. The whole event was bizarre, so she started with the basics. "Well, my friend Jason called. He wanted me to come over, but he didn't say why. I could tell by the sound of his voice that something was wrong. When I got to his house, I called him so he'd open the door. I hate ringing the doorbell. I'm always afraid his dad is going to answer the door. He's such a... crab ass."

Detective Sikes noted that as well.

She smiled.

"Go on," he said.

"But Jason didn't answer his phone, so I called a few more times, and then I just went inside." Detective Sikes didn't need to know how she got inside. "I was worried about Jason because of the last domestic fight his parents had." This should justify her breaking and entering through Jason's window, should that piece of info already be in his police report.

Detective Sikes nodded.

"So, when I got inside, Jason and his parents were in the basement, arguing. When I tried to get Jason's attention, something hit me in the back of the head, and here I am."

"Did you see who hit you?"

"No. From what I was told, I was hit with a TV. It hit me from behind. I never saw it coming. The thing is, I'm ninety-nine percent sure it was an accident.

Having no logical explanation to feed him, she shrugged.

"What about the bruises on your body and face?" he asked. "How did those get there?"

Nice. They saw the bruises. "I tripped when I went to fill Babu's prescriptions."

He made note of this. "Mrs. Cantinelli and her son Jason aren't pressing charges against Mr. Cantinelli. The side of Mrs. Cantinelli's face was red and swollen when we arrived on the scene," he said, looking at her like she might be lying about her bruises. "But she hasn't said a word about how it happened. If Mr. Cantinelli attacked you, I would strongly suggest you press charges because he's going to hurt or kill someone. It's just a matter of time."

"He didn't attack me. I'm sure of it."

"So that TV just flew up from its stand and hit you in back of the head?"

She nodded.

He handed her his card. "We're going to let Mr. Cantinelli go since we have nothing to hold him on. Maybe after your head heals, you'll be sure about that other one percent." He started to leave and then turned. "You know, if Mr. Cantinelli hurts or kills someone, you'll be partly to blame."

She knew this was true, but after what she had witnessed, she didn't think it was Mr. C.'s fault.

When the hospital staff took Jackie for a CT scan, all she could think about was that Dad was going to shit when he got his half of the bill, despite Mom's insurance.

Back in her room, Mom called from work.

"So, what happened last night?" she asked.

Jackie really didn't want to go over this again. "I don't know. Mr. and Mrs. C. were arguing. Things got crazy."

"I don't want you going to Jason's house any more. I never liked Bob. There's always been something seriously wrong with him."

"How do you think Jason feels? He's stuck with him every day."

"It's not your responsibility to save the world. It never was. I'm sorry I couldn't protect you, back then. I—"

"Mom, it's okay. Thanks."

It was late afternoon. Jackie was sitting up in the hospital bed watching a soap opera with the volume turned down, bored to tears, and wanting to go home. From the corner of her eye, she noticed a young man standing at the room entrance in sweat pants and a hooded, zip-up jacket. He said hello to the woman in bed one.

It was David! Not on official business. Not good. She disappeared beneath the covers, hoping he wouldn't spot her.

Controlling her breath to keep quiet and lying still, she pretended to be asleep. His presence grew stronger as he, no doubt, approached the bed.

Go away!

"Jackie?"

A hand squeezed her arm. The warmth of it penetrated the thin covers, rushed through her arm, and sent her stomach whirling like a periwinkle in the wind.

She threw back the covers. "Would you stop that?"

He jumped back. "Sorry."

She pointed to the wall where the white board hung. "Stand over there."

"Am I being punished?"

She shook her finger at him like Babu in scolding mode. "You…"

His hands folded in front of him, his head down, he ambled toward the wall. "I do not know what happened between us at the church, but I am sorry."

"Ha! Don't even think it was you. It was the candlestick."

Looking like a guilty schoolboy, he raised his eyes to look at her. "Then, why am I standing here?"

"Because you… you have this weird energy. It annoys me."

"Sorry."

"I don't know what the heck goes on in that church and what I picked up."

He smirked. "Obviously, too much. Father Dmitriev gave me an hour lecture on the dangers of getting too close to the patrons."

Her face burned, and she covered it with her hands. "I meant the candlestick."

"Honestly, I am very sorry I put you through that. I did not know you were so… sensitive."

"Father Dmitriev thought I was possessed back in the day. Now, I bet he's pretty much ready to burn me at the stake."

David nodded. "But that is only his opinion. I pray all the time over the problem in the church, and still it persists. Father Dmitriev has performed several exorcisms too, to no avail. We tried to keep the problem hidden from the congregation, but someone looked behind drop cloth. Now, the whole congregation knows. That is how I learned about you. Some church members came to me and begged me to ask for your help. They think God has blackened the icon to bring you back to church. You are still special to these people, despite what Father Dmitriev says."

This vision thing had gone too far. "I'm not what people say I am."

"They say that they felt energy around you. It made them feel good. I know what they are talking about, because I feel it too."

He feels my energy? "It's all in their heads."

David looked offended.

"How come the congregation never felt this way about me before I had the vision?" she asked.

"Maybe you were blessed the day you had it."

Ugh! There was no convincing David she wasn't who he thought she was. She had to come clean, tell him the truth. The whole school knew it. The congregation may as well know it too. Maybe then, David would leave her alone.

"I lied. I never saw the Virgin."

David's lips parted. He gazed at her, silently.

"I was scared. It was the first time this whole touchy-feely thing came to me. The vision of the fire was so vivid, I freaked out. Father Dmitriev made me feel like I'd carried the devil into the church, and everyone was staring at me like I was possessed. I was afraid that Father Dmitriev was going to throw me, Babu, and Grandma out of the church for good, so I made up the lie that the Virgin told me the church was going to catch fire."

"But it did."

"Well, yeah, but not because the Virgin told me it was going to catch fire."

"How do you know God didn't show you the vision?"

"Because I know what I am."

He looked at her like he didn't understand.

"I can read the emotion in objects and people. I know what's going on with them. I know what's happened to them."

"And you can predict the future?"

"No, I may have a feeling something's going to happen, but that's like intuition. Most everyone can do that. I just have extra help through the emotions I pick up."

"Then, if you cannot predict future, how did you predict fire?"

"I don't know."

"Would it be because God showed you?"

She grimaced. "And what if the vision came from Satan, like Father Dmitriev said it did?" She didn't really believe in Satan; she was just playing devil's advocate.

"That would mean that Satan has power within church, and that he showed you the vision to protect the church and to save a life. I do not think that is Satan's character."

"So what good did the vision do? I dropped the ball, and Stephanie died. And then everyone's on me like I'm all holy or something, when I'm not. I mean, I pretty much defrauded the church, and that's why I'm never going back there."

"Maybe God gave you this gift for a reason... to use for His good."

"I don't want to talk about this anymore."

"I understand." He took a step forward. "How is your grandmother?"

"Stubborn and not taking her pills."

He raised his brow. "Hmm."

"Don't say it."

He grinned.

"You will be proud to know, however, that I've been downloading Russian lessons. Maybe, someday, I'll be able to better communicate with Babu."

"Good. It must be hard for her not having anyone to speak with."

She was startled to see Madam Sophie standing by bed one, wearing her pink, quilted jacket and an olive-colored skirt that swept the floor.

"Oh, no," Jackie said, expecting hellfire to rain down on the room or for the ceiling to cave in.

David turned. He and Madam Sophie nodded at each other. Jackie guessed they were leaving it to her to make the formal introductions. She thought about just saying, "David this is Sophie," but to drop the title from Madam Sophie's name would be disrespectful—especially after Madam Sophie had been so kind to her. So, she dropped the bombshell. "David, this is Madam Sophie. And Madam Sophie, this is David Davidovich."

They stared at each other for a second or two.

"Madam as in fortune-teller, not prostitute," Madam Sophie said.

David blushed. "That did not cross my mind. I know who you are." Partially extending his arm, he held out his hand. Madam Sophie seemed hesitant about reaching for his hand as if she sensed that he was a seminarian and sparks might fly. But then she reached out and locked hands with him.

David pulled away. He looked nervous.

Madam Sophie eyed David up and down. "You're from the church. You are—"

"I am a seminarian completing my internship at Holy Resurrection."

"I would have gotten it if you gave me time," Madam Sophie said.

David flexed the hand that Madam Sophie had held.

"Madam Sophie was quite the Good Samaritan the other day," Jackie said, trying to ease the tension. "I was getting my butt kicked in town, and she came to my rescue."

Madam Sophie smiled, her crooked teeth showing.

"How did you know I was here?" she asked Madam Sophie, expecting her to have had some kind of a premonition.

"Newspaper," she said.

Jackie was kind of disappointed.

"Me too," David said. "I have to go. I have a basketball game with the neighborhood boys. Think about what I said." His gaze cut through Jackie. He glanced at Madam Sophie, a worried look on his face.

When David left the room, Madam Sophie looked curiously at her. "Problems at church?"

"Let's not go there."

"You want to tell me about last night?"

She really didn't. She was so tired of telling it, of filtering what she disclosed, but then she realized, with Madam Sophie, she could tell it all. She would understand. "Yeah," she said. "It was so weird. When I walked into Jason's basement, the room was hot, like there was friction or electricity in the air. And it was like the whole family was being controlled by some force. I mean, they weren't themselves. They were saying and doing the same things over and over like they were caught in a script. When I stepped in front of Jason, pictures fell off the mantel, the lights went off and on, and I was slammed in the back of my head."

"I warned you."

"What am I supposed to do? Lock myself in a padded room?"

"No. There are things you can do to protect yourself. You're a healer. You can protect yourself by zipping yourself up from the forces of evil and sending out healing energy to assuage those forces." She took a crystal out of her jacket pocket. "Take this."

Jackie shirked the crystal. "No. I'm good."

"It's just a natural object that will help ward off negative energies."

"No, thanks."

"The religious teachings of your church are so ingrained in your head, you can't even see a natural object for what it is. You can't even accept yourself for what you are." She slipped the crystal into her jacket pocket. "Come to my apartment. I'll teach you how to use your gift to protect yourself."

Father Dmitriev had called Jackie a heretic and a diviner. By the time Madam Sophie was done with her, he'd have sorcerer to add to the list.

"I'll pass."

"Call first," Madam Sophie said.

As she left the room, she passed Jason, who looked like he was about to shit when he saw her. "Was that Madam Sophie?" he asked Jackie.

Jackie nodded. Since she and Jason hadn't been talking, she hadn't gotten a chance to tell him about Sandra and how Madam Sophie came to her rescue. "I'll tell you about it later."

She was so happy to see Jason. She felt grounded, back to normalcy.

"I brought you something." Jason handed her the current edition of *Professional Photography*.

"Thanks." She set it on her lap.

"I'm sorry about what happened last night."

"It wasn't your fault. I'm sorry I couldn't help. Madam Sophie says I don't know what I'm doing."

He stared at her, slack jawed. "You're seeing Madam Sophie?"

"No. I'm not *seeing* her as in getting my fortune read. We're just friends."

His eyes widened.

"It's a long story. She's not a bad person. She's just... odd."

"Watch your back."

"Don't worry. I don't plan on seeing her again. So, how's your mom holding up?"

"She's not. Dad came home about an hour ago, packed his things, and left. Says the house is driving him crazy. He might be right. It was so weird. Ma and Dad were in the basement fighting. I came down to protect my ma, in case he flew off the handle. They kept saying and doing the same thing over and over. All I remember is walking over to them. After that, I don't remember anything until you were lying on the floor. My dad called the police. He told them he blacked out and thought he did it. He made them take him in."

"He did?"

Jason nodded.

"Well, if he comes home and goes berserk again, just come over to my house. My mom will understand. Unless you'd rather stay with Trish."

Jason dropped his head. "She shouldn't have told. I shouldn't have told."

"It's my fault. I'm sorry about what I said to you. I would rather die than hurt you."

Jason looked at her intently. "Me too." He leaned over and pressed his lips to her.

It was just a quick peck on the lips, but she was too stunned to say a word. She opened her eyes. Oh, God, she had closed her eyes!

Jason's mouth quivered.

Her heart was pounding. From one little peck?

He cleared his throat. "I need to see my dad. I'll call you later."

"Okay," she croaked, hoping the doctors came again soon because she needed her head examined now more than ever.

Chapter 26

Jackie spent another night in the hospital and was released the following afternoon. As soon as she stepped into the house, Babu dropped her needlepoint to her lap and crossed herself. Babbling in Russian, she hobbled over to Jackie in her slippered feet, grabbed Jackie's head with both hands, and kissed her on each cheek.

"I'll leave you to two to talk," Mom said and then disappeared into the kitchen.

Babu put her arm around Jackie. "*Prikhodi*," she said, leading Jackie to her room. She waved her hand at the bed. "*Sidi*."

Jackie sat down. Babu opened the bottom dresser drawer and took out the photo album she had showed Jackie the day she had passed out in the haunted bathroom. Babu opened the album to the photo of the three young women dressed in black. She pointed to the second woman and then tapped her chest.

"*Eto ya*," she said, and then, with a pitiful look in her eyes, she explained something to her.

"I'm sorry, Babu. I know that the woman in the picture is you, but I don't understand what you're telling me."

Babu sighed, looking tired and frustrated.

She had never read Babu. The only vision she had ever picked up from her was pure white light, and the only emotion she had ever picked up from her was peace.

Jackie slid the photo album from Babu's lap to her own and then held her fingers above the picture. "May I?"

"*Da.*"

Jackie touched the black-and-white photo and closed her eyes. In her mind's eye, she saw the three women, solemn and still. It was almost as if they were afraid to move, to even wriggle a nose or blink an eye—that, if they moved, evil would overtake them.

From the corner of her inner vision, a black mass floated into view, obscuring the three women. She waited for the darkness to pass, for the women to reappear, but the darkness hung in the center of her mind's eye, expanding and shrinking as if it were breathing. Concentrating, she tried to reclaim the vision of the women, but something seized her chest. In the split second of opening her eyes, a dark voice whispered, "Witches."

She stared at Babu, mouth hung open.

Babu, a frightened look on her face, took the chotki from her bed stand and pressed it into Jackie's hand. "*Molis'.*"

The chotki was lightweight and tickled Jackie's palm. It reminded her of the lock of hair she held after cutting her long tresses. She held it, knowing it had once belonged to her and thinking she could never reconnect it to her head. It was gone from her for forever.

"I understand, Babu. I know things aren't right with me, but I can't take your chotki." She tried to give it back to her, but Babu kept shoving it into her hand.

Jackie showed her the chotki and then patted her chest. "I have one of my own. I'll pray with my mine," she lied. She made prayer hands and then gave the chotki back to Babu.

Her forehead and eyes creased with worry, Babu took the chotki.

Jackie thought about how Madam Sophie kept trying to get her to take the crystal. She couldn't take that either. Somehow, it just felt wrong, as if she would be committing idolatry. How ironic. She couldn't take the chotki because it was no longer a part of her, yet she couldn't take the crystal because the teachings of the church were too ingrained in her. Madam Sophie was right. But she wasn't going to go to her for help. She didn't ask to be born this way. If all this misery was caused by the solar storm, she was sure the energy would eventually die, and everything would return to normal. Until then, she would just have to tough it out. Maybe, wear Mom's rollerblading helmet.

Chapter 27

At school, Jackie's locker was as good as new. It was chili-pepper red, like the other lockers around it, but slightly brighter because the paint was fresh. She tumbled the lock through its combination and took a deep breath before opening the door.

The only things inside were her own. She dumped her American History book and American Literature anthology inside, dug out her trig book, and slammed the locker shut before the pile of books and shit avalanched out the door.

Turning around, she found herself nearly face-to-face with Will. He didn't look happy. His thumbs were hung in his front jeans pockets, and he was wearing a tie and button-up shirt because of tonight's game.

He poked his index finger into her chest. "Stay away from Sandra."

She raised her hand and stepped back. "Whoa, you don't have to tell me. She's a psycho."

He glared at her.

He needed to know what a psycho Sandra really was, so she lifted the side of her shirt just enough to show him some of her bruises. "Courtesy of Sandra."

"That's nothing compared to what you did to her."

"Unless I have total amnesia, I don't recall doing anything, except rolling into a ball to protect myself. I didn't even touch her."

"You didn't have to. Sandra said you went with Madam Sophie up to her apartment. I know what you did. Everyone knows."

"Knows what? What did I do?"

"You put a curse on her."

"Curse? Did someone burn our science books and hurl us back into the Dark Ages? I went upstairs with Madam Sophie to put an ice pack on my face and take two Tylenol."

"John and Sean are afraid to leave their houses. Remove the curse."

"First of all, you're not my boss. Second of all, I didn't put a curse on anyone. I wouldn't do that; even if it could be done, I'm not like that."

"I was at the coffee shop when Madam Sophie drove you home. John, Sean, and I saw her take the wheel. They were spooked before the accident. Now they're really shitting bricks."

"Wait. Sandra had some kind of accident, and you think it's my fault?"

"It wasn't just an accident. It was a freaky accident like in the *Omen*."

Her shoulders tensed. "Is she alive?"

"Yeah. She's alive. But if I were her, I'd rather be dead."

She was afraid to ask, but she did. "Why?"

"Her car flew off the bridge and crashed into the bank. She was pinned at the waist. The steering wheel would have cut her in half if it budged another inch. She's paralyzed from her waist down."

Jackie's body grew cold. "I'd never wish something like that on my worst enemy. How could you think I would?"

"You're like one of those Wiccans or something. Everyone knows it. You read minds. You hang around that, that fortune-telling old bag."

"I don't hang around her. She helped me after Sandra beat the shit out of me. She's a nice person, you know. You shouldn't judge a book by its cover."

Will grabbed her arm.

"Ow! Let go of me."

"You take that curse off now! I don't care what you do to me, just leave Sandra alone."

She jerked her arm away from him. Crowds parted as she stormed down the hall.

"You're going to go to hell for this," Will shouted.

In the lunchroom, the three girls and one guy at Jackie's table, all which fell into the dork category, looked at her like she had some kind of disease. They whispered among themselves and then picked up their books and lunches and found other seats at the table by the stage.

Zeta sniffed her armpits. "I put on deodorant this morning. How about you?"

"Yep. Sure did."

"What do you think crawled into their lunch bags?"

"Me. They think I put a curse on Sandra."

"And not that Sandra's a dingbat who can't drive? She was probably texting at the time. That's not your fault."

"You knew about the accident?"

"Yeah. I didn't want to tell you. I figured you had enough to deal with, being in the hospital and all."

Jackie took a tiny bite of her Devilwood-spread sandwich. She wasn't even hungry. The bite of sandwich clung to the roof of her mouth. Trying to wedge it free, she wondered if any of her thoughts had created Sandra's accident. Madam Sophie said that she had the power to heal. What if she also had the power to throw curses?

Jackie thought through the things she was thinking at the time she and Sandra had their run in. Did she wish her ill, or dead? She wanted her to stop kicking, that's for sure. She also wanted to punch Sandra's face in, but she was sure that was Sandra's anger she was feeling and wanting to act out, not her own. And when Madam Sophie came to her rescue and threatened to curse all of them, how did she feel? She was glad, but only that it scared them away. She only enjoyed the power of Madam Sophie's words, not their intention.

Zeta waved her hand in front of Jackie's face. "Hey, Jackie. Hello. Are you okay?"

"Yeah, I'm okay. I was just thinking about Sandra."

"Don't let it get to you. You wanted people to stay away from you, and they are. There's a silver lining in every cloud."

"I don't want them to be afraid of me. Why can't anything just be in the middle? Everything in my life is always so extreme."

After school, Jackie drove to Mercy Hospital. If she could convince Sandra she wasn't a curse-casting witch, then maybe Sandra could convince everyone else, and they would stop being so afraid of her.

Sandra was sitting up in a Stryker frame, her eyes staring aimlessly at the wall. The curtain divider was drawn. The room, dim.

"Sandra," Jackie said.

Sandra jumped at the sound of her voice. "Get away," she spouted and then reached for the pager.

Jackie rushed to the bed and wrestled it from her hand. "No, just listen to me. I came to tell you that I didn't do it. I didn't put a curse on you."

"Then Madam Sophie did."

"That's ridiculous. Madam Sophie is a good woman. She would never do that."

"Nurse," Sandra yelled.

Jackie pressed her hand to Sandra's mouth to silence her. Sandra's eyes were about to bug out of her head. "Just stop," Jackie said. "I completely forgive you for what you did to me. I just want to be friends. Well, maybe not friends. Can we just stop being enemies?"

Sandra moved her head up and down.

"And I can take my hand off your mouth, and you won't scream?"

She nodded again.

Jackie removed her hand, but she was ready to put it back in case Sandra screamed. "So, you have no feeling from your waist down?"

Sandra shook her head.

"I'm really sorry this happened," Jackie said. "I'll definitely have Babu include you in her prayers. You'll be in my thoughts too."

Sandra pulled the covers to her chin.

"I'm going to go now. Can you tell John and Sean they have nothing to worry about? Maybe you can convince Will too. You know I don't like him. Maybe when I was thirteen, I did. Now, he's not my type. And I'm certainly not his type either. Having a conversation with his mother's thoughts at the Thanksgiving table put an end to our puppy love. Well, you take care." She wiggled her fingers and left Sandra to her silence. Jackie wondered if anything she had said to Sandra sank in.

Chapter 28

The hooks in the track rattled as Trish brushed back the divider curtain in Sandra's hospital room.

Sandra startled.

Trish leaned over the rail of Sandra's Stryker frame. "Don't listen to a word Jackie tells you. She's not the goody-two-shoes she wants you to think she is. I've seen her dabble with spells and work the Ouija board. Now she and Madam Sophie are like this." She entwined her index and middle finger. "She doesn't talk to me anymore. Not since she stole Jason."

Sandra, eyes wide, gripped the covers and shrank back, her head buried deep within the pillow.

"Don't worry," Trish said. "I'll do everything I can to stop her."

The curtain behind Trish ruffled against Trish's leg just above her knee-high sock. She turned to see the curtain blowing as if from an eerie breeze. The pitcher of water on the bed stand slid to the edge and crashed to the floor.

Sandra screamed.

Trish smiled and leaned closer to her. "You see? The evil follows her."

Chapter 29

Mom was at the kitchen table, on the phone, when Jackie came home. She glanced at Jackie and shielded the phone. "Jackie just got in," she whispered. "I'll call you later. Me too."

Jackie wished Mom would just quit and tell her exactly what was going on. Didn't Mom know she couldn't hide her emotions from her?

At the stove, Jackie lifted the lid on a pot. "I'm starving."

"You don't look well," Mom said. "You should have taken another day off. Where were you?"

"At the hospital."

Mom rushed toward her.

Jackie dodged the hand that was going for her forehead. "Mom, I'm okay. I went to visit a friend."

"You're as white as a sheet."

"I haven't eaten since lunch, and I barely ate then."

"Sit down. I'll fix you a plate."

She slumped into a chair and laid her head on the table. Her body was trembling.

Mom managed to wrap her hand around Jackie's forehead. "Hmm," she said. "Cool as a cucumber. Is everything okay at school?"

"I'm okay," she said, but the emotional weight of everything that went on that day—Will's accusations, people avoiding her like the plague, and the fear in Sandra's eyes—collapsed her chest. She fought back the urge to scream. She didn't want Mom to know how bad everything was.

"Can you eat?"

She wobbled her head to say yes.

Mom slapped some food onto a plate and warmed it in the microwave. Jackie took the plate to her room.

The food helped her regain a little energy, but her nerves were maxed out. She barely had enough strength to lift the fork to her mouth.

She was halfway through her mashed potatoes when her cell phone rang. She checked the display before answering. She didn't need to deal with anymore negativity today. But it was Jason, so she answered.

"Jas," she said, weakly.

"Hey. How'd it go at the hospital?"

"I don't know. Sandra wouldn't say a word, except to yell for help."

"I know you're having a rough day, but there's something I have to tell you."

She rolled her eyes. "What?"

"It's my ma, I think she's lost it, and I don't know what to do."

"Call your dad."

"I did. He's afraid if he comes home, he'll make matters worse."

"What's going on?"

"For the past hour, she's been sitting on the fireplace hearth in the basement, holding her head and rocking back and forth. At first, she was crying that Dad doesn't love her anymore. Something's not right about the basement. I'm scared, Jackie."

Chapter 30

Jackie knocked on Madam Sophie's door. She kept telling herself that she was doing this to learn how to protect herself so she could help Jason.

Madam Sophie opened the door, startling Jackie with her fortune-telling attire—her long Haitian dress, cornflower blue shawl, and crystal necklace. "Welcome, my child," she said and smiled, exposing her crooked teeth.

Jackie cautiously stepped inside. Her apartment, lit only with candles, reeked with incense, and the chairs at her fortune-telling table were pulled away as if she had been giving readings all day. Jackie's fingers trembled as she unbuttoned her trench coat.

"You're still not certain you want to be here," Madam Sophie said.

"I'm sure enough."

She took Jackie's coat and hung it on a quarter-moon hook. "Let's sit on the sofa."

Jackie had a feeling Madam Sophie wasn't happy with her answer.

On the couch, Madam Sophie took Jackie's hands in hers. A quiver ran down Jackie's spine. It reminded her of when Madam Sophie locked hands with her at the carnival. Back then she thought Madam Sophie was out to get her. She never would have believed that she'd be coming to Madam Sophie for help.

"You're a strong girl, yet vulnerable because of your ignorance," Madam Sophie said, dryly.

Jackie wished Madam Sophie would quit telling her how spiritually stupid she was. "I'm here now."

"Then, let me first tell you a little about your psychic ability. Through your senses and your unconscious mind, you can read more than the average person. We all have some psychic ability, but because most people brush off these sensations and revelations as coincidence and other things, they never develop their power. But your senses are very strong. You get these abilities from your great-grandmother."

She thought about Babu's light and shook her head. "I'm not like her at all."

"Shush," Madam Sophie said. "Like your great-grandmother, you have the power to heal. You can absorb and read incoming energy, and you can emit energy, healing energy. People sense this. They're drawn to you. That's why so many people were coming to you years ago. It wasn't the fact that you saw the Virgin that attracted them. It just made them notice you and invite the idea that you were special in this way."

"But I didn't see the Virgin."

Madam Sophie patted the top of Jackie's hand. "Yes, dear, I know."

Jackie's eyes grew wide. "How long have you known?"

"I knew back when people were petitioning against me. At first, I was angry that after all these years that I practiced my craft, I was being persecuted because of this child who came along and saw the Virgin. I watched you whenever I saw you in town or at the grocery store with your mother. Instead of feeling jealous, I sensed a frightened girl. A girl frightened of the gift she possessed and punishing herself for it and for the lie she told."

"My lie did a lot of damage. My parents got divorced because of it."

"If their marriage had any solid foundation, the incidents

your little lie had caused would have brought them closer together."

"But what about Grandma? She died of a broken heart because of me."

"That's what you called a heart attack as a child. She had a bad heart. It would have happened eventually. You need to accept what you are and quit blaming yourself."

"But I don't want to be a healer, I—"

"You already are," she snapped. "And through that gift, you will be able to help your friend Jason. With your positive energy, you can heal the house."

"The house? Seriously?"

"There are certain areas on earth and objects that contain imprints, or emotions, of past events, typically when something traumatic has occurred. The trauma leaves an imprint on surrounding objects. If the emotion is strong enough, the traumatic event that caused it plays out. The energy particles from the solar storm made these energy fields stronger."

"But, you said something the last time I was here about the susceptible. I thought you were talking about people."

"I was. Some people are more susceptible than others to the energy particles. It drives them crazy and makes them violent. It typically affects people who have these tendencies. The energy particles make the tendency stronger. Put them near imprinted objects, and they're powerless over their actions."

"So that's why Jason and his parents were caught in a script."

"They were caught in the energy left behind from some traumatic event that occurred in that house. The energy is affecting Jason's family and playing out through them. Heal the energy, and you will heal Jason's family."

"So, what do I need to do?"

"The first, and most important, thing you need to do is to learn how to protect yourself. I sense that you are in danger, more than when you were curled up on the sidewalk being kicked to death or when you were struck in the head. It's going to get worse for you. You need to be ready."

Normally, Jackie would have taken this as psychic mumbo jumbo, except that she thought Babu had been trying to tell her the same thing.

"Fine," she said. "Let's do it."

"Good girl." Madam Sophie rubbed her tiny, boney hands together. "Let's start with protection techniques. You need to learn how to spiritually zip yourself up to keep out the negative energy when you're in a highly emotional situation."

Jackie looked at her like she was nuts.

"It's just an imaginary zipper that you pull up from your pubic bone to your lower lip, like this." She pinched her thumb and index finger together and demonstrated.

"You're serious?"

"Of course, I'm serious. The area you are zipping is one of the energy pathways in your body. This area is capable of receiving negative energies. This is where your sickness is coming from when you're absorbing stray emotions. Zipping yourself up will allow you to block negative energies and to basically shut off your psychic ability. Try it."

"All right then." Jackie imagined a huge zipper running from her pelvis area to her lip. She pulled the imaginary zipper tab upward and imaged herself being safely zipped inside her body and all external emotions blocked out. If this really worked, she'd kiss Madam Sophie's butt on Main Street and give her an hour to draw a crowd.

"It will work if you believe it will work," Madam Sophie said. "Now, let's practice expelling the negative energies from your body. Sit up straight with both feet flat on the floor, your hands on your thighs. Take a deep breath. Hold it, letting your breath absorb the negative energy that is inside your body. Then exhale, imagining the negative energy flowing out your feet and into the floor."

Sitting erect with her feet flat on the floor, she did as Madam Sophie said. The breath she held grew denser and more tumultuous by the second. It pressed against her lungs. She held it inside until she could no longer contain it. She slowly pushed it from her lungs, imagining the airy beast sliding down her legs and seeping into the floor.

"Wow. I feel relaxed."

"Good. Let's work on turning your psychic power on and off. Rub your hands together like this." Madam Sophie moved her open hands back and forth against each other. "This will sensitize your palms before taking a reading."

Jackie rubbed her palms together several times and then stopped.

"Do you feel it?" Madam Sophie asked. "Do you feel the energy flowing through your palms?"

"Yeah, it's sort of tingly."

"Exactly."

"But, I don't want to be a fortune-teller. I just want to be able to fix Jason's problem."

"You won't be able to protect yourself if you don't learn how to turn your psychic powers on and off."

Madam Sophie had her practice on various objects that had belonged to clients of hers. With each object Jackie held, she had to tell Madam Sophie if the object exuded happiness or sadness, if the object belonged to a male or a female, and if any images, such as colors, symbols, or locations, came to mind. This was a cinch for Jackie. But after she held each object, she had to stop during the reading to zip herself up and to do the breathing exercise to cleanse herself of the energies she picked up. This was hard. She couldn't shake the mood of the impressions.

"You need to practice," Madam Sophie said, "on people. Start with a friend. Then, when you've mastered shutting off your psychic powers and cleansing yourself, come back and we'll develop your ability to heal."

"All right," Jackie said. She already knew the friend she was going to practice on was Jason.

Chapter 31

Before leaving Madam Sophie's, Jackie called Jason. "Jas, meet me at my house."

"I can't," he said. "I don't want to leave Mom alone. She's so depressed. I'm afraid she'll go into the basement and freak out while I'm not here."

"That's why I need you to come over. I think I can help her. I hate to say it, but you were right about something not being right in your basement."

"Ha! I knew it. But how do you know?"

"Madam Sophie."

"So you are seeing Madam Sophie!"

"I am now. She's teaching me how to deal with the emotions. And"—Jackie swallowed—"she says I can heal your house."

"Is this Jackie I'm talking to? What happened to all the denial?"

"I'm doing this for you... and to protect myself. Besides, it can't hurt to try. If it works, there must be some scientific basis as to why it works."

"Then, why don't you just come here and heal the house?"

"Because I don't know how. Not yet. I'm kind of in training, and I need your help to develop my... uh... abilities."

"I'm there," he said. "Dad's been staying at some dumpy hotel on the outskirts of town. If you can fix what's been driving us all nuts, then maybe he can come home. He's not the nicest guy to be around, but he is my dad, and he's never been that abusive. I mean, he hasn't been for a long time."

Jason showed at about seven thirty, when Babu was watching *Dancing with the Stars* and Mom was tucked away in her room. Jackie took him up to her bedroom and closed the door so Mom wouldn't know what she and Jason were up to. As far as having Jason in her room with the door closed, well, she didn't think Mom would care. Mom knew they were just friends.

They sat cross-legged on the carpet, facing each other.

"All right Jas. I want you to think of something, a single thing. I want you to feel it emotionally. Okay?"

Jason's fingers tensed. They looked like spider legs ready to creep across the carpet. "Okay."

"Then, I'm going to take your hands and read your thoughts."

"I thought you said you weren't psychic."

"In that way, I guess I am. I'm just not a fortune-teller. I mean, I can't predict the future."

"But you—"

"Just don't use the word *psychic*. Okay? If I didn't think I could help you in some way with this so-called talent, I wouldn't be using it."

He hunched his shoulders. "You can't change who you are. You can dye your hair, change your clothing style, but you'll still be Jackie. And that's not so bad. I think she's a great person."

Her heart warmed. "Thanks, Jas. Okay, then, let's start. Close your eyes and think of something you attach a lot of emotion to, like anger when your truck quits on you." She hoped he wouldn't concentrate on his emotional pain. She couldn't bear it. Not even for the short time she intended to read his emotions and then shut them out.

Jason closed his eyes.

"Nod when you're fully immersed in the feeling."

Jason's face was pale and innocent, his closed eyelids as big as quarters.

He nodded.

"Keep your eyes closed, and keep thinking about it," she said.

She worked her fingers beneath his hands. His hands were soft. His fingers wrapped around hers like tendrils. It was the first time, ever, that she had held Jason's hands. Sweat broke across her forehead and temples. She took in a few deep breaths and exhaled to relax, and then she closed her eyes and let the energy flow from his body into hers.

A taut vibration, like that from a bow sliding across the strings of a violin, grew in her gut. The vibration rose from its center and resonated in her heart. Her arms tingled, and her hands warmed.

The room was quiet, except for Jason's breathing and her heart pounding. It felt like her heart was between her ears because her ears were throbbing. An image of a beating heart flashed in her mind. Is this what Jason was thinking? She wasn't sure if she should ask, but Madam Sophie said she should spout out anything that came to mind, even if it didn't make sense.

All right. Here goes. "This may sound weird, but I see a heart beating inside my head."

Jason's fingers tightened around her hands.

The heart beat faster. Its warmth ebbed and flowed inside her, and she was immobilized by its rhythm.

"What do *you* feel?" Jason asked. His voice was the final paralyzing force.

Zipping herself up occurred to her, but even her will was subdued. Jason pulled her forward and pressed his lips to hers. Consumed with passion, she didn't resist. They rolled together onto the floor, smothering each other in passionate kisses.

A knock on the door broke the spell. Her eyes snapped open.

The handle wriggled. "Jackie, what are you doing in there?"

Mom asked.

"Nothing, Mom," Jackie said, her voice switching octaves. "We're just studying."

"Well, study with the door open, or come downstairs."

"Okay," she said. "Get off of me," she whispered to Jason.

Jason rolled off her. Kneeling before her, he looked at her with puppy-dog eyes. Jackie slowly raised her trembling body from the floor, using the bed for support. She hobbled to the door and unlocked it. When she opened the door, Mom was gone. She imagined the heat of her and Jason's passion pouring out of her room and into the cold hallway for everyone to see.

She dropped down on the bed beside Jason. "What were you thinking?" Dumb question.

"How I felt about you. I guess I got carried away with the kiss. But, you didn't resist."

"I was supposed to shut off the incoming emotions and then cleanse myself. That was the whole purpose of this exercise."

"Maybe, you didn't want to."

The memory of holding David in the church filled her head. "What just happened between us wasn't real."

"It was to me." His fawn eyes focused on the floor.

She wanted to touch him, but she was afraid to. "You have to understand, I get so caught up in other people's emotions, I don't know which emotions belong to me and which don't." She felt Jason's spirit slipping into sulk mode. "I need to learn how to control this 'emotions' thing. Just give me some time. Okay?"

"I promised I wouldn't get mad again, didn't I?"

"Yeah, you did. And we are friends, Jas, which means you're stuck with me, good or bad. Just, from now on, no more reading your thoughts."

Chapter 32

In American Lit, Jason sat slightly turned in his desk chair looking at Jackie. When their eyes met, his gaze lingered on hers. She looked away and fiddled with her pen, beating it against her notebook.

"Miss Turov," Mr. Davis snapped. "Do you mind?"

Mr. Davis looked like hell. His eyes were bloodshot, and he had bags under them as if he hadn't gotten a good night's sleep in days. There was something about his emotions that made her stomach tighten and fold into a fetal position. Something dark about him. And it had something to do with his wife passing.

"Sorry." She twisted the pen, squeezed it, and tried to bend it. Jason's energy kept floating her way. She coughed and cleared her throat.

"Is something wrong?" Mr. Davis looked agitated.

"No, Mr. Davis. Nothing at all."

Everyone was staring at her as Jason's thoughts flowed uninterrupted. He was thinking about their bedroom scene. She mentally zipped herself up.

The imaginary zipper held and protected her for about two seconds and then busted open.

"Stop it already," she said to Jason.

"Sorry, I can't help it," he whispered.

"Is something going on between you two?" Mr. Davis asked, crabbily.

Jason, slack-jawed, slouched in his chair. "No, sir."

The class laughed.

Jackie grimaced.

Mr. Davis tapped his finger on her desk. "I want to see you after class."

Great. She dreaded being near him with the awful emotions he was exuding, and she didn't want him in her business. She eyed the clock above the whiteboard. There were fifteen minutes left before the bell. Hopefully, he'd forget by then.

At the end of class, three classmates surrounded Mr. Davis with questions. Jackie slipped out the door.

At lunch, Jason sat down beside Jackie and scooted his chair close to hers. He was smiling. He dug into his crumpled lunch bag. His mother reused the bags until they disintegrated, and he ate the same lunch every day—salami on white bread with mustard and barbequed chips.

Zeta's eyes narrowed as she studied Jason. "What's up, Jas?" she asked with a smirk. "Bet I know what."

"Bet your mind's in the gutter," he replied.

"It lives there."

Jackie shook her head in disgust.

She startled when she saw Trish, who was standing at the head of the table, her lips rolled into a pout. Trish glared at Jackie and then walked up to Jason.

"What's this?" Trish asked Jason. "I thought you weren't talking to her." She said it like Jackie wasn't present.

He shrugged. "We made up."

"I'll bet you did." She turned to Jackie. "Bitch." She stormed out into the hall. Jason chased after her.

"Wow. Since when did Jason become such a Don Juan?" Zeta asked.

"Since he sidled up with Trish, I guess."

"You think they did it?"

"Trish did something to him. He's been awful frisky lately."

"Frisky," Zeta said. "Ha, like a puppy."

They both laughed.

Jason returned five minutes before lunch was over. He looked distraught, until he saw Jackie. Then, the color slowly returned to his cheeks.

"Sorry," he said to her as if she was expecting an apology.

She kind of missed the old, sullen Jason. He was... safer.

"Can we get together tonight?" he asked. "To work on your stuff?"

Zeta fanned her face. "This is really getting hot."

"That's not what he's talking about, are you Jason?"

"No, I'm talking about, like... your skills, so you can help me with my problem."

Zeta smacked the table. "Enough already."

"Zeta, would you just stop?" Jackie asked.

"We could do it in my basement tomorrow morning," he said. "My dad still hasn't come home, and my mom will be out running errands and doing her grocery shopping. It'll be safe."

Clutching her stomach, Zeta rolled with laughter.

"Stop it already, Z," Jackie said.

"Oh, I forgot. It's VQ I'm talking to." Zeta scooted back her chair and stood up. "Got to go. Don't do anything I wouldn't do."

"That doesn't leave much," Jackie said, trying to match her satire. When Zeta left, Jackie attempted to have a normal conversation with Jason. "I don't know if I'm ready. I still feel so vulnerable."

He clenched the hair draped over the side of his face. "Please, Jackie. I want my dad to come home. If we could at least find out what's been going on with the house, it may be a good start in solving this problem."

She sighed. "All right."

Chapter 33

When Jackie stepped into Jason's basement, the hair on her arms rose. "Do you feel that?" she asked Jason.

"What?"

"The energy."

"It's hot down here."

"Let me see your arms."

Jason pulled up his sleeves.

"Look, your hair is rising too," she said.

"Goose bumps? In a hot basement?"

"More like static electricity."

Jackie stepped farther into the room. The energy was strongest in the center. She felt agitated, like the air around her was brushing her the wrong way. She stopped and took a deep breath and imagined the air in her lungs sponging the negative energy inside her. Then she exhaled, expelling the negative energy–filled air. She inhaled and exhaled two more times like this.

Feeling less agitated and more in control, she walked toward the recliner.

Jason followed.

"Stay there," she snapped.

He raised his hands. "Okay, okay."

Jackie circled the recliner where the energy was the strongest and then sank down into its cushion. It was one of those swivel-rocker recliners. When she leaned her head back, the chair rocked a bit.

The recliner and the air around her made her feel agitated, jumpy. If she expelled the energy now, she wouldn't be able to get a good reading, so she let the energy overtake her.

Wanting to tear the stuffing out of the chair, she dug her fingers into the cloth arms. Jason stared at her. That poor, miserable, useless twit. She ought to just smack him. Her jaw tightened; the joints in her fingers grew rigid.

"What are you looking at?" she asked him.

He blinked.

"Don't you have homework to do?" she said. "You better go do it. You don't want to be a loser forever." A hole was opening up in the cloth as she wormed her finger into it.

Jason rocked from foot to foot, his hands in his pockets.

"Damn it, boy. What'd I tell you?"

A determined look formed on his face. How dare he defy her?

"Jackie, get up. Let's get out of here."

"I'm not your freaky girlfriend."

Jason tried to pull her out of the recliner.

Halfway out of the recliner, she freed her hands and plopped back on to the worn cushion.

"Jackie, get up."

"Quit calling me that."

He tugged her again. She jerked her hands away from him. He fell to the floor.

"Ha, you little shit." She wanted to kick a mudhole in his ass. She flew up from the recliner and drove the toe of her boot into his butt cheek.

"Ow!" He rolled away from her, jumped to his feet, and then rushed her.

They both fell into the recliner. Now, she was really pissed. Throwing punches into his sides, she whaled on him.

He pushed himself out of the chair. "Jackie! Get up!"

She lunged at him.

He jumped out of the way.

Her hands slammed into the rough fireplace stone, scraping her palms. She was stung by horror and surprise. He hurt her intentionally. How could he? He loved her, didn't he?

Even though she was emotionally hurt, the rage she had picked up from the recliner still drove her. She charged at Jason, knocked him to the floor by the stairs. Her heart racing, she came to her senses. She crumbled to the floor and sat next to him, her arms hung over her folded knees.

"You sounded like my dad."

"I'm sorry. I wasn't myself."

"Obviously."

"I told you, I didn't think I was ready for this. I'm still so vulnerable. What if I'd killed you?"

Jason's eyes were filled with hurt. "You may as well." He swallowed. "So now what do we do?"

"Go to Madam Sophie for more training."

Chapter 34

Jackie and Jason sat together on the tapestry love seat in Madam Sophie's parlor.

"My emotions got totally out of control," she told Madam Sophie. "I knocked Jason on his butt. I thought I was his dad."

Madam Sophie slid open the end table drawer. "You need to take this," she said, taking out the crystal she had tried to give Jackie the other day.

"I told you. I don't want to put my faith in an object. It just doesn't feel right to me."

"You're not going to be ready for the next step in solving Jason's problem if you don't learn how to protect yourself. This crystal will help."

"I'll practice. I promise. Just tell me what the next step is."

Madam Sophie returned the crystal to the drawer. "You need to research Jason's house. Find out what traumatic event occurred there."

"Then what? How do I heal the energy?"

"By neutralizing it with energy of the opposite polarity."

"I already know what the dominant emotion is," she said. "It's anger. Extreme anger."

"Yes, but you have to understand the person who put that energy there. Your positive energy will be strongest this way. You'll be able to envision that person and send the appropriate healing energies to him or her."

Jackie gave Madam Sophie the deer-in-headlights look.

"Trust me," Madam Sophie said.

"But, it's not like the person is there. I mean, it's just objects and energy. Right?"

"Their imprint is there. The whole traumatic event is imprinted on the surrounding materials. The ceiling, the walls, the floor. You must envision yourself reaching out to the person to whom the imprint belongs and send that person emotions of the opposite polarity. For example, if the emotional energy of the person was anger, you must envision sending that person energies of calmness, tranquility, and inner peace."

"How?"

"It's the opposite of reading someone's energy. Instead of acting as a sponge, you act as a floodgate, letting your thoughts and energies flow from your hands. It's just like when you practiced expelling the negative energies in your body. Let's have you practice on your friend."

Jason smiled.

"Not a good idea," Jackie said

"I thought he was your partner..."

"Was. He's fired."

"Now, now," she said. "Jason needs your help. There's no time for silliness. What I want is you to read Jason's emotional state and then send him energy of the opposite polarity."

"But how can you change the core tendencies of a person?" Jackie asked.

"Changing someone's emotional state is not the same as changing someone's core tendency. A person can be bad to the bone, but you can still send them energies to alter their emotional state."

"I guess. So, what is it you want me to do?"

"I want you to read Jason's emotional state. I'm sure you will find an emotion that needs healing."

Jason grew pale.

"No mind is safe from Madam Sophie," she told Jason. "So when I read you, no funny stuff. Just be yourself. Ready?"

Jason nodded and took a deep breath.

Jackie hesitated before taking his hands. She was afraid she'd fall under his spell and not be able to zip herself up. "I mean it. No funny stuff."

Jason grimaced.

She took his hands. They were soft, warm.

"Close your eyes, both of you," Madam Sophie said. "Jackie, open up to Jason's emotions."

Oh, jeez. Here it goes. Jackie closed her eyes and let Jason's energy flow from his hands into hers. The color purple washed over her inner vision, and the emotions of hurt and desire brewed in her chest. She sensed that Jason was at her mercy, like he was begging for her love. She wished he'd let up. She might like him in a romantic way if he were a take-charge kind of guy. Most of the time, she felt like his mom or his babysitter. Okay. So this was it. She would send him "take charge" energy. Whatever the results, it would be fun just to see if it worked.

"Concentrate on the positive energy you're sending," Madam Sophie said. "Jason, open up to Jackie's energy. Let it flow through your body."

"Yeah," Jackie said to Jason. "Take in the energy. Don't put any out there."

"Okay," he said, "but be easy on me."

Jackie focused on being in control. Then she let a "take charge" feeling fill her head and flow through her body and out through her hands. *In control, Jason. You will be in control. You will be strong, positive, and self-confident.*

She imagined Jason walking with his chest out and shoulders erect and flaunting his arm muscles—what muscles he had. She imagined him opening the car door for her, telling her to get in.

Sometimes she felt resistance in his hands, a blockage, and then an opening up as if he had opened up every pore in his palms to her. This was when he breathed in. She continued sending him these vibes, waiting for Madam Sophie to say time's up or something. Finally, after about five minutes, she let go of Jason's hands and flopped back into the couch. "I can't do this anymore. I'm exhausted."

"How do you feel, Jason?" Madam Sophie asked. "What's your dominant feeling right now?"

Jason raked his fingers through his angled bangs. He looked paler than before they started. He wiggled his fingers and took a deep breath. "I don't know. Confused, I guess."

After all that, Jason feels confused?

"Maybe Jackie should practice on you," Jason said to Madam Sophie.

"She can't," Madam Sophie said. "It won't work. I absorb and read everything, whether it's sent to me or not. I'll know quickly what she's thinking, and I'll resist letting it take control over me. Jackie, you must continue to practice this and your protective exercises before tackling Jason's house. Do you understand me?"

"But we don't have much time. Who knows what Jason's mom will do the next time she goes into the basement? I have to try it now."

"I'm telling you, it's dangerous."

Jackie's confidence wavered. "Why don't you come too? We can sneak you in when Jason's mom is running errands."

"Are you kidding?" Jason said. "My mom would freak. She thinks it's bad luck to have anything to do with horoscopes and fortune-tellers. She says it opens the door to the devil. She grew up Protestant."

"Jeez, Jas. You didn't tell her about me, did you?"

"She knows about your church vision."

"Obviously. But did you tell her the latest news? Does she know I'm—" She almost said it. "Overly sensitive to things?"

Madam Sophie shook her head. "Still denying."

"She just thinks you're going through normal teenage

growing pains," Jason said.

"Good," Jackie said.

"Be careful," Madame Sophie said.

When they left Madam Sophie's apartment, Jason held the door for her and then held the apartment building door open. Outside, he took her hand and he led her to his truck.

Inside his truck, Jackie smiled.

"What?"

"Nothing." She didn't want to tell him and spoil it. "Library?"

"Library." He placed both hands on the steering wheel and eagerly shifted the car into gear.

Chapter 35

In the Ravenwood Public Library, Jackie and Jason sat at a research computer. Jackie brought up the *Ravenwood Gazette* home page and then the news archive page. In the search area, she typed Jason's home address into the address field. There was a setting for the date range, but she wasn't sure how far back to start her search.

"Jason, how long have you lived in your house?"

"I don't know. I think we moved there when I was four. I know it was before I started kindergarten."

"Okay, so you're seventeen now, minus four. We'll start thirteen years ago and work backward with the dates. Hey, better yet, I'll look up local home sales first and find the name of the previous owners and the date they sold the house to your parents."

She entered Jason's home address in the search box for local home sales. Jason's house was listed along with the name of the previous owners, the date the house was sold, and the amount it was sold for.

"Holy shit, you guys paid almost two hundred thousand for your house."

He looked at her like, where have you been? "Our neighbors sold theirs last year for three hundred."

"Yikes! I'll never be able to afford a house at that rate, not even a garage. No wonder me and Mom live with Babu. I guess

David's got the right idea—free food and housing. Maybe I should become a nun and live in a monastery when I graduate."

"Who's David?"

"You remember. He's the seminarian who came to my door that day I pissed you off."

"You call him David?"

"Well, yeah, what am I supposed to call him? He's not an ordained priest. I can't call him Father David." That would sound weird. He was too young to be taken seriously as a priest. "You know he plays basketball with the neighborhood boys? He's pretty nice for someone who's going to be a priest."

"And what's he do with the neighborhood girls?"

"Jason, I know what you're thinking, and it's terrible. You don't even know him. How can you talk about him like that? You're jealous. You're jealous of a seminarian?"

"It's not as horrible as being in love with a guy who's going to be a priest."

"Oh, that is so ridiculous. I'm not in love, and I'm not joining a monastery. I was just saying—Come on. We're getting off track. I'm here to help you, remember?"

She navigated to the local news archive search engine and entered the previous owners' names and entered a date range equaling five years from when they sold the house.

"So, why do your eyes light up every time you say his name?"

Her fingers froze on the keyboard. "Oh, come on, Jas. That's just your imagination."

"No, it's not. Your mind's been elsewhere lately. Now I know where. So what is it you see in him that you don't see in me? What's David got that I don't?"

Okay. Now she was ready to spout it out—self-esteem—but she bit her tongue. This was going way too far. "We're never going to get anything done here."

Jason spun her chair around so that she was facing him and placed his hands firmly on her thighs. "Admit it. You felt something the other day when I kissed you."

Her shoulders tensed. "Do we have to talk about this now?"

He bit his lip, and then nodded. He tugged the seat of her chair, pulling her closer to him until their knees touched.

His heated emotions pressed against her. She swallowed. *Nice job on sending him feelings of being in control!*

"You feel it now, don't you?" he asked.

"I don't know what I feel. Nervous, I guess."

"I love you, Jackie. That's what I feel."

"Don't you think *love* is a dangerous word to toss around at our age? I mean, I don't even know who I am. Except that, currently, I'm a train wreck... a walking disaster. It's dangerous for you to even think about getting romantically involved with me."

"Making out with Trish was dangerous. I mean it was exciting, but I don't feel for her what I feel for you. I can't understand why you keep denying that you feel it too."

"It's not like I'm denying it. I do feel something for you. I mean, you're my best friend, and I can't imagine a day without you. And, I have to admit, I was jealous thinking of you with Trish. But I'm just not ready to move our relationship to the next level. Not now."

Jason's eyes grew watery.

Awkwardly, she wrapped her arms around him and hugged him to ease his pain. His heart beat in sync with hers, and his warm energy blanketed her body. Her heart radiated with love, but she didn't know if the love she felt belonged to her. Like in the church with David. It wasn't real. It couldn't be.

A tear escaped her eye and rolled down her cheek. Then, more followed. One after the other, tears dropped onto the back of her hands. She wiped the tears, hoping they'd stop.

She and Jason held each other for quite some time, and she cried quietly enough not to evoke the wrath of the librarians. She cried because Jason's passion and pain were flowing through her. She cried because she was totally screwed up.

Finally, with puffy eyes and Jason by her side, she quietly returned to her research.

Chapter 36

Sunday morning, Jackie walked up and down Main Street, camera strung around her neck, looking for places where emotions were soaring. Yesterday, she and Jason had discovered through their research that his house had belonged to Steve and Marianne Murphy. Steve had a history of violence: road rage, bar fights, and parking lot brawls. His wife, Marianne, and their three children had a history of bruises and broken bones.

Steve's days of violence ended when he bashed Marianne's head against the fireplace bricks. And, in a standoff with the local police, while Steve held his three children hostage, one of the officers, a sharpshooter from the Afghanistan War, got a clear view of Steve Murphy's head through the basement window and plugged him.

The anger Jackie had felt in Jason's basement, the frustration of not having anywhere to vent it but on someone else, and the fact that she had become Steve Murphy scared the hell out of her. The other day, she wanted to kick the shit out of Jason. What would she want to do this time? Bash his head against the fireplace? She needed to learn how to protect herself from Steve Murphy's violent energy. It occurred to her, last night, that maybe she could use her camera to disconnect from the emotions she picked up.

She spotted Tiffany's Antiques. A storehouse full of emotions, it was the perfect place to practice.

A bell on the door jingled when she entered. A woman in her fifties with a ruffled blouse and spiked blonde hair was sitting on a stool behind the counter. She looked up from the tattered paperback she was reading. "Good morning."

"Morning," Jackie said.

"Are you looking for anything in particular?"

"Actually, I'm not. I need to take photos for my photography class and was wondering if I could shoot some pictures of your antiques."

"Cool beans. Shoot away. Let me know if there's anything I can help you with."

"Thanks."

Jackie headed for the row of items against the back wall, a less conspicuous location should she totally lose it. A row of tall items—curios, chest of drawers, dressers, headboards, standing lamps, and coat racks—served as a cover. She touched her camera for reassurance.

The bell on the door jingled. A retired couple walked in. They were looking for antique pipes. The store lady led them to a display near the front of the store. *Yes!* This would distract the store clerk while Jackie did her thing.

Walking along a row of antiques, Jackie opened herself up to the object that held the strongest emotions. She was drawn to a curio made of cherrywood. She touched it, closed her eyes, and envisioned it coated in dust, sitting in the corner of an unused room full of objects no one cared about. Neglect was the prominent emotion. She removed her hand from its surface, took a deep breath, and imagined her breath soaking up the feelings of neglect that had settled inside her. Then, she exhaled, imagining the negative energy flowing out of her. She did this several times until she was cleansed.

That was easy, but neglect was a mild emotion.

She searched for something stronger. Her intuitive antennae went up as she approached a wooden headboard set.

She touched the headboard's scrolled design and closed her eyes. She envisioned a dim room with curtains drawn and an old man wrapped in dirty sheets, his mouth agape, his lips parched, and his eyes glassed over. The stench of death filled her nose. His son, his only living heir, visits with apathy. He asks the nurse how much longer his father has to live. The old man can't talk. He stares, eyes frozen open, glazed with death, and his mouth full of stink and rot.

A bad taste settled on her tongue and her insides felt hollow, as if a disease had eaten her organs and the marrow inside her bones. Her legs gave away and she collapsed. Lying curled on the floor, she couldn't get up. Her hand was no longer touching the headboard, but death was with her.

Breathe. Do the cleansing breaths.

She inhaled, but tasted the putrid air of decay. She coughed and gagged.

Quiet. Don't draw attention.

She tried to hold back the need to gag.

The camera. If she looked at the headboard through the camera's lens, maybe she'd be able to disconnect from the emotion.

She willed her fingers to touch the camera and bring it to her eyes, but her arm muscles wouldn't respond. She couldn't even crawl away from the headboard. Her heart raced.

The store lady and the retired couple were talking about antique pipes. No one knew that she was lying there, and if they did, what would they do, call an ambulance? Another day or two in the hospital was the last thing she needed.

Babu, help me.

She imagined lying beside Babu in her bed, her fingers entwined in hers, Babu's light flowing through her, cleansing her body of decay, pumping life into her dead muscles.

Jackie crawled a few feet away from the headboard. Her strength renewed, she took in a full breath. Holding it, she let it absorb the traces of death still clinging to her cells. Then, she expelled the tainted air. She did this several times until she was able to get up off the floor.

The store lady was ringing up the retired couple's purchase at the counter. "How's it going?" she asked Jackie.

"Fine, I think I got what I needed."

Babu's light. It was her crystal, her chotki, her talisman.

Chapter 37

As Jason drove Jackie to his house Monday evening, she sat silently in the passenger seat, except for her fingers lightly tapping the door arm. They hadn't said much to each other since they had left her house. They had awkwardly hugged on the front porch. It just didn't feel right to her. She didn't want to be Jason's girlfriend. She just wanted to be his friend, but she didn't want to tell him this. Not today. Facing Steve Murphy's violent energy was scaring her more than the thought of being romantic with Jason.

"Jackie?" Jason asked, jolting her from her thoughts. He was holding open the passenger door for her. "We have to hurry. Mom will be back from Bible study in about forty-five minutes. Are you ready for this?"

"I hope so."

In the basement, Jason lit an incense stick and placed it in a holder while Jackie rubbed her hands together briskly. Madam Sophie said the incense would aid in the healing process by making the energies flow more easily.

"Jason, no matter what happens, I want you to stay right here by the stairs. Don't come near me."

"But what if—"

"Jason, I mean it. Swear."

"Okay." He didn't sound that convincing.

She took the incense holder from Jason and entered the area where the negative energy was the strongest: the center of the room by the recliner and fireplace. The hair on her arms rose. The flyaway ends of her hair did too.

She placed the incense holder on the fireplace hearth and then sat down in the recliner and spread her fingers on the arms. She rubbed over the hole in the fabric she had created the last time she sat there. Then she focused on Steve Murphy, trying to recall the image of him from the pictures in the news stories she had read. She imagined that he was sitting in this recliner and she was inside his body.

Her finger wormed into the hole in the recliner arm, breaking the last of its bare threads. Heat ignited inside her. Sweat broke on her face, forehead, and scalp. Her fingernails clawed into the recliner's arms as she rocked the recliner back and forth in short, jerky movements.

Nothing ever goes my way. I work my ass off at the garage only to get stiffed out of a raise. My dickhead boss and his lame excuse that they ain't getting the customers they used to gripes my ass. Wouldn't stop him from giving himself a raise. His big house and built-in swimming pool. He ain't hurting. I'd like to take a lug nut wrench to the side of his head. I'd like to take a lug nut wrench to the side of Marianne's head. Marianne won't let it rest. Thinks I'm screwing up at work is why I ain't getting no raise. She's always bringing up things I done. I know she's messing around on me. She thinks I don't know. She thinks I'm stupid. I'm tired of supporting that...

Jackie's body trembled like a teakettle ready to blow its whistle. The objects in the room were trembling too: the pictures on the wall, fireplace tools, flat-screen TV. She wanted to rip the recliner to shreds with her bare hands.

"Jackie!" Jason yelled.

An object flew past her head and slammed into the wall

behind her.

Don't let Steve Murphy control you.

She closed her eyes and imagined she was sitting beside Babu on her bed. A candle was burning by the Virgin icon on her dresser, and Babu was squeezing a chotki bead between her thumb and index finger. Jackie wanted to scream and throw things, grab the chotki from Babu's hands and tear it to shreds, knock the candle over and set the room ablaze.

The fireplace tools clanked violently, and the pictures on the walls rattled.

"What's going on down here?" Mrs. C. asked.

"Mom, you're back," Jason said.

"What's she doing? What's she doing to my home?"

"Mom, she's trying to help."

"She's cursing it. Make her stop."

"She's not, Mom. She's trying to, uh, get rid of the negative energy."

Please go away. Let me finish. Babu is slipping away from me.

The recliner spun around twice, so fast that Jackie was pinned in place by its force.

"Get out," Mrs. C. screamed. "Get out of my house." She entered the highly charged area and stood before Jackie, her hands on her hips.

Jackie wanted to strike her, to bash her head against the fireplace stones. "Babu," she said with clenched jaws.

Mrs. C. slapped Jackie's face.

Jason tugged Mrs. C.'s arm. "Leave her alone."

"Get out," Mrs. C. screamed. "I heard what you did to Peggy's daughter, Sandra. Get out of my house, you witch!"

There was too much anger in this room.

Fight it. Think of Babu.

The soothing drone of Babu's Russian prayers and the gentle roll of her tongue over *r*s filled Jackie's head. Pure white light surrounded her, bright and clear like Christmas pin lights. It filled her head, her heart, and her body. The recliner shuddered. Objects flew over her head and smacked the wall behind her. The TV fell from the stand and crashed to the floor.

"How dare you let her into our home to work her magic?" Mrs. C. said. "She's destroying our family."

"She's not. Leave her alone."

"Get out!" Mrs. C. scratched Jackie's arms, trying to uproot her from the recliner.

Jackie fought the urge to sink her claws into her, to tear her to shreds like she wanted to do to the recliner. The recliner jerked hard to the right, throwing Mrs. C. backward and onto the floor.

The recliner spun. Jackie closed her eyes and envisioned Babu, the candle burning in her room and the icon of the Virgin. She envisioned Babu rolling the chotki beads between her fingers, and she listened to the drone of her prayers. Babu's energy squelched the anger and frustration. She breathed and imagined her lungs filling with Babu's light. Then, she exhaled, letting the energy flow out of her hands and into the recliner arms. She envisioned it flowing through the chair, into the floor, and spreading to the walls.

The fireplace tools clanked. The pictures on the walls rattled violently.

"Stop it!" Mrs. C. covered her ears.

Immersed in the light, Jackie continued to take full breaths and exhale, letting the calming energy flow from her hands.

The recliner slowly stopped spinning like a Tilt-a-Whirl ride coming to an end. Pictures fell from their hooks and crashed to the floor.

Everything became still, except for Mrs. C. crying for her to leave.

"I think I did it," Jackie said to Jason.

"I don't understand what's going on," Mrs. C. said between sobs.

"It's going to be okay, Mom."

"Make her leave," Mrs. C. said. "I don't want her in this house ever again."

"Mom, she—"

"It's okay," Jackie said. Dizzied from the spinning recliner and the scent of incense, she couldn't lift herself out of the chair. "I don't think I can get up."

Jason helped her.

She threw her arm around him and used him for support.

"Inviting devils into this house," Mrs. C. said. "Now I know that's what you do with that creepy makeup and your black fingernails. Devil's child. I'll have to get Pastor Phil to cast the devils out. Yes. That's what I'll do. And then Bob can come home."

Mrs. C. was still ranting when Jackie and Jason walked out the front door.

Jason drove her home and helped her up the stairs to her room. He helped her out of her coat. She kind of liked Jason taking care of her for a change.

When Jason left, she fell asleep and had a horrible dream. She dreamed that she was in Jason's basement about to be beat to death for witchcraft. Mrs. C. accused her of being a witch as the congregation from Holy Resurrection bore witness. Sandra was there, too, pointing at her from her wheelchair and telling everyone she put a curse on her. Father Dmitriev struck her first with a golden candlestick. David was there, too, but he couldn't save her because she had chosen the other side by taking the power to heal into her own hands. He stood there, helplessly, as the congregation came at her and Babu with anything they could readily pick up—umbrellas, canes, candlesticks.

Babu took her hand, and the basement walls disappeared, revealing the edge of a forest. "*Prikhodi*," Babu said, and they escaped into the dark forest where it was safe. But they were alone and hiding.

Chapter 39

At school, Trish—an extra dose of eyeliner beneath her eyes, lips painted blood red, and wearing her Catholic school-girl-gone-bad getup—shot Jackie a daggered look from her locker.

"I wish she'd just stop," Jackie said to Zeta. "What did I do to her? What did I do to anybody?" She slammed her locker door shut. "Everybody hates me."

"Hey, not everybody," Zeta said. "Don't count me in."

"I know. Thanks."

"Hey, did you help Jason with his problem?" she asked, carrying on her sick, running joke.

"I hope I did. I gave it my best."

Trish shot her another look.

"Beware the wrath of Trish," Zeta taunted, smiling and showing her devious eyetooth.

In study hall, Jackie sat at a different table than Trish. From several tables over, Trish's gaze bored into her. She couldn't study.

She had enough of this. This was childish. She had always been a good friend to Trish—a true friend—and now this was how Trish treated her?

Jackie strutted over to Trish's table. Ignoring Jackie, Trish doodled in her notebook.

"Trish!"

She turned her head slowly to look at Jackie. Her lips were drawn as tight as a Victorian purse string, and she had a vehement glare in her eyes.

"This is silly," Jackie said to her.

Trish's eyes widened as if Jackie had pissed her off by belittling her attitude.

"How about we talk about this," Jackie said. "Okay?" She straddled the bench, even though Trish didn't respond. "Why are you so mad at me?"

"You should know."

"If I did, I wouldn't be asking."

"Jason was mine, and you stole him from me. You never liked him until I did."

"Whoa. Jason and I are just friends, just like before. Nothing's changed." Why did she have that achy feeling in her chest, like she was lying?

"Oh, yeah? Is that why you two were all over each other in your bedroom?"

"Ah... that. How did you, uh, know...?"

"Jason told me. He said your kiss was incredible, that he never felt anything like it before. How could you? You knew Jason and I did it."

"No, actually, I didn't. I knew you guys made out. I didn't know you went that far. Anyway, to set the record straight, *he* kissed *me*."

"And then you kissed him back."

"I was, like, in a trance. I didn't know what I was doing."

"Yeah. Sure."

"Jason and I are just friends."

"Don't you think he deserves more than that? How dare you kiss him if you don't love him?"

Trish's words nailed her in the gut. She hadn't meant to kiss him. Or had she? She didn't know. She didn't know what was real when it came to her emotions. "I'm sorry. I'll talk to him. Honestly. I'll try to make this right." She couldn't make him love Trish, but she could be honest about her own feelings.

As Trish studied her, Jackie felt her distrust.

Back at her table, Jackie couldn't concentrate on her homework. She couldn't think logically at all. Solving life's problems was more difficult than solving trigonometry problems. There were just too many factors—human factors. But one thing was for certain: she had to have a heart-to-heart with Jason.

Chapter 40

In the lobby of the Starlight Hotel, three scroungy-looking guys in their late forties were sitting on dirty couches watching TV. So was this where you went when your life hit the shitter? They needed to add a Starlight Hotel square to the *Game of Life*. When you land on it, you leave your family pegs in the car, and go live in squalor.

The elevator was out of order, so she and Jason walked up a cruddy stairwell to the second floor. Afraid to touch the door handle, she pushed the stairwell door open with her shoulder, contaminating the arm of her trench coat instead.

"He's in room 2B," Jason said.

The hallway smelled like somebody, or everybody, pissed in it. She wanted to throw up. She covered her nose with her hand, the only way she could zip herself up to this.

Jason knocked on a grimy, yellow door. The number 2 was crooked and leaning against the letter *B*.

The door opened. Mr. C. looked like he had just come home from work. His hair was sweaty, and his shirt and jeans smeared with grease.

She was still angry with him for hitting Jason, for being the jerk that he was. Despite the violent energy in the house, he was still mean to the core.

"Hey, Dad." Jason sounded lighthearted, hopeful.

"Hey," Mr. C. said. "Come on in."

That was odd, Jackie thought. She didn't detect any tension with Mr. C. The energy in the room was tranquil, lonely, and remorseful.

"How's your Ma?" Mr. C. asked Jason.

"Psycho," Jason said.

Great. That'll get him to come back home.

Mr. C. raised his beer bottle to his lips and took a swig. Then he looked at them. "I don't have no pop or nothing, just water. Got one cup, though. You'd have to share."

"We're good." She didn't even want to sit on the couch, let alone put a dirty glass to her lips. She knew she and Jason would laugh about this later—if they didn't leave with a life-threatening disease.

"Dad, you need to come home. Mom's depressed without you."

"It ain't been good there," Mr. C. said. "I don't know what's been getting over me. I'm better off here."

"I don't know, Dad. Mom entertained Pastor Phil for two hours yesterday."

"That dirty, rotten snake."

"Mom wants you to come home."

"I know. She called yesterday evening crying. Said something about your friend here inviting devils into the house."

Oh, jeez. That'll get him to go home too. If I were him, I wouldn't go back either.

"What were you two doing in the basement to set her off like that?" Mr. C. asked.

"We were kind of trying to get rid of the bad vibes," Jason said.

Mr. C. leaned back into the couch and picked at the beer bottle label with his thumbnail as he studied Jason.

"We thought there might be some bad energy in the basement, since every family fight we had happened there," Jason said.

"Bad energy," Mr. C. repeated. "Huh."

"Yeah, and Jackie and I got to investigating and found that the former owner killed his wife in the basement."

"You know about that?" Mr. C. asked.

"You knew about it?" Jason said.

"Yeah. I got the house for fifteen grand under the asking price because of it. So you guys were working some kind of magic in the basement?"

"Oh, no, sir," she piped in. "No magic at all. It's all physics."

"Your ma said things were flying across the room. Is that true?"

They both stared at him, dumb-faced.

"They were flying that night you all had that fight," she said, "and I was hit in the back of the head. You didn't hit me. That's why I never pressed charges."

"So the basement is haunted?"

"No. It's just energy," she said. "The basement contains the energy from the murder and all the other violent events that occurred there. Think of it as writing data to a hard drive and then reading the data. You and your family were affected by the energy patterns stored there. It's like you were reading the patterns and acting them out."

"No, shit. I sensed that something didn't feel right down there. But why is this happening now? We've lived there for the past thirteen years."

"It has to do with the solar storm we had two weeks ago. It blasted magnetic particles to the earth and made the stored energy stronger."

"Sounds like something from *The Twilight Zone*." He took a swig of beer. "Pastor Phil, huh?"

"Yeah, Dad. You know how much respect Mom has for clergy. You can't let this happen."

Mr. C. nodded. "All right. Give me some time. But if we have another incident, I'm out for good."

On the drive home, Jackie wanted to talk to Jason about Trish, but there was this wonderful glow on his innocent face and his aura was bright. She didn't want to ruin his mood. It made her feel good inside. And she really wasn't sure if she wanted to give that up to Trish.

She *was* being selfish. Trish was right. Jason deserved the same love that he offered in return. But, romantic love or not, Jackie would give her life for him. What greater love was there? She supposed, though, Jason wasn't looking for a superhero, just a girl capable of loving him the same way he loved her. She didn't think she fit that bill. She was going to have to be straight with him. Tell him that Trish just may be the girl for him, if he'd just give it a try.

But not today.

Chapter 41

Jackie still couldn't get Babu to take her meds. Her cholesterol and high blood pressure pills had become a permanent fixture on the kitchen counter. By permanent, she meant they hadn't moved from between the blender and the toaster since she set them there.

As Jackie ran the hand mixer in the pot of potato chunks, she contemplated pulverizing Babu's dosage and stirring it into her mashed potatoes. With a little chicken gravy on top, Babu would never know the difference.

Mom had been no help at all. In fact, she'd been coming home late for the past few days. Like, nine o'clock in the evening late. And she wouldn't tell Jackie where she'd been. It was kind of funny that Mom thought she was keeping her love life a secret from her.

Jackie put two lean slices of chicken breast on Babu's plate and a heap of mashed potatoes. All right, so what's the worst that could happen if she did slip Babu's meds into her food? If she didn't touch her mashed potatoes and gravy because of it, she'd be all the better.

Jackie shook out a pill from each bottle and folded them in a paper towel. Then, she beat the paper towel with the edge of the rolling pin. She sprinkled the white powder onto Babu's mashed potatoes, whipped it in with a fork, and topped it with a well of gravy.

"Bon appétit!"

The front room was booming with the sound of *Wheel of Fortune*. Wireless TV headset, she reminded herself. Christmas. She set Babu's plate on the TV tray. Okay, so she first glanced at the TV to see what Vanna was wearing. Who could resist?

She sniffed the aroma of Babu's meal as it rose up with steam. Didn't smell like meds. That was good. Hopefully, it wouldn't taste like meds either.

"Enjoy, Babu," she said with a smile.

Jackie's cell vibrated in her hip pocket. She dug it out. It was Jason.

"Jas, what's up?" She casually leaned against the kitchen door frame and watched as Babu lifted a forkful of mashed potatoes.

"My dad's home," he said.

"Cool. How did it go?"

"When Dad walked through the door, Mom was speechless. They just stood there staring at each other for a while. For a minute, I thought she wasn't going to take him back. Then he dropped his bags and hugged her. They stood there holding each other for a long time, until Mom suggested coffee. Then they sat at the kitchen table talking. I'm just afraid they'll wind up downstairs and this whole thing will start up again."

"Thanks for your confidence."

"Sorry. It's hard to believe in something you can't see."

"Maybe I should come over, just in case—with Mom's rollerblading helmet, of course."

"My mom will freak if you step one foot in this house."

"And you're in love with a girl your mother doesn't approve of?"

"It's none of her business."

"It would be if we ever got married. It's not a good omen for parents of the young couple not to show for the wedding."

"You'd marry me?"

"Uh, no, that wasn't my point. I was just trying to... never mind. We really need to talk, you know. Your Mom won't even know I'm in the house. I'll sneak in through your bedroom window. You can play your music loud, like you always do."

"What about your car?"

"Come pick me up. I'll hide in the truck until you get inside and open your bedroom window."

"Hmm. I get to sneak you into my bedroom?"

"No funny stuff. We really need to talk."

"All right. Be there in twenty."

She tucked her phone back into her pocket. Babu was leaning back in the couch, the TV tray pushed to the side. She had eaten all the chicken, but she hadn't touched much of the potatoes.

"Babu, you're not hungry?" she asked, shaking her head and tapping her stomach.

Babu said something in Russian and waved her hand for Jackie to take the plate away. Jackie wondered if Babu could taste the medicine or if she was still angry that she wouldn't pray with her.

Defeated, Jackie took the plate. In the kitchen, she quickly washed it and the silverware and then stacked it all in the rack to dry. She did a paranoid check to make sure she had turned off the oven and burner. Then she grabbed her trench coat and satchel and waited for Jason on the front porch. She thought that maybe she should call Mom and see where she was. After all, she hated leaving Babu alone. But then again, she didn't want Mom to know she was going to Jason's. Mom didn't want her going there anymore, and ironically, Mom had this sixth sense when it came to Jackie lying to her. Hopefully, she wouldn't wind up in the hospital again, and she'd be home within an hour or two.

As soon as Jackie climbed into Jason's truck and pulled the door closed, Jason floored it.

"Whoa, slow down," she said. "This is a residential."

"Sorry."

The speedometer dropped from forty miles per hour to thirty and remained there until they got to Route 6, where it climbed to seventy.

"Where's the fire?" she asked.

"I want to be home in case something happens."

"Your confidence in me is unnerving."

He shrugged. "I just got a bad feeling."

Great.

As she and Jason approached his house, she hunkered in the passenger seat of his truck. Her stomach was churning. She hated doing underhanded things, especially when her reputation was at stake.

"I'll call you when I open the window," Jason said.

"All right."

Jackie slid down to the floorboard and dug her phone out of her satchel. Her stomach quivered. She didn't think she could bear another accusation hurled at her.

Her phone rang. Jason gave her the word. She slipped out of the truck and tried to close the door as quietly as she could. Then she did a hunkered rush to the side of the house. The crate was under Jason's window—where she left it—and Jason's window was open.

She balanced herself on the crate so it didn't tip over, and she hooked her hands on the ledge. Jason grabbed her arms. She pulled herself up so that her stomach was pressing into the sill.

Now, the tricky part. The last time she slid in head first to the floor. The window was too narrow to swing a leg around. "I need your help so I don't nose dive to the floor."

"Got you." He dragged her through the window and lifted her in his arms. Jackie was on her feet, instead of lying on the floor, which was good, except that Jason's fingers were locked onto the back of her trench coat, and his black shirt was unbuttoned an extra button. Sending him the self-confidence vibe was totally not a good idea. She wondered if he really did rush home because he was worried about his mom, or because he was excited about getting her alone in his room.

"All right. Let go. We need to talk."

His passion rifted through her. She stepped back, far enough, so that there was at least four feet between them.

Jason stepped toward her.

"No, Jas, stay right there so I can think without you influencing my emotions." She still hadn't mastered zipping herself up from him. And she didn't think Babu's light could help stave off his emotions either.

"All right," he groaned.

She cut to the chase. "Why didn't you tell me you and Trish did it?"

Jason hung his head. "It was just a tryst."

"Just a tryst? She's your friend too. How could you use her like that?"

"I didn't. I mean, I thought it was real at the time. I was so mad at you. She took advantage of me."

"Jason!"

"It's true. I was hurt and vulnerable. We sat on her bed while I poured out my heart. She held my hands and recited some kind of love poem. I couldn't help it. I kissed her as soon as her lips quit moving."

"Okay. So where does her taking advantage of you come in?"

"It's when she knocked me backward on the bed and sat on top of me, unbuttoning her blouse. I was helpless against her vixen underwear."

She held out her hand. "Stop." She was starting to wonder if this solar storm affected all their brains. "Trish supposedly is in love with you, and according to her, loves you more than I ever can. And she's totally pissed at me because she thinks I'm taking you away from her. I think you and I need to put what happened between us out of our minds, and you need to have a heart-to-heart talk with her."

"Why? I know you felt—"

"I just want things to be like they used to be for us—for all of us. I'm really tired of people hating me."

Jason stared at the floor and huffed. "Well, I guess it's better than not being with you at all." He looked at her with those huge fawn eyes. "Hug?"

She was suspicious of his intentions.

"As a truce," Jason said.

"Oh, all right," she said and opened her arms.

They awkwardly embraced.

The door flew open.

"Jason!" Mrs. C. yelled.

They stood there like they'd just been caught together with their pants down.

Now Mrs. C. was really going to hate her. She blew every chance of getting back on Mrs. C.'s good side.

"I told you not to bring her into this house," Mrs. C. said.

"Jackie doesn't mean any harm. She's not bringing in devils."

"That Sandra girl still can't walk. She'll probably be paralyzed for life."

"She didn't put a curse on Sandra, and she didn't bring devils into the house. She helped me to get Dad back home. She just wants to see if everything's okay."

"Get her out of my house!"

"Mom."

"Bob," Mrs. C. yelled.

"All right."

Before they could exit the room, Mr. C. was in the doorway. "What's going on?"

"Jackie's here," Mrs. C. said. "Jason brought her here against my wishes. I'm calling Pastor Phil."

"You're not calling Pastor Phil," Mr. C. said, "and she's not bringing devils into the house. Everything's fine. They told me everything."

"You didn't see it. It was like she was possessed, like Reagan in the *Exorcist*."

It's not like my head was spinning.

"The recliner was spinning," Mrs. C. said, "and objects were flying across the room!"

Okay, so the recliner was spinning.

"I know and they explained that," Mr. C. said. "It was just a matter of, uh—"

"Physics," Jackie said. "Magnetic energy."

"Yeah, magnetic energy. That's all," Mr. C. said.

"But Pastor Phil had to cast out the devils," Mrs. C. said. "He laid hands on all the objects in the room."

"I hope that was all he laid hands on," Mr. C. said.

"You think I would—"

"I think Pastor Phil would. Let's all go down to the basement and see if anything hits the fan. How's that? If nothing happens, you'll let this poor girl alone."

"But what if—" Mrs. C. said.

"If heads start spinning and shit starts flying, you can call Pastor Phil and his hands, and Jackie isn't allowed in this house ever again."

Jackie's mouth dropped open, but Mr. C. winked at her when Mrs. C. turned her head.

"To the basement," Mr. C. said.

They marched downstairs, single file. Mr. C., and then Jackie, Jason, and Mrs. C.

Mr. C. sauntered over to the family area. Jackie followed behind him.

She was afraid to ask him, but it was the only way they'd know for sure. "Mr. C., could you sit in the recliner?"

He gave her a worried look. "What if I go berserk?" he asked. "What if we all go berserk?"

She hadn't planned for that. Her shoulders tensed, and her fingers cowered into her palms. When fists went flying, would

Babu's light protect her? Probably the best thing to do in that situation, knowing what she knew now, was to cut and run and call 9-1-1. "Don't worry about it," she said, lying through her teeth. "I have everything under control."

Jason cleared his throat. His eyes were wide. He knew she was lying.

"Relax, Jas. Just stay near the stairs. You know the drill. And keep your phone handy."

"Yeah, sure." He backed up closer to the stairwell. Mrs. C. joined him.

Mr. C. rubbed his hands together. "Let's get this show on the road."

"Let's do it," she said, but she was hoping there would be no show.

Mr. C. sank into the recliner and closed his eyes.

Everyone was silent. After almost a minute, he opened his eyes.

"How do you feel?" she asked him.

"A little uncomfortable. Did someone do something to this chair? The cushion feels hard. I know I've been away from it for a while, but it used to feel like the recliner was wrapping itself around my body."

"Interesting," she said.

"It's always been his favorite seat," Mrs. C. said. "Like it was made for him. It came with the house, you know. It was practically brand-new."

"That explains why the energy was so strong. I thought it was coming up from the floor."

"Come on, honey," Mr. C. said to Mrs. C. "Come over here."

Mrs. C. unlocked her fingers from Jason's arm. She slowly approached the family area, looking around like something was going to fly.

"It's all right, Mrs. C. Nothing's going to happen," Jackie said, hoping she was right.

Jackie reached out her hand, but Mrs. C. didn't take it.

Mrs. C. sat down on the fireplace hearth and clamped her hands together between her knees.

She held her breath as she waited to see how Mrs. C. would adjust. The electric energy was gone from the room. The hair on her arms and head wasn't rising—a good sign.

Mrs. C. rubbed her hands over her arms. "It's cold down here," she said. "Lonely."

Jackie did detect a hint of loneliness. She sat down beside Mrs. C. on the hearth. "Does this room always feel that way to you?"

"Yes, I suppose." Mrs. C. stared contemplatively across the room, her head tilted. She wiped a tear from her cheek.

"Mrs. C., are you okay?"

She sniffled. "No. I feel so sad."

"Why, Mrs. C.?"

"I just don't think Bob loves me anymore." She put her hand to her chest. "My heart aches so much."

"Sharon, you know I love you," Mr. C. said. "I never meant to hurt you. I'm sorry." He started to get up from the recliner.

Jackie motioned for him to sit back down.

He did.

The last time she had been here, she only concentrated on the anger. But there was so much sorrow in this room too. Poor Mrs. C. She wanted to cry with her.

She put one hand on Mrs. C.'s arm and the other on the fireplace and moved her hand around the stones until her palm tingled. Blood on the stone appeared. It ran in narrow streams to the hearth where it formed a thick pool. The left side of her head just above her temple ached.

My husband bashed my head against the fireplace, Jackie thought. *My own husband.*

She had this achy feeling at the bottom of her throat, and it felt like her heart and chest were going to explode. The heartache was too much to bear.

No. You have to be in control. Think about Babu.

She envisioned herself snuggled with Babu on the couch as Babu told her a story. The sound of her voice—the rolled *r*'s and soft consonants—ignited her heart with love.

"Why don't you love me anymore, Bob?" Mrs. C. asked. "No one loves me." She burrowed her head in her hands.

"But, I do," Mr. C. said.

With one hand on Mrs. C.'s arm and the other pressed against the fireplace, Jackie envisioned Babu's love radiating from her body and flowing into the hearth. "Mr. C. loves you very much," she said. "He left because he didn't want to hurt you. Jason and Mr. C. love you. Jason called me every day, worried to death about you. He wanted to help, but he felt helpless. He loves you so much, and so does Mr. C., and nothing will ever get in the way of that. Do you feel the love they have for you? Do you feel it flowing into your body, warming your heart?"

Mrs. C. sniffled. "They love me?"

"Yes." She wrapped her arms around Mrs. C. and rested her head on Mrs. C.'s shoulder, hoping Mrs. C. wouldn't start hollering for her to leave. She continued sending Mrs. C. vibrations of love. "They love you very, very much."

Mrs. C. laughed and then sniffled. "I believe they do. I feel it."

"Here, Mom. Here's a tissue," Jason said.

"Thank you." She blew her nose.

"I'm sorry I yelled at you," Mrs. C. said to her. "I don't know why I did. I was just crazy."

Mrs. C. stood up. Jason gave her a huge bear hug. Mr. C. got up from the recliner and joined his family, wrapping his arms around Mrs. C. and Jason.

This was good. Their love would strengthen the positive energy in the room.

Jason looked at Jackie and motioned for her to join the group hug.

She may as well. No use adding any negative thoughts to the room.

She gave Jason a quick side hug.

"Thank you, Jackie," Jason said.

She couldn't believe she did it. The whole situation had been so surreal. She never would have imagined that this was what she'd be doing with her so-called talent. It was kind of cool, though, being able to help a friend. She smiled at Jason and hugged him once more.

Chapter 42

Saturday, Jackie worked from nine in the morning to two in the afternoon at Photo Junction. Since she had learned how to zip herself up from negative emotions by thinking of Babu, dealing with customers wasn't that bad. Only once in a while would a newbie come in, and she'd have to show them how to take the memory card out of their camera and use the photo selection machine. She typically picked up their insecurities about using technology and found herself anxiety-ridden. But today, she was able to block that out. And she was still glowing with the thought that Jason's home life was back to normal—well, as normal as it could be. She was happy she had been able to help.

She closed out the cash register and handed the afternoon shift over to the next capitalist slave. Then she headed to the coffee house where all was well in the universe.

Walking down the sidewalk, she scanned the area for Sandra and her team of hooligans, but then she remembered that Sandra was wheelchair bound and no longer a threat to her. Not that this made her feel any better. It made her feel worse. Her hospital visit hadn't helped. Everyone still thought she had put a curse on Sandra. They avoided her and whispered behind her back.

Inside the coffee house, the smell of espresso beans and the rich caramel and cranberry colors on the walls soothed her soul.

She ordered a mocha frappé—low-cal of course—but she still had the barista add the whipped cream, her all-time favorite soul food. Heading toward the couch by the window, she spotted David, dressed in blue jeans and a T-shirt. He was sitting at the back table by the paintings from local artists, a backpack at his feet.

Her stomach tightened. *New plan.*

Before she could turn for the door, David glanced up from his paper.

Doh!

He stood up. "Jackie, how are you? Come, sit down. You have time, yes?"

"Uh, no. Actually, I was just going to mosey on home." Her heart was pounding as if to a heavy-metal drumbeat. *Get a hold of yourself.*

"How are Russian lessons going?" he asked.

"Good, good. Although, I'm speaking Russian like a two-year old. 'Jackie want soup. Soup is hot.'" *Dork!*

His upper lip slightly curled as he smiled. Another attractive feature, damn him. "At least you are communicating," he said.

"Yeah, but not enough to really talk to Babu."

"*Sadis, pozhaluysta.*"

The Russian flowing from his lips mesmerized her, and she stood there with her mouth open, like a dope.

"Sit, please," he said.

"I... I know what you said. You kind of caught me off guard." She slid the rickety wooden chair from the table and sat across from David.

"How have you been? Staying out of the hospital? Yes?"

"I'm trying. I was only there to visit a... friend." She looked away from him.

"A very kind gesture."

"Yeah." If only it were taken that way. If David knew what people thought of her, he wouldn't be talking to her. He would have avoided her when she walked in the door.

"Have you thought about what I said? About using your gift for good?"

"You're wanting me to come back to church, aren't you? How's that going anyway?"

"Our prayers and exorcisms still have not helped. I believe God is waiting for you."

She shook her head.

"Have you asked Him to help you with your gift?"

"Uh, no." She assumed asking Madam Sophie for help didn't count. "I have used my gift to help Jason."

He raised his eyebrows. "Jason?"

"My friend. Best friend, actually."

"Oh," David diverted his eyes to the table. "Does he wear dark clothing like you?"

"Well, yeah. So do my friends Zeta and Trish."

He nodded and was silent for a bit. "Do you still believe in God, Jackie?"

She swallowed. "Yeah, I guess do. I just don't think He wants anything to do with me."

"He does."

"Seriously, He doesn't."

David tapped her black fingernail. "So, you have chosen the dark side?"

She curled her fingers, hiding her fingernails in her palms, leaving only her thumbnails exposed. "I'm not on any side. I'm, like, in the middle."

"A fence-sitter?"

"No. I..."

"Perhaps if you chose a side, God's side, your life would be easier. I would love to see you every week at church."

"Believe me. I don't belong there."

David laid his hand on top of hers. Her stomach did a double flip. His energy was strong—positive and powerful. "Never believe you are an evil person," he said. "You have good heart. I feel it."

She slipped her hand from his and wrapped her fingers around her icy mocha. The cold, sweaty cup cooled her hands—and her insides.

Feeling someone's gaze on her, she turned to see Jason staring at them. He was standing at the counter by the cream and sugars. From the hurt look on his face and the tension in the room, she sensed he'd been standing there a long time. "Jas," she said nervously. "Join us." Great. She just made it sound like she and David were a couple.

Jason sauntered over to their table, never taking his eyes off David. Of all the days for David to wear jeans and a T-shirt.

"Jason. This is David Davidovich. He's the seminarian I told you about."

David reached out, but by the look on Jason's face, he didn't want to be friendly at all. Instead of shaking David's hand, he snatched a chair from a neighboring table and sat on it backward, resting his folded arms on the back of the chair.

"Don't let me interrupt." Jason looked at David and then at her.

She moved her lips to explain, but nothing came out.

"I was just telling Jackie, that she needs to choose a side," David said.

"Oh?" Jason said.

"Good or evil." David met Jason eye-to-eye.

"Jackie's fine the way she is," Jason said. "She has special powers, you know."

She dropped her forehead into her hands and closed her eyes. "Please don't go there," she mumbled.

"Did you tell him how you used your powers to heal my house?" Jason asked.

She took in a deep breath and then sighed. "I kind of mentioned it."

"She said something about using her gift to help you," David said.

"She used her power to—"

"Stop," she said. "All I did was touch the recliner and the fireplace and neutralized the traumatic energy."

David's brow wrinkled.

"Jason's family had a problem in their house. It was caused by a traumatic event. That solar storm we had a few weeks ago made the energy from the event stronger. I simply neutralized the negative energy by sending it energy of the opposite polarity."

David fiddled with his coffee spoon. "And you learned this from?"

She squinted. "Madam Sophie."

David shook his head. "I am worried about you. She is probably not helping you out of the goodness of her heart. She wants you to be like her."

"And I'm worried about you. You're beating yourself up because your prayers aren't working, when all you have to do is..."

"What?"

She reluctantly finished her sentence. "All *I* would have to do is touch the iconostasis and neutralize the energy."

"And this power you have comes from where?"

"From... me. Honest, there's no hoodoo involved. It's just the manipulation of energy."

"So you are just going to touch the iconostasis and fix it all by yourself—without the help of God or Satan?" David asked her.

She nodded. "That day I had my first vision, I thought I heard the candlesticks cry. I think it's related. Besides the fire, has there been any other traumatic event in church?"

"I would not know. At least not in the past two months, the time I have been there. We would have to ask Father Dmitriev."

"That's out of the question."

David scraped the coffee cup handle with his thumbnail.

"Perhaps you are right."

"I'll prove to you that what I do isn't evil. That it's all scientific. But you absolutely have to promise that, if I come to the church, Father Dmitriev won't be there."

"I don't know how you are going to prove it, but I will give you the benefit of the doubt. I believe that God has a purpose for you and that is why the iconostasis is charred. I will make sure Father Dmitriev is busy elsewhere."

"Good. Oh, and since you like to bargain, if you could do one more thing for me. Visit a friend of mine, the one in the hospital, and tell her what you think of me. The good stuff."

"Fair enough," David said, "but if your science project doesn't work in church, which I do not believe it will, could you do something for me?"

"What?"

"Return to church."

Ugh, that backfired. "Sure," she said, reluctantly. It was going to work. It had to.

"Then, I will ask Father Dmitriev to take my rounds at the hospital. It will have to be on Thursday."

"Okay. Jason and I will do some research. I'll call you to confirm we're ready."

"You mean I get to go too?" Jason asked.

"Of course, Jas. We're *friends*. Remember?"

"Yeah, that's right. Good-ol' friends. Chums for life." He patted her arm like she was his football buddy.

"All right, Jas. Knock it off."

Jason unstraddled the chair and stood up. "So we get to play Ghostbusters, huh?"

"Yeah, except there aren't any ghosts, just stray energies," she said, just to make sure David understood they weren't doing witchcraft.

"Jackie," David said, "there are lost souls, the unbaptized, who have not made their way to heaven. There are also demons loose on earth. You should not be so dismissive of these possibilities."

She sighed. "Sure. Just let Jason and I do some investigating. I'll call you when we know something."

Outside the coffee house, Jason said, "You'll call him? You have his number?"

"I have his business card. That's typically how professional people advertise their services."

"A seminarian?"

"Yeah. He visits the elderly, translates like he did for Babu, serves as a mentor to the neighborhood youth—you know, stuff like that."

Jason didn't hold the truck door for her, and he was sulking when they climbed inside.

"Come on. Get real. This guy's going to be a priest. He's the last kind of guy I'd ever fall in love with." Her stomach churned.

"Yeah, I guess you two are just friends—like you and me."

"Yeah, I guess we are. Besides, he's too old for me. I think he's like twenty-four or something. I'm only seventeen."

"Almost eighteen."

"Yeah, but not until spring. He's, like, old." Which made him even more attractive to her, but she didn't tell Jason that.

"So how are you going to prove it's all scientific?"

"Well, David believes that Satan has no power in the church. Therefore, if I do heal the iconostasis, he'll have to believe the energy to heal came from me."

Chapter 43

In the library, at the research computers, Jason rolled his chair close to Jackie. "So where do we start?" he asked, his sad, puppy-dog eyes begging for her love.

Maybe if he didn't act so pitiful, it would work out between us. What happened to the friendship they used to have? They definitely needed a break from each other. Maybe that would bring him back to his senses.

She rolled her chair closer to the desk and placed her fingers on the keyboard. "Well, I was thinking we could search the news archive on the *Ravenwood Gazette* website for Holy Resurrection. Maybe something significant will pop up."

Jason rested his elbow on the desk and leaned his head against his hand. He pinned his gaze on her. She wanted to tell him to knock it off, but then he'd get hurt, and he'd be doubly broody all day.

She entered "Holy Resurrection Russian Orthodox Church" into the search text box and then pressed enter. A long list of archived articles appeared on the screen. She scrolled through them and read the headlines. Most of the articles were reports on church events: bake sales, benefits, special masses, marriages, and baptisms. The only article about an unusual event was of the fire. She clicked the headline and skimmed the article. All the information in the article was everything she already knew: Stephanie Yarrow caught her sleeve on an altar candle while cleaning the church, and the candle tipped over, catching the iconostasis on fire.

"What I can't figure out is, how... well, what I felt when I touched the candlestick, how it relates to the charred iconostasis."

Jason rolled his chair even closer to hers. Their knees touched. "What'd you feel?"

"It's not important."

"Obviously it is, if you're researching where it came from."

She swallowed. "It was like, desperation. Like a hunger for someone." She lowered her eyes.

"For David?"

She threw her hands up. "For I don't know. The feelings were just there, and I picked them up."

"I can tell you where those feelings came from."

"It came from the candlestick."

"Sure. And you just happened to be at the church with David?"

"He set me up. He refused to convince Babu to stay in the hospital unless I promised to come to the church."

"He knows Babu?"

"No. Well, now he does. He was translating for her. He was on the translator's call list at the hospital."

"What else went on while we weren't talking?"

"Enough! It'll teach you not to get pissed at me and run to Trish."

Jason wrinkled his mouth. His silence allowed her to think.

"I wonder if Stephanie's grandparents still live in town. They raised her. I don't remember her mom and dad. I remember Stephanie spent a lot of time in the church, and she wasn't quite stable mentally. Grandma used to talk about how Stephanie was thirty-something and still living with her grandparents. I hope that doesn't define mentally unstable, because it'll probably happen to me."

"You think we should talk to them?"

"Actually, I was thinking of talking to the house."

Jason looked at her like she'd totally lost it.

"As in, pick up emotions and images."

"Yeah, right. Do you know where her grandparents live?"

"I haven't a clue. Maybe my mom would know." She noticed the research librarian at the desk across the room paging through a huge book, a pair of square-framed glasses resting on the bridge of her nose. "Or, we could ask the research librarian. Put our parents' tax dollars to work."

At the research librarian's desk, she asked, "Can you tell us how to find someone's address?"

The research librarian inserted a bookmarker into the open book and then closed it. "We can search the Yellow pages database." She poked the bridge of her reading glasses to push them closer to her eyes, and then she positioned her fingers on the keyboard. "What's the name of the person you're looking for?"

"Stephanie Yarrow," Jackie said.

The librarian's eyes grew wide behind the lenses of her glasses. "She's dead. She died in that church fire."

"Yeah. We know."

"So why do you want to know where she lives? She obviously doesn't live there anymore."

"I wanted to talk with her grandparents. I remember she used to live with them. Me and my friend Jason are doing a report for our journalism class."

"Well, I guess I can just tell you. We don't have to look it up. They live at 9416 Orchard Street. I remembered their address from staring at it so many times when I was your age. I used to fantasize about living there."

The librarian jotted the address down on a piece of paper and then handed it to Jackie.

"Thanks." *That was too easy.*

The house on Orchard Street was a huge, cobalt blue Victorian with a yellow front porch. Definitely a looker. Jackie rang the doorbell. She hadn't planned what she was going to ask. She really just wanted to get inside the house. Mosey around. Pick up some of Stephanie's emotions. See if they matched what she had sensed in the church.

A woman in her thirties, with a baby on her hip, answered the door. *Maybe Stephanie had a sister.*

"Hi. My name is Jackie Turov. Me and my friend Jason are doing a piece for our journalism class about the fire at Holy Resurrection, and we'd like to ask some questions about Stephanie Yarrow. We want to write a more humanistic story than the newspaper article we read. We were told Stephanie's grandparents live here."

"They died about two years ago," the woman said. "We bought this house last year from their daughter."

"Oh." Jackie's heart sank. Now what? There was no way this woman was going to let them in to look around, not without a really good excuse.

"I'm sorry I can't be of any help." The baby fidgeted in the woman's arms and tugged her hair.

Jackie stared at the doorbell. "S'okay." Maybe she could get insight from Stephanie's mom. She might even have some of Stephanie's personal belongings. "Would you know where the daughter is?"

"Florida, most likely. She'd been flying back and forth taking care of funeral arrangements and the estate."

"Would you have her number?"

"Not really. My realtor handled everything."

Jackie's brow creased in frustration.

The woman adjusted the baby on her hip and then reached out her hand. "My name's Debbie, by the way." She and Jackie shook. "I heard the Yarrows were good people. It's really nice of you to want to do a humanistic piece."

"Thanks, but I guess we're out of luck." Her mind raced to make up some story that would require seeing the inside of the house for herself.

The baby let out a shrill cry. "Sorry. Feeding time." A three-year-old girl came out of nowhere, hugged he woman's leg, and stared up at Jackie. Debbie's shoulders dropped. "Gotta go. Nice meeting you."

"Yeah, you too," Jackie said, stunned that she had gotten nowhere.

The woman closed the door.

Jackie looked to Jason and sighed. "Back to the library, I guess." Just as they turned and started down the steps, the door opened.

"Hey," the woman said. She peered out from the half-closed door, the baby's head pressed against her chin. "My best friend Nancy used to be their caretaker. Maybe she can help."

Jackie's hope returned. "Really?"

"Maybe. Let me text her. I don't know why I didn't think of this to begin with. I guess, when you're home with kids, your brain turns to mush."

"She lives nearby?"

"Pretty much. Twenty minutes from here."

Nancy led Jackie and Jason to the kitchen where they sat at the breakfast island on white stools. The kitchen was immaculate. And Nancy looked just as clean in her nurse's smock and pants. Even her gym shoes were spotless.

"I wasn't sure I wanted to do this interview at first," she said to Jackie. "The Yarrows were good people, and the way their granddaughter died was horrific. I just can't believe she'd be that careless, being pregnant and all." She covered her mouth as if she didn't mean for that to slip out.

"She was pregnant?"

"Yeah. You're not going to put that in your report, are you? Mr. and Mrs. Yarrow didn't want anyone to know. They paid off the editor of the *Ravenwood Gazette* to keep it hush-hush."

"I don't know. It certainly adds a new twist," Jackie said, just to make it sound like they were really researching a story for their journalism class.

Nancy sighed. "Oh, well. I guess it doesn't matter if anyone knows now. She's dead, and so are her nearest relatives."

"Why would they—Oh, she wasn't married, was she? And she was a Russian Orthodox working for the church."

"You got the picture," Nancy said.

"What about the baby's father?"

"Are you kidding? That secret died with her."

"Was she dating?"

"No. Stephanie wasn't all there. She was delusional. Her mother had her when she was forty-seven. By the time Stephanie was in high school, her parents were retired. They moved to Florida and left her in Ravenwood to live with the grandparents. Father Dmitriev gave her a job at the church. Something that she could handle and would allow her to bring in a small income."

"That's cruel," Jason said. "Her parents left her behind?"

"It's not like you think. Stephanie would never have been able to adjust to the move and to a new location. She had to have everything the same every day. She was kind of ritualistic. It kept her as sane as she could be. Plus, she was always close with her grandparents, and they, being in their eighties, had someone else to watch over them when I wasn't there."

"Did you interact with her before the fire at any time?" Jackie asked. "I mean like, how was she dealing with the pregnancy and all?"

"I don't know. I barely saw her. She spent most of her time at the church. When she came home, she went straight to her room. I remember her room was like a shrine. Talk about carrying your work home with you."

Her room! It would tell them everything they needed to know about Stephanie's emotions.

Jackie stood up and reached out her hand. "Thank you so much for answering our questions."

With a loose, reluctant grip, Nancy shook her hand. "Could you not put my name down as a source? I don't want anyone to know I was the one who let the cat out of the bag. I work with people every day. A lot of them confide in me. I don't want to lose their trust."

"Sure. No problem. My lips and pen are sealed. Just one more thing, though. Which room was Stephanie's?"

Jackie and Jason drove back to Ravenwood to Mr. and Mrs. Yarrow's old house. Debbie was surprised to see them. The baby was still on her hip—poor Debbie.

"Hi, it's us again." Jackie said.

"Problems?" Debbie asked.

"Uh, no. We just wanted to thank you. We talked to Nancy and got a good interview. I was also wondering, though, if you would show us around the house. We like to give our articles a feeling of place and character."

She looked at them like they wanted to come in to steal something or case the place. "I don't know. I was just about to start dinner and put the baby to bed. When's your paper due?"

"Tomorrow," Jackie said, before Jason blurted something less urgent, like next week.

"All right. I hope my kids will be just as involved in their homework when they go to school."

"Thank you."

They stepped inside the foyer.

"This is the living room," Debbie said, pointing to the right.

Jackie had a pen and paper in hand, but what she really wanted to do was walk around and touch things. She also desperately wanted to go to Stephanie's room, but Debbie might get suspicious if she acted too eager. "You know, I'm kind of the touchy-feely kind. Can I just walk around and take in the atmosphere?"

Debbie bounced the baby on her hip. "Sure," she said. But she was still looking at them like they might steal something.

Jackie touched the back of the couch, but she could tell the furniture belonged to the new owners. She walked across the wooden floor. Stepped around toys. She detected chaos, but a happy chaos. She touched the bricks on the fireplace, closed her eyes.

Sickness festered in the walls. The grandparents were very ill before they died. She could taste it and smell it. Bitter and foul. She moved her hand around the bricks while she breathed deeply and exhaled slowly, expelling the negative energy.

"Boy, she's really a creative type, isn't she?" Debbie said to Jason.

"Can I see Stephanie's old room?" Jackie asked.

"I wouldn't even know—"

"It's the last bedroom on the left," Jackie spouted.

"You really did your homework."

"We want a good grade. Actually, we need a good grade. We got an *F* on our last assignment."

As they walked up the stairs, Jackie ran her hand over the railing. Too much data, too many hands. The wallpaper in the hallway was old, yellowing, and dense with sickness and despair.

"That wallpaper's got to go," Debbie said. "We started remodeling downstairs first. The kitchen cost a fortune. You know, they still had gold appliances?"

Jackie didn't care if they had a coal cookstove and an icebox. She just wanted to see Stephanie's bedroom. She stepped around Debbie and touched the door handle to Stephanie's room. It was cold, somber.

"May I?" Jackie asked.

"Sure," Debbie said. "Excuse the mess. It's serving as a storage room right now."

Jackie pushed the door open. Boxes were stacked against the walls. Some were blocking the window. On one wall, there was a white spot in the shape of a cross. If Stephanie had been praying to it, her energies and emotions would have gathered there.

"Could Jason and I move some of these boxes? I'd like to get a closer look at that mark on the wall."

"Sure," Debbie said, a tone of suspicion in her voice.

She and Jason pushed two stacked boxes away from the wall. Then, she placed her hand over the white spot.

"All right," Debbie said. "What are you doing now? You're not writing an article, are you? Are you psychic? Are you the Holy Resurrection girl?"

Busted! Jackie pretended not to have heard her.

"Yes, but she doesn't call herself psychic," Jason said.

"So why are you really here?" Debbie asked.

"To get answers," Jason said.

"To what?"

"We can't say."

"This won't affect the baby, will it?"

"Uh, no, I don't think so. She's just reading right now."

"She does other things too?"

"She heals negative energies with her hands."

Freak her out, why don't you? "Jas, come on now. I'm trying to focus—and no, this won't hurt the baby."

The wall was cold. Most likely due to the heat vents being shut off in the room. Jackie opened up to the stored energy. A ribbon of fear fluttered through her heart, and words poured from her mouth.

"Theotokos Virgin, I'm so scared. Please, help me. Please take it away." Jackie dropped to her knees and clasped her hands in prayer. "Mother, please, tell me what to do. You were pregnant too out of wedlock. Please guide me. Send your angels down to help me, to aid me, like they did for you." She wrapped her arms around her stomach and rocked back and forth. "Theotokos Virgin, rejoice, Mary full of grace, the Lord is with thee—"

"Jackie!"

Jason's hand on her shoulders nudged her into reality.

I'm Jackie, she thought. *And I'm not pregnant.* She took a deep breath to soak up the negative energy then exhaled to release it.

"Is she okay?" Debbie asked. "Maybe I should get the baby out of here."

"I'm okay," Jackie said, but the thought of being in Stephanie's predicament sent chills down her spine.

Jason grabbed her arm and helped her to her feet.

"She was scared and sad," she said to Jason. "She may have been desperate, hungering for love when she was at church that day. I mean, she was all alone with this."

"You think she committed suey?" Jason asked.

"I don't know. But I can't help but think it's my fault she died."

"You were twelve, and you were scared. You didn't even know what was happening to you. Besides, what's done is done. You can't change the past."

"True. The only thing I can do now is put the energy to rest." That is, if her "science project" worked in church.

What if it didn't?

Chapter 44

When Jackie came home, Babu was in the kitchen slicing carrots for soup, her chubby arms bulging like sacks of potatoes from her housedress sleeves. Since Jackie had been involved in saving the world, she had slipped in taking care of Babu. She kissed Babu's cheek as carrot slices dropped from Babu's knife into the soup pot on the burner.

"I can do this, you know," Jackie said.

Babu brushed her away. She was back to the way she liked it—in control and manning her kitchen. Jackie let her be. Mom was right. There was no changing Babu. Jackie had quit trying to get her to take her meds. She didn't know how Babu knew when she slipped them into her food, but she did. Jackie thought what Babu was really mad about was that she had refused to pray with her. There was no changing herself either.

In her room, Jackie dug out David's card from her satchel. Her heart fluttered when she read his name, handwritten above Father Dmitriev's.

You're not calling to ask him out, she told herself. *You're calling him to update him on what you found out about Stephanie.*

She keyed in his number. As the phone rang, her heart beat faster. She took a deep breath, held it for about ten seconds, and then slowly exhaled. She did this several times until her heart rate slowed—well, until it slowed enough so that she wouldn't go into cardiac arrest from hearing David's voice.

"David Davidovich," he said.

"It's me, Jackie." Great. She sounded like she was out of breath.

"Jackie?" The sound of his voice made her forget why she had called.

Control. "I have some horrible news to tell you."

"You've chosen the dark side?"

"Ha, no. It's Stephanie. She was pregnant when she died."

"Wait," he whispered. "Let me find a better place to talk."

His footsteps echoed as if he was walking through a church or rectory hall.

"Jackie?" he said in a low voice.

"Yeah, I'm here."

"So, you are sure about this? I mean, how do you know?"

"Her grandparents' caretaker told me. And, I felt it when I was in her room. She was scared and desperate. She prayed to the Virgin for help."

"So now what?"

"Well, now that I know what she was going through, I'll be able to put myself in her place and counteract the energy."

David was silent.

"You still there?"

"Yes."

"Are you good with this? You know, if Father Dmitriev catches us, he's not going to recommend you for priesthood. You'll be out the door looking for another career. You do realize what you're risking?"

"I do. I trust God will prevail. Are you good with what we bargained?"

She gritted her teeth. "I... I would give it a try... if it came to that," she said, her jaw clenched.

"It is all I ask. Then I will see you Thursday, at five?"

"Yes."

Wednesday at school, Jackie was still parting crowds and

getting fearful glances. She really hated this. She had wanted everyone to stay away from her, but this was ridiculous. In study hall, she caught Trish glaring at her. Jackie thought about going over there, telling her that she talked to Jason, but at this point, she didn't really care. Trish was being childish about this whole thing. Let her suffer. Let her think that Jackie and Jason were a couple.

In American Lit, Jackie was so happy to see Jason, she wanted to hug him. He must have seen it in her eyes because when he talked to her there was a content smile on his face and his aura was bright. Yesterday, working through the Stephanie Yarrow investigation, it felt like they were a team again.

While Mr. Davis explained the symbolism in *The Awakening*, Jackie wrote a quick note telling Jason it was on for Thursday. She crumpled the note and dropped it to the floor. He picked it up, read it, and mouthed something to her.

"What?" she whispered.

"What time?" Jason whispered back.

"Is there something going on here?" Mr. Davis asked.

"No," Jackie said abruptly.

"Don't you two see enough of each other after school? Do I have to separate you?"

The class was laughing.

"No, we won't disturb the class anymore," she said.

"You're not disturbing the class. You're disturbing me. Makes me feel like I'm not as interesting as Jason."

The class roared.

Jackie shrugged. "What can I say?"

Mr. Davis stared at her with his bloodshot eyes. The lines around his mouth and eyes had deepened since the beginning of the semester. He looked as if he had aged ten years. His aura was pure black. Cramps tugged her stomach lining. She wished that whatever was going on with him would get resolved because he was really being a pain in her butt lately.

Chapter 45

Thursday morning, Jackie awoke with a killer headache. She felt like the back of her head was being squeezed in a vice. When she sat up in bed, the blood drained from her face and the pressure in her skull made her feel like throwing up. She made a dizzied rush down the hall and to the bathroom.

Kneeling on the cold bathroom tile, she dry heaved over the toilet.

Caffeine. She needed lots of caffeine.

In the kitchen, she held her head until the coffee was finished brewing. She poured herself a cupful, leaving it black instead of diluting it with cream like she normally did. She needed the full effect of the caffeine, and she needed it fast.

It tasted like shit.

At the kitchen table, she took a few more sips of the bitter brew and then leaned her head back slightly and closed her eyes. Minor relief.

"Meditating?" Mom asked.

Jackie's eyes snapped open. Mom was already dressed, which was unusual because it was six in the morning and she didn't start work until nine. She was in some get up—yoga pants and a camisole.

"Headache," Jackie said.

"Probably stress. You really haven't been yourself lately. Is something going on with you?"

"Uh, no. Nothing's been going on." If she only knew. "I just woke up with a killer headache."

Mom looked worried. "On a scale of one to ten, how bad is it?"

"I don't know. It hurts too bad to think. Oh, God, I think I'm going to puke." She rushed to the sink and spewed coffee like dragon fire. She tore off a sheet of paper towel and wiped her mouth. "Ten."

"I'm calling Dr. Zinba," Mom said.

"The neurologist?"

"He said to call him if you experienced any debilitating headaches."

"Mom, it's been like two weeks since I was hit in the head. This can't possibly be related."

Mom pressed her phone to her ear. "Quiet."

Jackie dropped her forehead into folded arms on the counter. Pressure squeezed her temples, making her sicker and terribly nauseated. She raised her head, sauntered to the table, and collapsed into a kitchen chair. Of all the days for this to happen. She hoped she'd be well enough by five.

"His office doesn't open until nine," Mom said. "I'll call his emergency number."

Babu shuffled into the kitchen.

"Morning, Babu," Jackie moaned. She was too queasy to get up and pour Babu a cup of coffee.

Babu grabbed her arm. *"Chto sluchílos' s toboy?"*

Jackie figured Babu wanted to know what was wrong with her because there was a concerned look on her face. "Nothing, Babu. *Nichevo.*"

She touched the back of Jackie's head. *"Golova balit?"*

Jackie nodded.

Babu wouldn't let go of her arm. If Babu was a healer, Jackie didn't want Babu expending all her energy on her. In Babu's condition, it might kill her.

"Babu, I'm okay."

"Take her to the emergency?" Mom asked someone on the phone.

Babu made the sign of the cross, and then bowed her head in prayer. Her fingers tightened around Jackie's arm as she prayed.

"Dr. Zinba's answering service says to take you to the hospital," Mom said to Jackie. "Dr. Zinba will see you there."

"No," Jackie moaned. "Not again." She wondered how long this was going to take. She was anxious enough about going to the church. Since it was hard for David to get rid of Father Dmitriev, she couldn't screw this up by not being there when she said she would. Although, if she was too sick to do the job, she might fail, and then David would expect...

Babu let go of Jackie's arm leaving a red imprint of her fingers. Her grip had made Jackie forget her headache momentarily, but then a sharp pain, which vibrated clear to her eyebrows and settled between her eyes, reminded her. She squinted.

"Get dressed," Mom said.

"All right." She supposed the sooner they left, the sooner they'd be back. And maybe they'd have something good to give her for this headache. She just hoped it was nothing a few pills couldn't cure. "Babu, I have to go to the doctor."

Babu put her hands on Jackie's shoulders and shook her head. *Net, net.* She pushed Jackie's shoulders, trying to get her to sit back down.

"Babu, I have to go. This could be serious. Remember when I was hit in back of the head? Maybe something—"

"*Net. Sidi. Sidi.*"

"I'll be okay."

In the emergency waiting room, only two other people were ahead of Jackie. Mom had checked her in. She had heard Mom on the phone with Dad the other day, explaining her last hospital visit. She thought he and Mom were going halves on the balance of that one. Wait until the balance of this one is added. It's not like either of them make bank.

It wasn't long before she was called into triage. The triage nurse gave her two Tylenols. She could have done that herself at home. She wondered how much those two tiny pills were going to cost her parents.

Despite the fact that there were only two other people ahead of her, she and Mom still wound up waiting an hour before she was admitted into the emergency area. It kind of took the meaning out of the word *emergency*.

Finally, a nurse led them to one of those tiny treatment rooms with a curtain for a door. Jackie put on a hospital gown and climbed into the bed. She waited another hour to see Dr. Zinba.

"You're back," Dr. Zinba said when he saw her. "What brings you here today?"

"Headache," she moaned.

"How long have you had this headache?"

"Since I woke up."

Dr. Zinba leaned over her and shined a penlight in each eye. "Does the light bother you?"

"No, my head just hurts like hell."

He slipped the penlight into his jacket pocket. "Can you tell me what month this is?"

"October."

"Day of the week?"

"Thursday."

"Sit up at the edge of the bed and relax your legs."

Jackie pushed back the covers and sat up at the edge of the bed. Dr. Zinba tapped her left knee and then her right knee with a reflex hammer. Each leg involuntarily flew up accordingly.

"I'm going to arrange a CT scan for you this morning, and then we'll go from there."

She waited an hour to get a CT scan and another two hours for Dr. Zinba to interpret the results and give her the verdict.

"No sign of bleeding or a hematoma," Dr. Zinba said. "Everything looks good. Has the Tylenol kicked in?"

"No," Jackie groaned. She couldn't believe that with all this high-tech, expensive equipment, they couldn't cure a headache or find out what was causing it.

"There's a possibility blood seeped into your spinal fluid from the head trauma you experienced. A continuous flow of blood in the spinal fluid can be fatal. I suggest we do a spinal tap."

"Holy shit!"

"It's a simple, but tedious procedure," he said. "We simply insert a needle in the lower lumbar region and extract a sample of spinal fluid. However, to be honest with you, there's always the danger that the needle will hit a nerve and cause paralysis."

She covered her face with her hands and thought about Sandra. Maybe it was her fault. Maybe karma was at work here, and she was going to get what was coming to her because of Sandra. Babu didn't want her to leave the house. Maybe she sensed something bad was going to happen to her—again.

Settle down, she told herself. *You're getting all superstitious.*

She was sure the doctor who did this operation wouldn't intentionally cause paralysis—but there was always that chance. She could just bleed to death. All right, she guessed the spinal tap was on. She couldn't imagine having a headache like this until she died.

She uncovered her eyes. "Let's do it," she said. "Mom?"

"I guess we have no choice." Mom squeezed Jackie's hand.

Mom's hand was warm, and Jackie picked up a sense of stability from her.

"One more thing," Dr. Zinba said. "Your mother will have to sign a waiver that basically says you won't sue if something goes wrong."

"That gains my confidence." Jackie looked at the clock on the wall. It was already eleven. She needed to be out of there by at least four thirty. She had told Jason everything would be okay—that she'd be out by ten and she'd get some rest and be as good as new for tonight. Boy, was she being optimistic. "How long is this going to take?"

"It shouldn't take longer than fifteen minutes to prep you and take a sample. Then we'll send it to our lab for processing. Maybe an hour, maybe two, depending on how busy the lab is."

Eleven, twelve, one, she counted. "And, what if there's bleeding?"

"Then we check you in and clean you out."

Why me? Why today? "All right, let's get this over with."

A half an hour later, Dr. Zinba came in with an assistant. Jackie sat up at the edge of the bed and bent over. The assistant cleaned and disinfected the area on her back near her tailbone. She had to keep still; if she moved, she might cause her own paralysis. So this was on her now.

It didn't take long to take the sample. Dr. Zinba's assistant stuck a large square Band-Aid on her back.

Then they waited.

And did they.

Mom went for coffee. Jackie was starving. Her stomach rumbled; her head ached. She asked the nurse for two more Tylenol, and she lay back. The hospital was cold and unwelcoming. She thought she smelled death, which, to her, was the mixture of antiseptics, blood, and urine.

Mom brought her a bag of salty chips. Jackie could see the salt, but with the killer headache, she couldn't taste it. The chips had a flat, nothing taste.

Finally, Dr. Zinba came into the room. Jackie tensed, anticipating the verdict.

"It's clean," he said. "Are those Tylenol working?"

"Clean? Now what?" she asked.

"Follow up with your family doctor," he said.

Her mouth dropped open. "After all that?"

It was two o'clock by the time Jackie got home. Babu was so happy to see her, she smothered her in a bear hug.

"I still don't feel good, Babu."

"*Prikhodi*," Babu said and led her to the kitchen. She ladled out a bowl of chicken soup and set it before her.

"Thank you so much. *Spasibo bol'shoye*."

The soup warmed her cheeks and dulled the pain. Afterward, she curled up by Babu in her bed. Whispering prayers, Babu brushed back Jackie's bangs. Jackie closed her eyes to sleep.

Jackie awoke from a dream about being burned alive. In her dream, she was in Holy Resurrection Church, bound, like Joan of Arc, to a stake, kindling at her feet, mouth gagged, and hands tied behind her back. Father Dmitriev lit the hay with a long candle. The nave was filled with people from school, cheering the fire on. Behind her, hanging upside down from the top of the iconostasis, their hands tied behind their backs, one leg crossed behind the other forming a triangle, were Madam Sophie and Babu.

Chapter 46

Jackie slipped out of bed, leaving Babu sound asleep, snoring. She was groggy, but her head wasn't aching anymore. It felt more like one dull pain capped over her head, like she was wearing a tight hat.

In the bathroom, she splashed cold water on her face and brushed her hair, but the wispy strands fell flat. The headache had drained the life out of her, and her dream had put her over the edge. Screw it. She changed into black jeans, a black T-shirt, and combat boots, hoping it would put her in a kick-ass mood.

In the front room, she peeked out the window for Jason. She had told him not to beep the horn. She didn't want him to wake Babu. She didn't know where Mom went, but Jackie was hoping to slip out of the house before she came back so she wouldn't make her stay home.

As soon as Jason pulled his truck to the curb, Jackie was out the door. When she slid into the truck seat, Jason stared at her. "You look like hell," he said. "You don't have to do this, you know. I mean, you're not just doing this because David wants you to, are you?"

"I'm doing this to prove a point, and because I want to know what happened to Stephanie. She's the reason I'm in the social mess I'm in now. And I have to do this today because David said it wasn't easy to get Father Dmitriev out of the church."

"Fine."

They drove to Holy Resurrection in silence. Jason parallel

parked in front of the church.

"We're about ten minutes early," she said. "That'll give me some time."

"Time for what?"

"Time to find out what really happened. I want to do this without David around." She didn't need the drama.

Jackie tugged the church door handle. Jason followed her into the entrance area. It was quiet, and a faint scent of incense wafted in the air.

She hesitated at the nave entrance. Maybe Jason should wait here. The nave was for baptized, repentant believers. But then, who was she to tell Jason he couldn't enter? "Come on."

He followed her across the polished floor. The candles in the choir areas and above the Holy Doors were lit. The only thing glaringly out of place was the drop cloth draped over the left side of the iconostasis.

"This place is weird," Jason said.

"Not your typical-looking church, is it?"

"How come there are no pews?"

"Some of the Orthodox churches have them, but Father Dmitriev never permitted it."

"So this is where it all happened," Jason said, dreamily.

"Yeah. This is it. You see that wall with the pictures on it? That's the iconostasis. That's what I saw catch fire. It started right there, behind that drop cloth." She climbed the platform steps and fingered back the covering, revealing the charred icons. "Voila. My reoccurring nightmare."

"Freaky."

"I'm going to take a reading and try to figure out what really happened to Stephanie. No matter what happens, stay right there. Okay?"

"I know the drill."

She wrapped her fingers around the candlestick and pressed her other hand to the iconostasis. Cold metal and canvas tingled against her palms. She inhaled and opened up to the energy. Two emotions poured through her—desire for Stephanie's lover and sorrow because he wanted her to abort the baby. The emotions met in her heart and twirled together, and a powerful cyclone churned inside her. Funneling into Jackie's head, a vision formed: Stephanie lighting the candles in front of the icon of the Virgin of Vladimir, bowing her covered head, and praying, "Holy Mother, tell me what to do."

"Jackie," Jason yelled.

Something clutched Jackie's wrist. Her eyes snapped open. It was Father Dmitriev.

"Enough," he bellowed.

Emotions fizzled, and the vision dissolved. Looking at Father Dmitriev, her nerves prickled. She was no longer Stephanie Yarrow, but a frightened child, helpless before Father Dmitriev's accusing eyes. "I was..."

"Working your witchcraft again. You may have fooled the congregation, but you've never fooled me." He squeezed her wrist. "I told you never to come back."

Her wrist grew hot, just like it did when he had grabbed it that day of the exorcism. Her trench coat sleeve caught fire. She screamed and batted her arm.

Looking bewildered, Father Dmitriev released her sleeve.

The fire consumed her coat, enveloping her in flames. Like acid poured on raw flesh, her body burned.

It's not real. Go with it. Burn.

She fought the pain as voices surrounded her. Jason's, Father Dmitriev's, Stephanie's. Closing her eyes, she saw the blow to the head. The tipped candle stand. The flames consuming Stephanie, spreading to the iconostasis. The horrifying truth.

Jackie was awestruck.

Let it go. Breathe.

She envisioned Babu surrounded in white light stepping out from the flames. Jackie reached for her. Babu wrapped her arms around her and surrounded her with protective light. The fire died.

With arms spread open, Jackie touched the candlestick and iconostasis.

"Stop this," Father Dmitriev said.

"Let her finish," Jason said.

Jackie imagined Stephanie before the iconostasis holding her baby, reveling in its tiny features. Her heart filled with joy and love. The energy radiated from inside her, flowed through her hands, and into the candlestick and iconostasis. She fed the energy with deep inhalations and released it through exhalations. Ignoring Father Dmitriev's accusations, she opened her eyes and watched the charred icons regain their color and the faces of the Virgin and the saints emerge.

Father Dmitriev's face was ashen, his eyes stricken with fear as he stared at the iconostasis, its icons restored. He turned to her. "What are you?"

She dropped her arms to her sides. "A girl with a vision."

"You have the devil's eye and power." He pointed his finger at her. "There shall not be found among you any one that maketh his son or his daughter to pass through fire, or that useth divination, or an observer of times, or an enchanter, or a witch, or a charmer, or a consulter with familiar spirits, or a wizard, or a necromancer. For all that do these things are an abomination unto the Lord."

She stepped toward him. "I'm not an abomination. You are."

"How dare you insinuate such a thing?"

"The baby was yours. She came to you for assurance, but you wanted her to get rid of it. When you placed the Eucharist on my tongue, you were planning. You were thinking about how you were going to kill her."

"I should have cut your tongue out." Father Dmitriev hissed.

"She's fine as she is." David was standing at the side door of the iconostasis, his phone in his hand. "Is what she says true?"

"Stephanie was going to talk," Father Dmitriev said. "What was I supposed to do?"

"Burn Stephanie and your child alive?" David asked.

"Yes. If it would save this church from embarrassment."

"You mean if it would save *you* from embarrassment."

"I am this church! What's done is done. There's no proof. Jackie can conjure up all the visions she wants. There's no physical evidence. And who would believe that I set my own church on fire? If you say anything more about this to the bishop, I'll tell him you've been keeping company with psychics and witches. You'll be thrown out of the church, with no chance of ever becoming a priest."

"She's not a..." David's eyes grew wide as he looked at the iconostasis. "How did you..."

"I told you how," she said.

"She has the devil's power," Father Dmitriev said, "that's how!"

"It's just physics," she said.

Staring at her, David lowered his phone.

"You're going to keep this secret?" she asked David.

"I have chosen my profession. And you... Let God be his judge."

"What did you expect from me? I told you how this worked."

"Perfect." a girl's voice said. "Jackie's fallen from grace."

Jackie turned. Trish was standing among the choir benches.

"Trish," Jackie and Jason said at the same time.

"My demonic friend wanted to be here himself to do this, but this place is kind of off limits for him. We have to do this by proxy instead."

"Do what?" Jackie asked.

"How's your headache, Jackie?" Trish held up a cloth doll with a pin sticking into the back of its head. "I can't believe you made it. You weren't supposed to. You weren't supposed to find out the truth. We didn't want you feeling all good about yourself and choosing the other side. But it looks like you've made the right choice. Now it's time to say good-bye."

With another pin, Trish jabbed the doll's leg.

A sharp pain thrust through Jackie's leg and hung there. "Ow!" Jackie grabbed the back of her knee. The pain was so intense she could barely stand.

"This is so cool," Trish squealed. "Isn't it fun to have powers, Jackie?"

Trish dangled the doll over a flame of one of the choir candles. Sweat trickled down Jackie's forehead. She couldn't believe that what Trish was doing was actually working. Trish was messing with her head, that's what she was doing. Jackie took a deep breath to absorb the negative energy and then exhaled.

Father Dmitriev marched over to the candle rack and reached for the doll. "Enough of this. Give it to me."

Trish raised it above her head. Dancing around him, she kept jerking it away from Father Dmitriev. "Want it?"

"Stop this nonsense," Father Dmitriev said. "This is a house of God."

"Sounds more like the House of Horrors from what I overheard." She turned to look at Jackie. "I hope you burn in hell," Trish said and kicked over the candle rack.

Father Dmitriev tried to catch the rack, but it fell against him. Candles toppled from the rack holders, catching his cassock on fire. Some of the flames caught onto the Oriental carpet beneath his feet.

Father Dmitriev, letting out nervous screams, swatted at his sleeves, but the flames consumed his cassock. Jason snatched one of the nave carpets and beat it against Father Dmitriev.

Trish tossed the doll into the fire.

Jackie's skin seared. Shrieking, she dropped to the floor and rolled. She conjured thoughts of Babu, but in her mind's eye, Babu burned too.

Before she could roll again, David was on his knees at her

side. He pressed his hand to her forehead, but all she felt was her skin melting beneath a hot iron. She jerked her head away. "Make it stop! Make it stop!" She had to keep moving. She thrust her head from side to side. The pain was too much. She wanted to get up and run.

David gripped her shoulders. "Please. Let me help you."

He began to chant in Latin.

She kicked and writhed and gnashed her teeth.

His energy, warm and exhilarating, seeped into her. In her mind's eye she saw a single flame, a wick from a thin, red candle burning. The pain she felt was suddenly quelled.

Jason shoved David's shoulder. "Get away from her. She's fine."

David didn't budge. He gazed into her eyes.

"Get up," Jason yelled.

She couldn't move. She was spellbound by David's energy, hypnotized by his gaze and the cosmic ring that glowed around his hazel, gold-flecked eyes.

David slowly rose.

It had taken a lot of will power for her to let go of his sleeve and to sit up.

Jason stooped beside her and touched her shoulder. She only knew this because she could see his hand. She couldn't feel it. "You okay?" he asked.

"Yeah." David's energy gripped her until sirens cut through her haze.

Father Dmitriev was lying on the floor, his body twitching, covered in white foam. David, kneeling on a half-hardened puddle of candle wax, hovered over him.

"I put out the fire," Jason said to her.

"Where's Trish?" she asked, trying to divert his attention from the look on her face.

Jason grimaced. "She ran off. Can you stand up?"

"I don't know."

Jason put his arm under hers and helped her up.

Police, firemen, and paramedics rushed into the church.

Two paramedics tended to Father Dmitriev.

She was leaning on Jason when Detective Sikes approached them.

David sauntered over to them. Her eyes briefly met his.

"Jackie, what a surprise to see you again," Detective Sikes said sarcastically. "How come when something big goes down in this town, you're involved?"

She shrugged.

"I'm Detective Sikes," he said to David and reached out to shake his hand. He glanced at the paramedics tending to Father Dmitriev and then turned his attention to Jackie, Jason, and David. "Want to tell me what happened?"

They each volunteered information, but none of them mentioned anything about the voodoo doll, just that Trish tried to burn the church down and that she had totally lost it.

"So why are you all here?" he asked.

"Uh... we," Jackie began.

"We were just doing a little investigating." David handed Detective Sikes his phone. "There's a recorded confession of the fire on this phone. Not of this fire, but of the fire that burned Stephanie Yarrow and her unborn child alive."

Jackie dropped her jaw. He was risking his chance of becoming a priest. What changed his mind?

Detective Sikes called over one of the police officers. "Evidence," he said to him.

The officer pulled a plastic baggie out of his shirt pocket and held it open. Detective Sikes dropped the phone into the baggie.

"What's going to happen to Trish?" Jason asked Detective Sikes.

"She's a minor," Detective Sikes said. "It'll be up to the juvenile court system to decide. They may sentence her to time at a juvenile detention center, or they may just release her on probation. Fleeing the crime scene, though, isn't going to help her case."

"Neither is being a psycho. Can we go now?" Jackie asked Detective Sikes.

"Sure. If I have any more questions, I'll have someone bring you down to the station. Same goes for you too, young man," he said to Jason.

David looked at her with parted lips.

"I have a few more questions for you," Detective Sikes said to David.

"Could you wait just one minute?" David said to him. "Jackie, can I talk to you before you leave?"

Panic rose in her chest. She shook her head. "I'm done here."

Jason glared at David and put his arm around her shoulder. "Let's go," he said to her. As he escorted her out of the church, she picked up really bad vibes from him.

Chapter 47

In the truck, Jason clenched the steering wheel like he was squeezing someone's throat. His aura was super dark.

"All right, Jas, say it," Jackie said.

"Say what?"

"What's on your mind?" Her intuition told her it had to do with David.

"You should know."

"Oh, come on. Don't assume I know everything."

"You can read my emotions, so you tell me."

She swallowed. Why was he making her say this? What if she was wrong and she opened up a whole can of worms? No, this could be the only thing that would make Jason not talk to her. He was jealous of David.

"Is it something I did in the church?" she asked.

"You're getting warm."

She tapped her fingers on the truck's door arm. "Is it something that made you... jealous?"

"You're getting hot."

She stopped tapping. "Jason, quit playing games. Tell me, because as I remember, I was caught up in Trish's thoughts."

"Don't play innocent."

Ouch. Those "take charge" feelings she had sent him were still working.

"It was afterward, after Father David broke the spell," he said.

"Don't call him Father. He's not a priest."

"Looks like you changed his mind. He gave the police that recording."

"That doesn't mean..."

"I saw the look on your face after he let go of you. I saw how he had to unlock your fingers from his gown."

"It's a cassock, not a gown. He's not a drag queen. And I don't remember." She knotted her fingers together. "I wasn't myself."

"Then who were you? Are you going to tell me that you were only feeling what David was feeling, that you were just this empty vessel being filled with David's emotions?"

Her shoulders trembled. Why was he doing this to her? Hadn't she gone through enough today?

He parked in front of Jackie's house.

She jerked the door handle, but the door didn't open. She hit the lock-unlock button. Jason hit it too. "Jason, unlock the door."

"No."

"I need to lie down. Please, stop playing games."

"I want to know. Do you love him, or me?"

She stared at the handle that kept failing to open the door. "Please, Jas."

"You're not leaving this truck until you tell me."

She sighed. "Why is this so important now, at this very minute? Why can't it wait until tomorrow?"

Jason rested his forehead on the steering wheel. "Because you're my best friend, and I'm suffering so bad right now because I feel like you're being torn away from me. I know I can't make you love me, not romantically, but it's killing me because I feel like I'm losing you."

Tears pricked the corners of her eyes. She wanted to touch him, but she was afraid to.

"He pushed me down the stairs when I was three," he said.

"Who?"

"My dad. He pushed me down the stairs. That's why the stair

thing."

"Oh." She didn't know what more to say. He kind of caught her off guard with that one.

"You said you'd listen if I ever wanted to talk about it." He raised his head. He looked so innocent, so fragile.

She was a monster for hurting him.

"Yeah. Thanks. I mean, thanks for confiding in me."

"It's easier now that Dad's acting differently. He's been going out of his way to be a nice guy. He helped me replace the catalytic converter on my truck. Before, the only thing he'd do was tell me to park this piece of shit out of his way."

"Good. I'm glad it's working out for you."

"Thanks for your help."

"You're welcome." She pressed the lock-unlock button. The sound of it unlocking was a relief, but the sound of it locking was not.

"You didn't answer my question," he said.

Ugh! She took a deep breath. "I told you before. I don't even know who I am or what my true feelings are."

Jason looked at her with contempt. He hit the button and unlocked the door.

Great. Was he letting her go just for now or for good? She opened the door just a crack. She wanted to tell him she was sorry for the way she acted around David. She wanted to tell him how much she cared about him, and how she hated herself for hurting him.

"You were right about one thing," he said. "You are a liar."

His words slapped her in the face, and the impact made her eyes sting. Pushing open the truck door, she tried to hold back tears.

"We belong together, and you know it," he said.

She got out of the truck and slammed the door, not because she was angry at him, but because her emotions were out of control.

She ran up the front lawn steps, tears streaming down her face.

On the front porch, she dried her face with the edge of her trench coat and tried to get a hold of her emotions before she went into the house. Her hands shook as she worked the key into the door lock. As she turned the doorknob, the handle turned on its own evading her grip, and the door opened.

"Jackie," Mom cried out. "Where were you? I was so worried."

Jackie's eyes were tender and the skin beneath them, raw. She knew it looked like she had been crying.

Mom opened her arms. "Come here, sweetie." As Mom hugged her, she noticed a man, about thirty-something—early thirty-something—sitting on the living room couch with a boy, who couldn't be older than two, on his lap.

"Mom," she said, her voice muffled because half of her mouth was pressed against Mom's arm. "Who's that?"

Mom took Jackie's hand. "Let me introduce you. Jackie, this is my friend Andy and his son Mathew. Andy, this is my daughter Jackie."

Andy reached out to shake her hand while his son tugged at his beard. "I'm so glad to finally meet you. Your mother was a little hesitant about introducing us."

"Insecure," Mom spouted.

He laughed.

Jackie stood there like a dope, her mouth hung open. She knew Mom had a boyfriend, but she hadn't expected him to be this young.

"What funny, Daddy? What funny?" the little boy said.

Andy lifted his boy's shirt and blew raspberries onto his plump tummy. "That's funny."

Jackie's eyes grew wide, and she looked at Mom.

Mom shrugged and smiled.

"Andy, it was nice meeting you too," Jackie said. "Uh, sorry I look like"—*watch your mouth, little boy in the room*—"heck. I'm sure

Mom told you I had quite a day with my headache."

"How is your headache?" Mom asked.

"Gone, miraculously."

"What could have caused such a headache?" She turned to Andy. "You should have seen her this morning. She couldn't even keep down coffee."

"Migraine," Andy said. "My ex-wife used to get those all the time."

"If you'll excuse me," Jackie said, "I need to soak in the tub."

"Yeah, sure," Andy said. "I'm glad you're home safe. Your mother was worried to death. She's quite a woman, you know."

"Yeah." *She must be for landing you, even though you come with a side package.*

Babu hobbled from the kitchen. When Babu saw her, she clenched her hands together, closed her eyes, and mumbled.

"I'm still alive," Jackie said to Babu.

Babu crossed herself, and weakly smiled at her. The light around Babu was dim, and she looked tired.

In the bathroom, with cold cream packed on her face, Jackie slid into the warm tub water until it touched her chin. The water rocked her shoulders and splashed against the sides of the tub. The sound of moving water echoed in her ears and rang with Jason's voice calling her a liar. She closed her eyes to let Babu's light overtake her, but her thoughts shifted to Mom and her boyfriend—her *young* boyfriend.

No wonder Mom had been acting so strangely. Why was she trying to keep it a secret? Was Mom trying to protect her, or was Mom confused, like her? Maybe she just wasn't sure about how she felt, or maybe she was afraid it just wasn't real.

Jackie hoped it was real for Mom. She wished Mom the best. She really did. As much as she wished her parents would get back together, that things would be back to the way they were before she had her first vision, and that her father would love her as she is, Jackie was old enough to know that was never going to happen. Mom may as well move on.

What's real for me?

What's real was David set her heart soaring whenever she was around him. And whenever she left him, she carried his energy. She felt it now and knew she couldn't possibly be reading his vibes because he wasn't physically with her.

And Jason—her best friend in the whole world, her other half—she needed him in her life. And it was her wanting that, not him feeding her those thoughts because he wasn't here right now either.

What was real was she didn't belong with David. She could never become the person he wanted her to be. It was Jason who accepted her as she was. It was Jason with whom she felt comfortable and whom she couldn't imagine living without.

In bed, dressed in her black fleece, Jackie called Jason. Everything that had happened to her today—the whole voodoo doll incident and Father Dmitriev fessing up to his crime—seemed insignificant compared to the tension between her and Jason.

When Jason didn't answer, she swallowed back a heavy feeling in her throat. A sharp pain shot through her heart.

She called him again. This time, she let it ring longer. She wouldn't blame him if he never talked to her. He was right. She was a liar. She hadn't been true to her feelings. She had been so afraid to connect with other people and to accept herself as she was.

No answer.

Screw it! She tossed the phone to the foot of the bed and

plopped her head into the pillow. Let him be angry. She was tired of being judged. She was tired of judging herself.

"Jackie," Mom yelled.

"What?"

"Your friend is outside, on the lawn," she said.

Jackie scrambled out of bed and into the hall. "Who?"

Mom looked up at her from the bottom of the stairs. "He's... well... take a look."

What friend? Her stomach knotted.

Downstairs, Jackie parted the living room curtain. In the gray dusk light and drizzling rain, stood Jason, a lit candle in one hand and a sign that read, "Heal me" in the other.

"Huh."

"Is everything all right?" Mom asked.

"Maybe."

Jackie threw on her trench coat and ran out the door.

"Your shoes," Mom said.

Jackie's bare feet smacked against the wet steps and trotted through the cold, sopping grass. She stood in the drizzling rain before Jason, her coat open, her hands clenched.

The candle's flame illuminated the glassy whites in Jason's eyes. His face was pale; the hollow in his throat, deep. Drops of rain dripped from the tips of his wet hair and rolled down the shoulders of his leather jacket.

She squeezed her hands until her nails cut into her palms. "I lied, Jason. I lied because I was scared."

Jason drew the sign close to his chest like a shield.

"I'm still scared."

"Heal me." Jason's face was wet. From rain or tears, she couldn't tell.

She closed her eyes and dug deep for the only words that were right to say. Forcing them from her lips, she faltered at first, but then they came out coherent and clear. "I love you."

She opened her eyes and assessed the damage.

"It's killing me," he said.

She touched his face. "I'm so sorry."

The sign slipped from his hand and fell to the wet grass.

She wrapped her fingers around his and blew out the candle. Together they released it and let it fall to the ground. She slipped her arms around Jason and absorbed the pain she had caused him. She just wanted him to stop hurting.

They stood in the rain, holding each other until Mom opened the front door and said, "Why don't you guys bring it inside? But not in your room!"

Chapter 48

At school the next day, Jason walked Jackie to her locker and kissed her on the lips. "See you in class."

"Yeah, see you," she said.

"Jeez, Jackie," Zeta said.

"What?"

"What kind of kiss was that? I mean, put some heat into it."

She shrugged her shoulder. "We're at school."

"Yeah, right." Zeta huffed.

"Just leave it alone. Everything's good."

"Is it? And what went on at that church? How come I always miss the good stuff?"

"Good stuff? Didn't you hear about Trish?"

"Did I! Her mother called me last night and blamed me for Trish's behavior, for like an hour."

"Was Trish home?"

"She was until the police arrested her. Her Mom said something about taking her to a juvenile detention center. I should have known Trish was losing it when she brought that Ouija board over to Mr. Davis's house."

"She did?"

Zeta looked over Jackie's shoulder. "Hey, jock-face. What are you looking at?"

Jackie turned around. John shot her a sly look and huddled with Sean, Will, and some other jocks in front of the haunted bathroom. They must have heard about the latest Holy

Resurrection incident. Her nerve endings tingled, and the hair on the back of her neck rose. They were planning some kind of mob action against her. She knew it.

"Jackie, are you all right?" Zeta asked.

She nodded and took a deep breath, held it, and exhaled, imagining the negative energy flowing out of her body. She did this again until her nerves stopped tingling and she was in control. "Time to deliver," she said to Zeta. "Wait here."

Smiling deviously, Jackie walked toward them. "Step aside," she said. "I have work to do." They didn't move, so she pushed her way through them and tore the yellow ribbon that was stretched across the bathroom entrance.

The bathroom was as cold as a mocha frappé and fogged in a misty blue. Standing in two inches of water, she touched the overflowing sink and opened up to the stored energy. Water ran over her fingers, and the mirror moved inward and outward, shrinking and stretching her reflection. Lightheaded and spacey, Jackie struck the mirror to make it stop. Her fist slammed against stainless steel, the pain bringing her back to reality.

She closed her eyes and envisioned Julie Dickenson striking her fist against the mirror and the mirror shattering. The mirror was made of glass. Julie picked up a long, jagged shard and ripped it across each wrist. Blood pouring out her wrists, she panicked and held her wrists under the running water, trying to keep the blood inside.

Julie Dickenson never intentionally committed suicide, Jackie concluded. She was high. She wasn't thinking logically, and her addiction fed her feelings of hopelessness.

Jackie placed both hands on the sink and immersed herself in Babu's light. No situation was hopeless, she told herself. With a little clear thinking, there was always a way out. She let feelings of hope filter through her fingers and flow into the water and the porcelain. She imagined it spreading through the sink and water pipes. She did this until the water running out of the faucet slowed to a trickle and then stopped.

When she came out of the bathroom, she startled at the amount of people packed into the hall. They stared at her as if they'd been waiting to see if she'd come out unscathed. She was scared at first, but really, this is what she wanted. Let them believe what they wanted to believe. They couldn't hurt her anymore.

She ripped the Out of Order sign from the cinder block wall, crumbled it in her hands, and tossed it at Will. He blocked it with his hands, and it fell to his feet. The crowd around him jumped away from the crumpled paper as if it were packed with a curse.

"Tell the janitor the haunted bathroom is back in order," she said to the crowd. "Oh, and one more thing. If any of you ever pick on Pete again, I swear I'll curse you with a serious case of dorkdom."

With a huge grin, Zeta handed Jackie her books. "Way to go!" They walked down the main hall together, laughing at the expressions on everyone's faces.

In American Lit class, Jason was already seated when Jackie entered the room. She squeezed his arm when she passed him. His energy was strong and happy, his aura, bright.

Mr. Davis slouched in his chair, looking haggard as usual, his aura, a washed-out purple. He began the lesson by tossing his textbook copy into the garbage can by his desk. *Thump!* The class fell silent and all heads turned toward Mr. Davis.

"'The School,'" Mr. Davis said tiredly. "Who read 'The School' by Donald Barthelme?"

A few hands flew up immediately. Some hesitantly went up. Mr. Davis leaned his weight onto the arms of his desk chair and stood up. The chair rolled recklessly backward and hit the wall beneath the whiteboard. "Not that it really matters if you read it or not." He careened to the front of his desk and leaned slovenly against it. He rubbed his unruly beard. His bloodshot eyes stared over the heads of the students. "I mean, the fundamental question here exists whether you read the damn story or not. Is it death that gives meaning to life, or is it life that gives meaning to life?"

Mouths dropped open; eyes grew wide. Jackie sensed that everyone was too frightened by Mr. Davis to answer.

Mr. Davis narrowed his eyes and then stumbled down the aisle. His eyes were focused on Jackie, but he stopped at Jason's desk. "Hey, you look happy today." There was a foul odor coming from Mr. Davis's mouth, like alcohol—a serious amount of alcohol. She could smell it from where she sat. Mr. Davis was trashed. Drunken trashed. "You two are inseparable," he slurred. "It's one of the things I've grown to count on." His eyes grew watery.

What on earth was going on with Mr. Davis? He had been nutty ever since they covered "The Yellow Wallpaper."

And then it hit her.

"Yes," she said to Mr. Davis.

He glared at her with bloodshot eyes. "Yes, what?"

"Remember when we discussed 'The Yellow Wallpaper' and you asked me if I thought objects can have an effect on people?"

Mr. Davis looked at her and squinted.

"The answer is yes."

He came closer to her, his lips slightly parted like he wanted to tell her something.

Despite his stench, she tugged his jacket sleeve to pull him closer to her desk. "I can make it stop," she whispered, "if you want me to."

He laid his hand on her shoulder and nodded. His exhaustion softened her muscles, and a deep sadness settled into her bones.

Chapter 49

At the juvie home, Trish slipped out of the dinner hall, toting, in her hoodie pocket, a mouse she had snatched from the computer room and a black crayon she lifted from the activity center. She smiled curtly at the hall monitor and then hurried to her room to get there before the other girls returned.

Inside the closet, she pulled the tattered string hanging from the light and closed the door. The half shelf in the center of the closet, about twelve inches deep and twenty-four inches long, was perfect for what she needed. She removed the shelf from the brackets and set it on the floor. She slipped the mouse out of her pocket. Holding the mouse and pulling its cord tight, she rubbed the cord over the sharp edge of the shelf bracket, cutting through plastic and working harder to cut through wire. She tossed the cord to the side.

Sitting cross-legged on the closet floor, she set the shelf on her lap and slipped the black crayon from her pocket. Starting at the upper-left of the board, she wrote the word, "Yes." In the upper-right corner she wrote, "No." Then, she wrote the alphabet, *A* through *M* in the upper half of the board, and *N* though *Z* beneath it. Beneath that, the numbers, *1, 2, 3, 4, 5, 6, 7, 8, 9, 0*. Near the bottom of the board, "Good-bye."

She placed the mouse on the center of the board and lightly rested her fingertips on its curved surface. The mouse was lightweight and slid easily. Although she couldn't see through it, it would do the job. She closed her eyes and concentrated on the recipient of her intended message. "Where are you? Show yourself, you two-faced, lying devil."

She waited for an answer. It was subtle at first, but then she was sure she heard it, the deep-throated, vibrating breathing of her fiendish friend.

"I made that voodoo doll for you," she said, "just like you told me to."

The mouse moved with a force beneath her fingers, a force greater than her unconscious mind could maneuver. Trish opened her eyes and breathlessly read each letter: *C-H-I-L-D-S-P-L-A-Y.*

"You promised me Jason. It's not my fault the young priest saved her."

Y-O-U-F-A-I-L-E-D

"Let me try again. Just get me out of here. You need me, you know."

N-O-T

She whipped the mouse against the closet door and then crossed her arms and pouted. "You're not getting one over on me," she seethed. "I'll get the whole Vatican on your ass if I have to."

But until she got out of here, she was stuck. And there was no way she could warn Jackie—even if she wanted to.

Chapter 50

On her way to Mr. Davis's house, Jackie decided to stop by the rectory. Maybe a bad idea, but she needed to tell David not to bother talking to Sandra. Now that she had this evil Jackie persona working for her, she didn't want him blowing her cover. Maybe, too, she just wanted him to know where she stood.

She rang the rectory doorbell, but no one answered. She was just about ready to phone David when he opened the door.

"Jackie," he said, barefooted and sounding pleasantly surprised. His black shirt was misbuttoned and half tucked into his black slacks.

"Your shirt's misbuttoned," she said, trying to hide the fact that he had her ruffled.

He looked down at his shirt and then smiled at her sheepishly. "Sorry. I was not expecting company. With Father Dmitriev gone, I have been a little lax on my dress code inside the rectory."

She held up her hand. "No problem."

"Come in, please. I was just going through bills in Father Dmitriev's office. The Bishop is in the process of finding a new rector. Until then, I need to, how you say, be man of ship."

She smiled. "Yeah, that's it."

He directed her to the sofa. "Sit down, please. I am slowly figuring out where Father Dmitriev keeps things." David unbuttoned the first misaligned button on his shirt.

Her mouth went dry. "Well, it's good practice for when you

become a... priest. Is that still on?"

His fingers worked to button his shirt. "Father Dmitriev's recorded confession was all the church took seriously." Correctly buttoned, David sat down in the winged chair. He leaned forward, resting his arms on his thighs and entwining his fingers, his bare feet planted solidly on the floor.

Her stomach back flipped every time she looked at them. Shouldn't he have to have those covered up?

"Why'd you risk it?" she asked. "After I chose, what you call, the dark side."

"Because through God I was able to save you from Satan. I still have faith in you."

She raised her eyebrows. "Thanks, I guess. But really, it was so surreal, to be burning because of a stupid doll. I must have been reading Trish's mind, her fantasy of me burning. That's what Father Dmitriev did to me when I was twelve. He was thinking about what he was going to do to Stephanie, while giving Holy Communion. I read his mind."

"But how did the burning stop? This time, I mean."

"Maybe when Jason pulled the doll out of the flames, Trish no longer believed I was burning, and I read her mind."

"What about when you were a child? How did the burning stop then?"

"I don't know. I remember Babu holding me and praying and..." She swallowed. "Well, maybe it was Babu's love that saved me. And maybe, when you, well, it was your..." she lowered her eyes. "Well, you know... your Godly compassion for me that made me quit thinking that I was burning."

"I suppose there will always be logical answer. That's why believing in God is a matter of faith."

"I have faith in myself now. We're square on our bargain, aren't we?"

David nodded.

"Oh, and forget about talking to my friend about me. I don't care what people think anymore."

David narrowed his brow and studied her.

Feeling awkward, Jackie stood up and fought the urge to take one more look at David's gorgeous feet. "Good luck with being the man of the ship."

"Wait, Jackie, there is something I need to ask you." He walked over to her. "I was wondering, what are your plans when you graduate high school?" He sounded nervous.

Holy shit. Where did that come from? Did her mom put him up to this? "Actually, no plan yet."

"You are graduating this year? Yes?"

She glowered. "Yeah."

"You must have put some thought into it?"

"No, well, a little, I guess. I thought maybe I'd be a photographer, but I kind of had reservations since I have a hard time being around people. I mean, I thought I'd keel over if I had to deal with all the emotions bombarding me at a wedding or some other major event. My second choice was recluse. But, I have a lot more options now that I know how to control myself. I just haven't thought about it."

His fingers tensed. "In the spring, I will have finished my internship here."

"Congrats. Glad to hear someone's on a career track. You're probably glad to finish with school."

"Actually, I am not." He flexed his thumbs.

"You one of those people who enjoy being a lifetime student?"

He shook his head. "It's just that, when I am finished, I will be ordained."

"I thought that was a good thing."

"It was, until..."

"You found out the truth about Father Dmitriev? That must have been a real downer to your faith in the religion."

He stepped closer to her. "No. My faith in the church and God is strong."

His eyes were desperate, and she was sensing emotional pain.

"As an Orthodox priest, I can marry. As long as I do it before I am ordained."

Oh, shit! She swallowed. "You're having second thoughts?"

"I want to be a priest, but I can't help but feel... it is very strange, but—"

Her cell phone rang, scaring the hell out of her. "Sorry."

She read the display. It was Jason. She walked over to the window and peeked out to see if Jason had followed her. There was no sight of him or his truck. Good. He didn't need to know where she was.

"Hey, Jas." Her voice cracked. She cleared her throat. "What's up?"

"Hey, I thought maybe we could stream a movie tonight?"

"Sure. Your pick this time."

David was listening to her conversation. She hoped he wouldn't say a word. All she needed was for Jason to hear David's voice, and her relationship with Jason would be over in a heartbeat.

"Come over at seven," she said. "I need to pay Mr. Davis a visit first. I'll pick up some snacks on the way home. Love you," she whispered. She ended the call and turned to David. "Sorry. That was Jason."

"I heard."

She reached out her hand. "Thank you for your help. If it wasn't for you, I never would have learned the truth."

He looked at her hand as if contemplating whether to take it. Then, he gently touched his fingertips to hers. She wondered if Russian men didn't shake hands with women. Embarrassed, she pulled her hand away, but he took it, and in one deft move, he pulled her to him and pressed his lips to hers.

She was about to have a coronary. Spitting the Eucharist onto the church floor wasn't enough. No. She was lip-locked with a seminarian in a church rectory. What an encore. Cleansing breaths and zipping up were totally out of the question.

With her lips pressed to his, a candle's flame lit in her mind. She tried to shake the image.

Think about what you're doing. You cannot do this!

The image faded. The blood in her body started to circulate, and the neurons in her brain began to fire. She shoved him. "Stop," she yelled.

She was shaking. What the heck was with him—his energy, the image?

"I am so sorry," he said. "I cannot control how I feel about you... I cannot explain...I... I think I am in love with you."

"No. You can't be. You're going to be a priest."

"But I can't help but think that we were brought together by a divine force..."

"We don't belong together." She stepped back several feet from him. "I am what I am. I can't change."

"In time..."

"I won't."

A pensive look washed over him. "I understand."

Relieved, she sighed. "Good."

Before stepping out the door, she turned to him. She had to know. "So, what are you going to tell the congregation about me?"

David's eyes slightly brightened. "That there's still hope."

She bit her lip and turned away. She quickly descended the rectory steps and didn't look back.

"I'm Jackie Turov," she said to herself. "A psychic and a healer."

With chin raised, she walked to Mr. Davis's house on a mission.

Chapter 51

Mr. Davis opened the door in a rumpled T-shirt and a pair of plaid boxer shorts. "Jackie." He stared at her. The bags under his bloodshot eyes and the skin around his jaws were sagging—the effects of no sleep and large doses of alcohol, no doubt.

"I thought you'd be expecting me," Jackie said.

Mr. Davis held onto the open door. "I didn't think you'd come."

"Well, here I am."

He stared at her like she had caught him with his pants down, which she kind of did.

"I'd like to help," she said, "but you have to let me in."

He furrowed his brow and then swallowed. Finally, he opened the door further and stepped out of the entranceway. She took it as an invitation to enter.

Inside, the living room was completely trashed: the sofa heaped with clothes and books, and the coffee table cluttered with empty beer bottles, a half bottle of rum, class essays, and Mr. Davis's infamous red pen.

Mr. Davis, slumped-shouldered, said, "I just wanted to talk to my wife. To tell her I'm sorry she had to suffer. That I miss her."

Jackie drew a blank at first, but then it all came together. "Oh. And you let Trish bring over her Ouija board?"

"She showed up at my door with it. She was trying to get me

to switch her class hour. She convinced me she could contact the other side." He pointed to a closed door off from the living room. "We did it in there, where she died."

Jackie wondered what havoc the solar storm could have wreaked in that room. "So, what's going on?"

"I didn't want to ask you to come, but it keeps asking for you."

"What does?"

"It won't let me sleep. Alcohol helps, but now, I think I'm going to lose my job."

Poor Mr. Davis must think he's being haunted. She touched Mr. Davis's arm to console him.

The bedroom door flew open.

Mr. Davis startled and stared horrified at the open door.

"Trish?" she called out and took a step forward.

Bam! A powerful force slammed into her and knocked her to the floor. She sat there, jaw-dropped, legs outstretched. Something clamped around her ankles, like two invisible hands, and jerked her forward. She fell backward. Flat on her back, she was dragged across the living room floor, her satchel slipping off her arm. Frantic, she clawed the carpet to keep from being pulled into the room.

But she was.

And the door slammed shut.

She sat in the dark, her heart racing. The force released her ankles, but then something slithered across her lap. Afraid to move, she sat still, every muscle in her body frozen. The something slithered around her side and her back, and coming full circle, it cinched her waist and squeezed her ribs. She could barely expand her lungs to breathe.

A tall votive on the dresser lighted, illuminating a picture of the Virgin imprinted on the glass. Across the wall by the bed, moved a shapeless shadow. It morphed into a shadow of a snake. Slithering along the wall, it divided into two snakes. Entwined, the snakes crept from wall to wall, circling the room like creatures on an eerie carousel.

The dresser mirror glowed and then lit with a scene of people holding candles and singing in front of a huge icon of the Virgin of Vladimir on her front lawn. Flowers, tiny icons and statues, and stuffed animals were propped around the icon.

A hot breath warmed her neck, startling her and sending a chill down her spine.

"Heal me," a demonic voice hissed. In the mirror, she saw herself at twelve in the grocery store on her hands and knees, heaving chunks onto the polished floor, the woman with the scarf tied around her shaved head bent over her.

The scene changed to Father Dmitriev placing the Holy Eucharist on her tongue. It looked like there was two of him, superimposed. One of him had demonic features—a stretched face, pointed beard, and eyes deep-set and glowing. She screamed out in pain as the Eucharist seared her tongue. Father Dmitriev and his demonic double pointed their finger at her.

"She's possessed," they said in unison.

With fear washed across her face, she pointed to the iconostasis. "The Virgin," she said before the disbelieving congregation. "She spoke to me. She showed me a sign."

The demon mocked in a girlish tone, "The Virgin. She spoke to me. She showed me a sign."

A multitude of voices laughed.

"Liar," the demon said gruffly.

The image changed to her and Trish in the school hallway, a vehement crowd gathered around them.

"You're nothing but a fake. She lied," Trish said to the crowd. "She never saw the Virgin." Trish's features contorted, and her eyes burned red as she glared at Jackie.

Jackie closed her eyes and envisioned Babu and her light. She imagined the light pushing against the serpent wrapped around her body.

"Babu is a witch," the demon whispered.

Her eyes popped open. It read her mind.

A multitude of voices whispered around her, but she couldn't understand what they were saying. In the mirror, Babu and Madam Sophie were hanging upside down from the iconostasis in Holy Resurrection Church, their hands tied behind their back, one leg crossed behind the other forming a triangle.

"Babu is a witch. Babu is a witch," the multitude of voices said.

The scene switched to Babu standing at a meager wooden alter. Crippled and sick villagers were lined before her. The two women from the photo were at Babu's side, praying as Babu laid her hands on each of the sick.

The mirror turned dark, and all reflection was lost. Then out of the darkness, three figures emerged, dressed in black dresses and headscarves. They were standing in front of a wooden building, just like in Babu's photo album.

The voices whispered, like gossip, and then grew louder, and the rhythm of the words grew faster.

Babu ran from the churchyard, escaping an angry mob, some waving their fists and staves. She ran into the forest, just like she and Babu did in Jackie's dream.

"You persecuted her because she was a healer."

"Babu is a witch," the demon said.

"You're lying."

The two snake shadows circling the room had multiplied, and the walls were crawling with a multitude of serpentine figures.

She closed her eyes and envisioned Babu sitting in her bed, a country quilt spread over her legs, her chotki entwined in her fingers, and a white light surrounding her as she prayed. "Babu's not a witch. She's a devout woman," she whispered.

The serpent constricted, squeezing her body. She envisioned Babu's light filling her, protecting her from the serpent. The serpent's grip loosened slightly, but only to slither around her neck and constrict again.

Struggling to breathe, Jackie sank her fingers into the taut, smooth flesh wrapped around her neck. She couldn't fight it. Not with her own strength. Not with Babu's light.

Where was Mr. Davis? Why wasn't he helping her?

She kicked, trying to scoot backward toward the door. If she banged her head against it, maybe Mr. Davis would open it and break the spell.

She could barely move.

Dizzy and weak, she let her fingers slip from the serpent, and her arms dropped to her sides.

I'm going to die. A silent acceptance washed over her.

Wheezing, she remembered and reached for her coat pocket. The boa constrictor–sized serpent bulged under her arm, shortening her reach. She flopped onto her back. Raised inches off the floor, she bent at her waist. Her fingers brushed the cloth of her trench coat as she searched for the pocket opening. Pulling her coat pocket within reach, she was able to slip her hand inside.

The lightweight rope tickled her palm. Yes! It was still there. Thank you, Jason.

She pressed her thumb and index finger to a chotki knot and frantically prayed.

The serpent's strength slowly weakened. It loosened from around her and slithered off. She hit the floor. She lay there clenching the chotki and gasping for air.

The votive flame went out, and the door opened.

Slowly, she got up from the floor.

Mr. Davis stood at the open door, his eyes looking more bloodshot than before. "Is it gone?" Mr. Davis asked.

"How the heck would I know?"

"I thought you knew about these things."

In the living room, she grabbed her satchel, which was lying crumpled on the floor, and she beelined to the front door.

Mr. Davis trailed her. "Will it come back?"

"Probably, but not for you."

Chapter 52

The encounter with the serpent had left a bad taste in Jackie's mouth, like metal on her tongue. Her senses had dulled too. She wasn't picking anything up, no emotions, that is. This would have been a good thing to her in the past, but now, she just didn't feel like herself.

Her throat had been sore since the incident, as if the demon had stuck its head down it to peer inside her. What had happened at Mr. Davis's house contradicted all she had believed in, shattered the values she had laid in place to make her believe that she was okay and the rest of the world was insane.

Chapter 53

Over a week had gone by and still, every day, Jackie awoke feeling blah, like something inside her had died. How long would this feeling last? She wished it would pass. Perhaps it was true that once you had tasted evil, you could never get the taste out of your mouth.

She didn't tell anyone about the incident, not Jason, and not Zcta. To tell them would be like saying, "I'm not the person you thought me to be. My thoughts are false. My world is false."

She had buried the chotki in her bottom dresser drawer. It had been a tool for the moment. A last resort. But what did she know about God? He was miles away from her heart. She hadn't known Him since she was a child. Perhaps she really never knew Him at all.

What she needed was to restore her balance. She needed Babu's light, but Babu wouldn't come near her. For some reason, she frightened her.

She would have to heal herself.

Legs folded Lotus-style, her hands resting lightly on her knees, palms up, she tried to envision Babu's light, but the light was dim. Maybe it was because Babu was afraid of her.

She envisioned another light. One that she made up as being somewhere buried inside herself. It was as tiny as a pinhead, or maybe more like a pinhole with light creeping through.

She breathed deeply, taking in the minuscule amount of light, and then she exhaled, casting out the negative energy. Every time she took in a new breath, her senses grew duller.

Her cell rang. She jumped.

It's just a phone call, not a demonic presence.

"Hey, girl," Zeta said. "Where you been hiding? It's Halloween. Did you get your costume?"

"Got it."

"Jason and I will be over at five."

"All right."

"You okay?"

"Dandy."

"Something going on between you and Jas?"

"No."

"I hope not. That boy can't say one sentence without including your name."

Jackie sighed.

"You're not thinking of breaking up with him?"

"No, we're good. It's me. I just don't feel like myself lately."

"It's the party."

"No, I'm okay with the party. Don't worry about it. I'll be fine."

"You don't sound convincing."

Jackie wasn't convinced either.

Chapter 54

Zeta adjusted the wings on Jackie's Halloween costume so that the tips extended above Jackie's shoulders. Then in one gruff move, Zeta bent one of the wing tips downward.

In the freestanding oval mirror in her room, Jackie beheld herself. Calf-high boots with straps and buckles, opaque-black tights, a silken and vixen mini dress, and two black wings—fittingly, one broken.

"I thought you were going as a zombie nun." Zeta was dressed like a zombie school girl—her hair disheveled, her face white with thick black circles around her eyes, her white blouse sleeves cut at different lengths and ragged, and her over-the-knee socks torn.

"Fallen angel seemed more appropriate," Jackie said.

Jason sidled behind her and wrapped his arms around her waist. He was dressed like a zombie priest, although he kept telling her that he was only a seminarian. "It's okay that we don't match," Jason said. "You can fall into my arms anytime." He kissed her neck. The gentle tickle of it shivered down her nape and across her shoulders.

"Would you two get a room already?" Zeta rolled her eyes.

"We already have one." Jason squeezed Jackie tighter.

She pressed her fingers into his arms to keep them from constricting and suffocating her. "We have a party to go to, remember?" she asked Jason's reflection in the mirror.

His dark zombie eyes were glossy and burning with desire.

She spread his hands apart, breaking his hold. His hands fell to his sides. Facing him, she took one of his hands into hers and gently kissed it. She wasn't ready for what was on his mind, and she didn't want to hurt him by telling him that. She had already made him suffer long enough with not being able to touch him all these years, but she was still scared to truly open up to him. Perhaps it was because she had shut everyone out for so long, she didn't know how to behave in any other way. It didn't help that this blah-ness was making her feel even worse.

"Let's get out of here," she said.

Downstairs, Mom was kneeling at the coffee table beside two-year-old Mathew, picking candy out of his pumpkin bucket and inspecting each piece. The room reeked of sugar and chocolate.

Amused, Andy sat in the armchair and watched Mom work. Jackie still couldn't get over how Mom landed a guy ten years younger than herself. She guessed Mom was still young at heart, even though her divorce and drinking weathered her a bit.

"Jackie, remember how I used to do this for you?" Mom asked.

"Ugh. Don't remind me. My bucket sitting on top of the fridge taunting me. You divvying out a few pieces a day."

"That's because I loved you and didn't want you getting sick. What time you coming home?"

The question threw Jackie off guard. "At curfew, like always, unless you're bending the rules."

"No. It's just that Andy and I are going to watch *Night of the Living Dead*. Thought you'd like to join us. Zeta and Jason, you're welcome too. It'd be like a family night."

Zeta and Jason shrugged as if considering it.

"I don't know how long we'll be out," Jackie said.

"If it's nine thirty or ten-ish we could wait."

"We're good. You guys go ahead."

Mom looked uneasy.

"Mom, really. Maybe some other time."

"All right, then. Be home by curfew."

"Yes, Mommy."

Babu hobbled out of the kitchen with a cup of coffee in each hand. She looked at Jackie and shook her head. Jackie found this odd. Babu had always accepted Jackie's goth-ness. Ever since that night Jackie came home shaken from Mr. Davis's house, it was as if Babu had been afraid to get close to her. If Babu was like her, Babu must have sensed that she had made contact with a demon, the same one that persecuted her back in the day. But, it wasn't like they could discuss it. The simple Russian phrases Jackie knew could never describe to Babu what she had witnessed or what she saw in the mirror. But Babu knew something was amiss before it had happened and had tried to warn her.

Babu gave one coffee to Andy and set the other on the coffee table near the heap of candy Mom had already inspected.

"Bye, Babu." Jackie forced a smile, trying to look happy and normal so Babu wouldn't worry.

Babu signed the cross in the air and said something to her—or to God—in Russian.

"Take care of my daughter," Mom said to Jason, a warning look in her eyes. Mom may not be psychic like her, but even Mom knew what was on Jason's mind.

"I will, Ms. Turov," he said meekly.

Jackie yanked his arm and dragged him out the front door. Zeta followed, laughing.

The party was walkable, just a block past Dad's house. Only his upstairs bedroom light was on. Avoiding trick-or-treaters, no doubt. Jackie hoped he knew that without candy, the scant bit of Halloween decorations he put out wasn't going to keep his house from getting TP'd. She might even do it herself!

Jackie still couldn't wait to see the expression on everyone's face when she walked into the party. She had gotten invited through Zeta, who got invited from someone in her art class, who was invited by the girl who lives there. And of course, Jackie invited Jason. No big deal. These parties were all word of mouth.

The front yard was full of teens in costume with red plastic cups in their hands. Music pounded, vibrated through Jackie's body, but beside that, she felt nothing, sensed nothing. She would have thought she was perfectly normal for once, if she didn't feel so blah.

The crowd of teens standing in front of the house parted for her, Zeta, and Jason. In fact, for her it parted wider.

Inside, the house was packed with people, which made it harder for them to clear a space. Will glared at her from the stairs. He was wearing a blood-red tunic trimmed in black—an executioner's costume. And he had his arm around some other girl. *Shouldn't he be with Sandra?* Jackie gave him a look, like "what's with you and the new chick?"

Sean, dressed like a football player—what else—punched Will's shoulder. He was sitting a step above Will. Will turned and whispered in Sean's ear. John, dressed like a clown, joined the conclave.

Jackie touched Zeta's shoulder. "I'm going to tell them to kiss my—"

"Just let it go," Zeta said.

"They make me sick. The self-righteous sons of—"

"Jackie, let's just have fun. Ignore them."

"Come on, babe," Jason said. "I'm not dressed for a fight." He straightened his priest collar.

"Fine. And never call me babe." Jackie knew if there was a fight, she'd win. She imagined crumpling Will and Sean like tinfoil. Her face burned.

"Wow," Zeta said, "I've never seen you get so angry before.

Come on, let's grab a beer."

"There's beer?" Jason asked.

"Boy, you don't get out much," Zeta said. "You've been hanging out with Jackie too long."

Jackie gave Will and his henchmen one last searing look and then followed Jason and Zeta into the kitchen. The floor was sticky from spilled beer and liquor. It made a tacky sound as Jackie walked across it. The table was covered with bottles of hard liquor. By the fridge, the trash was overstuffed with plastic cups, paper plates, napkins, and empty booze bottles. A keg sat near the sink.

Jason and Zeta took a cup from a tower sitting on the countertop. Jason tapped beer from the keg. Foam ran over the edges of his cup.

"First time?" Zeta asked. "Give me that." She dumped the foam in the sink and showed Jason how to properly tap beer.

"Hey, freak," Will said. "No one invited you."

Will, Sean, and John blocked the kitchen doorway leading out to the front room. Will clutched his executioner's ax like a security blanket.

"You talking to me?" Jackie asked, her blood heating to a boil.

"Jackie," Zeta said, caution in her voice.

Jackie took a few steps toward them and stared Will in the eyes. She was about a foot or more shorter than all of them—and about fifty pounds lighter—but she didn't care. She could take out the whole bunch.

"Go home, witch girl," Sean said. "No one wants to be in the same room as you."

If Jackie could shoot daggers out of her eyes, she would have. "I can do anything I please." Her voice came out dark and heavy.

She cleared her throat. Will, Sean, and John stepped back. A figure in a red velvet cape and hood watched them from the stairs.

"Just leave," Will said to Jackie.

"Make me." Her voice came out sounding weird again. She swore her hair was standing on end. She was so pumped with energy.

"Want me to carry her out?" Sean asked Will.

"Do it," Will said and pushed Sean.

Jackie shot a look at Sean, who stumbled toward her like he had been knocked out of bounds. The veins in her arms pulsed.

Sean sailed backward. Flying through air, he slammed into Will and John.

"Holy shit," John said. He and Will helped Sean up from the floor.

Everyone was mumbling and staring at her like she had been the one who threw Sean. The figure standing on the stairs dropped its hood.

"Trish," Jackie said. Their eyes locked on one another. A voice inside Jackie told her that Trish had to be stopped.

Trish ran out the front door. Jackie followed her out into the yard and around the house. Jason and Zeta chased behind her as Trish moved briskly down the sidewalk.

Bright pink lights flashed up ahead. Two squad cars, a fire truck, and an ambulance were parked along the curb. Trish paused by the ambulance. Her face was pale, her expression distraught. She cut between the fire truck and ambulance. On the other side of the street, she disappeared into a dark gangway.

"They're inside your Dad's house," Zeta said, out of breath.

"What?" Jackie asked distracted by Trish's disappearance.

Jason squeezed Jackie's shoulder near her broken wing. "Go on. We'll wait here."

Jackie realized the paramedics were at her dad's house. "And do what?"

"See what's up," Zeta said. "He's your father."

The word "father" slammed into her chest.

A paramedic held open the front door while two others carried out a gurney with a man strapped to it. It was her dad.

A woman wearing pajama bottoms and a coat followed them, crying.

"Maybe you can ride in the ambulance," Jason said. "Zeta and I will meet you at the hospital."

"She can have my ride," Jackie said referring to the frantic woman following the gurney.

Zeta squinted. "What's wrong with you?"

"Ha. That's the same question Dad kept asking when I was twelve. 'What's wrong with you, Jackie? Why can't you just be normal?' I'll tell you what's wrong with me. He's my father. He was supposed to stand up for me. And what did he do? He left my mom and me. So, no, I'm not getting into that ambulance with him."

"Wow," Zeta said. "Where did that come from?"

Jackie's chest was on fire, her forehead rolling with sweat.

"You think you should call your ma?" Jason asked.

"Yeah. Maybe I will." Even though it shouldn't be any concern of hers, it would be fun to see how she dealt with this.

At the hospital, Jackie, Mom, Jason, and Zeta sat in the waiting room, along with that other woman. Mom was being polite to her, but Jackie could tell Mom was bothered by the fact that Dad had replaced her with someone else. Jackie wondered what Mom told Andy. He was probably wondering if Mom still had feelings for Dad. So what if Dad had an aneurism and was now in a coma. It wasn't like he'd be crying over Mom. He always blamed Mom for being weak and too sentimental. And he was right.

"Don't worry," Zeta said to Jackie. "I'm sure he'll pull through this."

Jackie drew back her head; her chest jutted slightly. Did Zeta really think she was worried?

Jason rubbed Jackie's hand. She wished he'd knock it off.

His face lit like he had just been hit in the head with an amazing idea. "Hey. Why don't you try healing your dad?"

Jackie's chest felt like it had been pierced with a hot iron rod. She gritted her teeth.

"What?" Jason asked.

"Yeah, Jackie," Zeta said. "Why not? What do you have to lose?"

"I'm going to lay my hands on a man who wanted nothing to do with my so-called gift? I don't think so."

Mom leaned over. "You really *can* heal?"

"Yeah, where have you been?"

"I thought you were just..."

"You can say it, Mom. Psychic?"

"You're good with that now?"

"I'm pretty much dealing with it now. I'm dealing with a lot of shit, so don't get me started."

"Sorry." She turned to Zeta. "What's wrong with her?"

"You're asking Zeta what's wrong with me? I'll tell you. All my life, I've been protecting you, keeping silent, because you were too weak to deal with my problems. Now you want to know if I'm good with it? Well, I'm not. And I'm not good with the idea of healing a man who has never accepted me as I am." She stood up. "I'm going home. I've had enough for one evening. Good night, folks."

She walked down the hall, alone. Mom cried.

"Wait up," Jason said.

She stopped. "Forget it, Jason. It ain't going to happen tonight."

"What?"

"You know. Go home and take a cold shower."

"I wasn't even thinking that. I'm worried about you."

She rolled her eyes. "Get over it."

"You're not acting like yourself," he said. "Something's

happened."

"It's called apathy."

"No. I used to feel this energy around you."

"What? Are you me now?"

"I'm not dead. It's what people open to you felt back in the day."

"Is that why you asked me to heal you?"

He nodded. "But now it's you who needs healing."

She turned abruptly and left him standing there.

Jackie wandered the streets looking for Trish. She was like a fly in the ointment. Meddling in things bigger than herself. Stuff she didn't understand. She needed to stay away.

After walking in the dark for an hour, Jackie asked herself why she even gave a shit. Trish hadn't any power over her. Not anymore.

When Jackie came home, Mom was at the kitchen counter pouring a huge glass full of gin. Jackie was tired, and a bit of sympathy for Mom slipped into her gut. Her stomach felt queasy and panging with regret. She considered apologizing to Mom, but she couldn't, and she couldn't even get her feet to move toward the kitchen.

Mom's a big girl. She'll be fine.

Babu's door was halfway open. Lit candles packed the dresser. Just Jackie's picture sat on the dresser among the many candles. The bed was empty.

Dressed in black, Babu appeared in the doorway, her eyes full of pity and sadness. She kissed the cross on her chotki and then closed the door in Jackie's face.

There's something terribly, terribly wrong with me.

In her room, Jackie sat on the floor. Eyes closed and open hands on knees, she took a deep breath, held it, and imagined the breath absorbing the apathy inside her. She exhaled, imagining it shooting out her nose and mouth. She was tired, but she did it a few more times. Then she tried to imagine Babu's light, but all she could see was Babu kissing the chotki cross and shutting the door in her face.

The crystal!

Maybe Madam Sophie had been trying to give her the crystal for this very reason.

Chapter 55

In the morning, Jackie went to Madam Sophie's. Why wasn't Madam Sophie opening the door? Jackie knew she was in there. Her "Psychic Reading $20" sign burned in the window, which meant she was open for business. Jackie's body heated, and her nostrils flared. She pounded the door. "I'm not leaving until you let me in."

She continued to pound and make threats.

The door opened.

"I need that crystal."

Madam Sophie gripped the edge of the door.

"Aren't you going to invite me in?"

Her shoulders lifted and tightened.

"What's wrong with you? What? Are you through with me? You got Jackie to work her magic, and now your job is done?"

Madam Sophie slowly stepped to the side.

Jackie swept past her, scanning the room for the crystal. "Where is it?"

"It won't work for you."

"You said it would keep me safe. I need it." She slid open the end table drawer. Empty.

"I think, my dear, it's too late."

"You knew this was going to happen?" She stepped toward Madam Sophie, whose eyes were wide, with pupils like eclipsed moons.

"Not this, I only wanted you to use your power, to quit denying your talent." She used a kind, friendly tone.

"You let me believe it was all physics."

Madam Sophie took several steps backward. "It's what you wanted to believe, and it was the only way."

"You lied about the solar storm?"

"No. It was partly true. The solar storm did affect Jason's house, the church icon, and the things you healed. Although, its power wouldn't have lasted as long as it did, not without another power. The solar storm enabled it to come through. It's been playing with you. Slowly crushing you so you'll never find your own light."

"Fix it."

"I can't. You must go. Don't come back."

"I know you can."

"I can't."

"Liar!" Jackie's body trembled like a volcano ready to spew. The anger inside her, hot as lava.

Jackie had backed Madam Sophie up against the wall. She wrapped both hands around Madam Sophie's throat. Her knuckles turned white as she squeezed. She didn't want to do this, but she couldn't stop herself.

Madam Sophie's watery eyes bulged. "Let the anger go, Jackie," she said, her voice raspy. "You know how to protect yourself. You have the skills."

"Quiet, witch," Jackie hissed.

Madam Sophie closed her eyes. "When the time comes"—she coughed—"you must open up to him. Let him into your heart."

"He already is." Jackie laughed involuntarily and let go of Madam Sophie's throat.

Madam Sophie slid down the wall, one hand on her throat and the other covering her head as Jackie left.

Chapter 56

Trish, in her hooded cape and fingerless gloves, pounded on Jason's door. His dad, dressed in a navy blue mechanics outfit, opened it. He looked surprised.

"You're not Jackie," he said.

"I need to see Jason."

"Well, I don't know if he..."

Jason appeared behind him. "It's okay, Dad."

"All right, then," he said and left them alone.

Jason blocked the doorway with an outstretched arm. "What do you want?"

"I need to talk to you about something... in private."

Jason looked at her with distrust.

"I'm not here to entice you. Listen, I know now that what I did was wrong. I shouldn't have pressured you to love me and to work those spells."

"You what?"

She waved her hand. "Never mind that. I'm afraid something's wrong with Jackie, and it's my fault."

His lips formed a tight, and his hand slipped a little down the door frame.

"You saw what happened at the party," Trish said. "It wasn't me who threw Sean."

He glanced behind him and then closed the door. "Come on." He led her to his truck. "Spill it," he said.

"Well, I guess you've noticed that Jackie isn't herself lately."

Jason burrowed his hands in his jacket pockets and nodded.

"It's because she isn't. There's something inside her, something I invited with my Ouija board."

"Like a demon?"

Trish nodded. "With me, it traveled at my side. But with Jackie, it's inside her."

"Why Jackie?"

"It wants to kill her. Something to do with Babu."

"For real?"

"How do you think I was able to work the voodoo doll? I thought it was helping me to win you over. But it was just using me."

"We can't let it hurt her. How do we get it out?"

"I don't know. Maybe that priest can help."

"No," he snapped. "We're not calling him."

Trish raised her hands in defense. "Sorry."

"Maybe Babu can help. Jackie always says she has this light about her."

"You know how to speak Russian?"

"No."

"The priest does."

Jason kicked the toe of his boot into the dirt. "He's not a priest. He's a seminarian, and he can still take Jackie away from me."

"Whoa. Jealously is truly a green-eyed monster."

Jason glared at her.

"Sorry. I completely understand. That's how I got us into this mess. But I'm telling you, if you want to save Jackie, you have to let go."

"I can't. Maybe Jackie will know what to do."

"Jackie doesn't have much control, and I doubt it will let her do anything to overcome its control over her."

A rebellious look washed across Jason's face.

Trish shook her head. "You're hopeless, you know?"

"No. I have hope."

"Fine. Maybe we can use the Ouija board to send it back. Maybe it's like a two-way door."

"Why are you helping her?"

She shrugged. "I don't know. At first, I wanted to get even with that demon. But now, maybe I just want to gain your trust. I don't want you to hate me."

Jason grimaced. "I'll talk to Jackie. She has it in her to fight this thing. She'll know what to do."

Chapter 57

In school, Mr. Davis was looking like his old self—starched and ironed shirts, a crease down his jeans' legs, hair slicked back, and reeking with cologne. He wouldn't call on Jackie whenever she raised her hand, in fact, he didn't acknowledge her at all. Sometimes, she'd catch him looking at her, and then his eyes would avert from hers.

He was curious about Jason, sometimes even acting protective of him, like the way he lingered by his desk, touching his shoulder in a fatherly waay.

Come father me. I dare you.

Jason was quiet around her, contemplative, and cautious. They walked together down the hall to their lockers. As she reached for her locker, Jason touched her arm.

"You okay?" he asked.

"You mean, am I worried about my dad? No. I'm fine."

"Not that. Just tell me what to do. I'll help you."

She knocked him against the locker and pinned him in place. His body froze. He looked so fragile, like she could break him with a touch. She ran her fingers over his youthful face. "You want to help me?"

The color drained from his lips and cheeks, turning them corpse-like. "What happened at Mr. Davis's house? You never told me. You've been acting weird ever since that night. Even Babu thinks you're acting weird. I noticed the way she stays away from you. And at the party, you threw Sean across the room, without even touching him. Everyone's talking about it."

"I didn't do it. Trish did. She's the one dabbling with demons and Ouija boards."

"That's not what Trish said."

Her mouth dropped open. "Are you cheating on me with Trish?"

"No." His voice trembled. "I-I just talked to her. She came to me. She's worried about you too. We want to help you, but we don't know what to do."

"Stay away from me."

Alone, Jackie walked home from school. Piss on them. She didn't need friends like Zeta, Trish, and Jason. They needed to mind their own business.

Flies buzzed in her head. She grabbed her hair wanting it to stop.

At home, she banged on Babu's locked bedroom door. "Let me in!" She wiggled the door handle. It was locked. She ought to just kick it in. She wanted to knock those candles to the floor. She wanted to ignite this house and burn alive with it.

Pacing the between the dining room and front room, she noticed that Mom had left an empty gin glass and a half-filled bottle of gin on the coffee table.

I think I'll get soused. She hadn't eaten in three days. The alcohol would give her a boost.

She plopped down on the couch and put the bottle to her lips and guzzled. Mom was going to shit when she saw her drunk. She'd probably cry. Ha!

The gin bit her tongue. It burned her throat, warmed her stomach. It rippled through her taut nerves, relaxing them. She guzzled the rest of the bottle. Her muscles went numb.

For a moment, she felt free. As if what had gotten a hold of her had let go. The weight of her anger had lifted.

Then, blackness.

Chapter 58

The room burned with a yellow glow. Shadows flickered on the ceiling. Jackie was in bed. Two voices, a male and a female, spoke Russian in low tones, and strangely, Jackie knew what they were saying. She must be dreaming.

She tried to wake up; she struggled to move her arms and legs, but they were bound. Babu and David, at her bedside, stared down at her.

"Let me up!" she demanded.

"No, no angry," Babu said in Russian.

"Untie me!"

"Babu said not to get angry," David said.

"I understood her. Say something to me in Russian."

"I am sorry, Jackie, but I have to do an exorcism on you," he said in Russian.

"What? No! No exorcism!" She jerked at the restraints, which felt like leather belts.

"Look at how she suffers," Babu said. "She no eat. It is my fault. The demon do this to punish me."

"You are familiar with this demon?" David asked, surprised.

Babu nodded. "When I young girl, I was forced to honor it."

"Who forced you? Your family?"

She lowered her head. "No. Bad people. But I hide from them. I stay in cabin in woods. One day, I find priest wandering forest. He was cursed by sorcerer, by the bad people. His skin, rotting, he forced to leave his village. I take him into my cabin. I wanted to help him. He wouldn't let me use my herbs or my gift to heal him. He trusted his Christian God to save him. I saw the light in his eyes when he spoke to me. He not give up. He get worse and worse. I took care of him as he lay dying. I could not do nothing. I put my hands on him and prayed to his God that He would work through me to heal him. Healed, the priest brought me to his church to heal others who were sick or who had been spoiled through witchcraft. But the demon put thoughts in their heads that I was working witchery. They dragged us—me and the two sisters who assisted me—out into the church yard, and they beat us with sticks and staves. I ran into the woods, past the priest, my friend, whom they hung from a tree."

David wiped the tears from her face with his cassock sleeve.

"I am coward. I ran into the forest while my friends were left to die." Babu crossed herself. "Forgive me."

Jackie fought back an urge to laugh. What was wrong with her? She loved Babu. The thought of the demon manipulating her and Babu made her furious.

"I will free her and rid the earth of this demon." He took up his Bible.

Jackie wanted to tell him to perform the exorcism, but her lips wouldn't move. Jackie's insides tightened like her organs were being squeezed. Sharp pains shot through her body.

The door flew open.

"Don't you dare touch her," Jason said.

Trish, dressed in a dark cloak, a Ouija board tucked under her arm, followed behind him, and Zeta behind her.

"Holy balls of fire," Zeta said. "This is like a scene from *The Exorcist*."

"It's the only way," David said to Jason.

"She's mine now. I'll take care of her."

"And what will you do? Call on Satan to expel his demons? I can't believe you walk in here with a Ouija board. You people, dabbling in the occult, that's how this started."

Trish stepped forward. "I brought it through with this. I'll send it back with this."

"You think you have power because of your voodoo doll stunt? Without the demon, you have no power."

Babu put her hands on Trish and Jason's shoulders. "Please," she said in Russian, "let David do his work."

Somebody do something, Jackie thought. Her spine slowly arched until she was bent backward and staring at the headboard. Her body raised above the bed. The restraints cut into her wrists and ankles. And then she crashed to the mattress.

Babu clasped her hands together, "Kill me instead," Babu begged.

David swung an incense burner over Jackie. The thick smoke caught in her throat, and she coughed. Then he took up the holy water dispenser and splashed water onto her face. The droplets burned like acid and ate through her flesh. She screamed. The bones in her face twisted and pulled. She raised her head and said to David in a dark voice. "Do you like me now?"

It's not me talking. I can't control my mouth.

"I love Jackie," David said, "not you, demon."

"Trish, do the Ouija board," Jason said.

"Okay, okay, but I'm not sure what to do."

"I thought you had a plan."

"I didn't plan for this."

"I don't freaking believe this," Zeta said, her voice shifting octaves.

"Give me this." Jason snatched the Ouija board from Trish's hand. "Give me the pointer."

Trish dug the pointer out of her cloak pocket and gave it to Jason.

Jackie laughed at everyone.

The Ouija board ripped from Jason's hands, flew through the air, and smashed against the wall repeatedly until it splintered.

David continued to pray without distraction. He cast the sprinkler at her. The droplets ate into her arms, her neck, and her face.

Madam Sophie had told her to let him into her heart. He was in, and she knew it. But maybe she wasn't talking about the demon. It was inside her, controlling her, but it wasn't in her heart. Maybe Madam Sophie had meant someone else. Was it David she should let in? He quelled the demon's power over her before at the church, though it didn't last. She still had fallen victim to its power. Was it Jason? There was no way he had any power to fight the demon at all.

"Heal yourself, Jackie," Jason said. "Please. I know you can do it. Fight him."

Her neck abruptly twisted. She stared at Jason and hissed. She couldn't control herself.

"You want to eff with someone," Jason said, "eff with me."

That a boy, Jason, stand your ground. She couldn't believe how much he loved her. She was so sorry for the way she had treated him. *Only you know me, Jason, and I know you.*

"You think she can hear us?" Zeta asked Jason.

"She'll hear me if I send her my thoughts."

Yes, come to me so I can talk to you. If I could send you my thoughts like I did when we were practicing, I could tell you how much I love you, before the demon destroys me.

Jason took her hand. She couldn't stop her own hand from crushing his. He closed his eyes. His face squinted in pain.

She read him. He asked her what he could do to save her. She just wanted him to go and save himself, but not until she told him how she felt about him.

She tried to shut her eyes, but she couldn't control her body. The only thing she had power over was her thoughts. She thought about Jason and how much she loved him. That he was her best friend in the whole wide world. The love burning in her heart grew stronger. She felt the light. It was similar to what she used to pick up from Babu.

I love you, Jason, she continued to think. *You are my best friend in the whole world.* She opened her heart to him and focused on sending him the energy of love. The energy grew stronger with each thought she sent to him. The light burned inside her and radiated through her hand to Jason.

Her head dropped to the bed.

Something hit the wall. Jackie rose up. Jason was crumbled on the floor by the door, his face sallow, and his eyes yellowed and glaring at her.

Oh, shit! She had sent him the demon. "David, untie me! It's not in me anymore!"

David stopped reading from the Bible and looked at her hesitantly.

"Someone untie me."

"No. It's trickery," David said.

"No tricks. It's in Jason. Look."

Trish and Zeta quickly unbuckled the belts that bound her.

Jason lunged from a sitting position at David, knocking him and his Bible to the floor. Jason's fingers tightened around David's neck. "How strong is your faith, seminarian?" Jason said in a dark, demonic voice.

Babu threw her hands to her face. Jackie could no longer understand the words she was saying. Babu looked up at the ceiling, pleaded in Russian, and then made the sign of the cross.

Freed from her bonds, Jackie jumped out of bed and fought to hold Jason, concentrating on taking the demon back.

"What's up with Babu?" Zeta said.

Babu was holding a crystal paperweight in one hand. In her other hand was a pewter letter opener. Babu pointed the letter opener at the floor. She chanted in Russian. The crystal slowly lit until it brilliantly glowed with a pure white light.

"Holy shit," Jackie whispered.

Jason looked up at Babu, relaxed his fingers from around

David's neck and chanted in Latin to counter Babu.

The light flowed from the crystal through Babu, into the pewter opener, and to the floor. The spot on the floor where Babu directed the light appeared to open. It swirled with red and green clouds of energy.

Babu looked at Jackie, and Jackie knew what she was saying. Babu had unlocked her mind to her.

"Help me restrain, Jason," Jackie said to Trish and Zeta.

Trish and Zeta rushed to help. David latched on to Jason to hold him.

Jackie put one hand to Jason and the other to the edge of the swirling energy. She envisioned the demon flowing through her, out her arm, and into the portal.

Jason struggled to free himself from Zeta, Trish, and David, but the demon, more concerned with stopping Babu, continued chanting.

The light flowing from the crystal weakened. Jackie opened up her heart. She thought about Jason, about Babu, about how much she loved them. The love burned inside her, and the light grew stronger.

Jason's body contorted, and a shrill scream projected from his mouth. The demon, in the form of a black mist, was sucked out of Jason. It ripped through Jackie and funneled through her fingers into the energy hole.

The light in the crystal went out, and the portal closed.

All was quiet.

The crystal fell from Babu's hand and hit the floor, breaking the silence. Babu dropped to her knees.

Jackie rushed to Babu, and kneeling beside her, threw her arms around her.

Jackie hugged Babu and whispered, "I heard what you told David. No more secrets, for either of us."

David helped her lift Babu from the floor.

Jason touched Jackie's back. "I got your message."

"I didn't mean to send you the demon."

"It's okay. Really. And I understand now." He looked at David and then at her.

Oh, no. Here it comes again, the jealousy.

"You love me, but as a friend," Jason said. "You tried to tell me before, but I just didn't listen. I wanted it to be something more, but it can't be. Your heart told me so."

"I said all that?"

He nodded.

"I didn't mean to lie. I really believe we belong together."

"It's okay. Everything you've said about me is true. I am shy, and I guess, in a weird way, I like to suffer. It's like the only thing I expect in life."

"Are we still friends?"

"Best and always." He hugged her.

Babu groaned.

"I gotta help Babu," Jackie said. "We'll talk later."

"Sure." Jason slipped his hands into his jacket pockets. He followed Trish out the door.

"You gonna be all right?" Zeta asked her.

"Yeah."

Zeta looked around the room and then struck her forehead with the heel of her hand. "Why didn't I take pictures?" She walked out the door, grumbling about missed opportunities.

Jackie and David walked Babu to the bed. "You need to rest," Jackie said to her. "I know how much energy it takes."

Babu smiled weakly and lay down.

David quietly gathered his Bible, incense burner, and holy water sprinkler while Jackie picked up the crystal and letter opener. By the blank expression on his face, it looked like he had been knocked off-kilter.

Their tools in hand, she and David stood at opposite ends of the footboard silently looking at one another.

Babu waved her arm in the air and bantered something in

Russian.

"What did she say?" she asked David.

"She said they are just instruments. The real power comes from the heart."

Chapter 59

The heart monitor and ventilator bleeped as the thin blanket spread over Jackie's dad narrowly rose and fell with each breath he took. He wasn't the same man who came to her door in his Carhartt jacket and cleared away the toilet paper, devil spears, and shrine. The hard lines on his face had softened. With a ventilator tube in his mouth, he was asleep, at peace.

His hand was open and lifeless beside him, a plastic clip on his index finger. She gently laid her hand in his and closed her eyes. Her memory took her back to when she was five and she, Mom, and Dad went to the beach. He led her to the water, her tiny hand swallowed by his, her toes caressing the wet sand, and the sun warming her shoulders. Her heart warmed, too, with love, and the love burned as brilliantly as the sun. The warmth from her hand spread to his. When the water washed over her feet, Dad lifted her onto his shoulders. As he slowly submerged in the water, Jackie knew she wouldn't drown. He was her pillar, her support.

"I forgive you, Dad," she whispered.

The love inside her grew more intense, turned to light, and flowed from her hand into his. Goose bumps rose on her arms and the tiny hairs stood on end as the energy in her palm and fingers grew stronger. A white light illuminated her mind's eye, and she was at peace.

Dad's fingers twitched. His eyes opened and stared blankly at the ceiling. She gently set his hand into a gathering of bedsheet and blanket and then grabbed her coat from off the chair.

Out in the hall, she found his nurse. "He's awake," she said.

A surprised look on her face, the nurse jumped up from her station and rushed to his room.

Jackie let her go in on her own. She and Dad would recover their relationship one step at a time. Forgiving him and waking him from his coma were the first steps.

When she turned, David was standing at the end of the hall, his rumpled cassock as lax as the jeans and gym shoes he was wearing, his hair tousled, a backpack slung over his shoulder. He smiled, his eyes gleaming.

Jackie couldn't keep the corners of her mouth from turning up into a smile or wipe the glow from her face. *What the hell was wrong with her? What was it about him?*

"That's a new look for you," he said.

She knew he was talking about her white blouse with the flared sleeves, and the fact that she had curled her hair. She'd been hoping to make a good impression on her dad, had he been awake, and had borrowed the blouse from Mom.

He glanced at her black pants and combat boots. "Well, it's a start."

She threw up her hands. "What can I say?"

"How about, that you will have coffee with me?"

She wrinkled her mouth. They absolutely did not belong together. And if she said yes…

"It's okay," he said. "I understand. I just thought that…"

The energy she felt whenever she was around him was tugging her now, drawing her to him. She couldn't explain it.

"The crystal thing… what Babu and I did… you're good with it?" she asked.

He pressed his eyes closed momentarily and said, "I am good with it."

"Well, then, sure. Coffee would be wonderful."

He extended his elbow. She linked her arm in his. His energy channeled through her, making her body quiver. She didn't fight it. Instead, she hugged his arm and let the energy flow.

Far, far away, in a remote Russian village, a red candle burned. Beside it, two faceless cloth dolls, a red ribbon binding them tightly together.

About the Author

JoAnne Keltner is a novelist and freelance editor. She has published YA titles Obsession (Musa Publishing, 2013 ed.) and Goth Girl Virgin Queen (Solstice Publishing, 2015). She currently lives in Raleigh, North Carolina, where she enjoys gardening, tending to her chickens, and spending time with family. Every evening you will find her obsessively streaming popular series.

www.joannekeltner.com

71107722R00200

Made in the USA
Columbia, SC
26 August 2019